THE MOST TERRIFYING PSYCHIC WAR IN THE
ANNALS OF SCIENCE FICTION!

THE DUELISTS

On the one side was the SYNDICATE, a brutal
organization of power-hungry men who tyrannized
the world by means of a super-drug known as PSI-40.

On the other was the ANTIS, the secret, underground
organization led by the mysterious Killjoy.

THE DUEL

When they clashed, it was a battle of tremendous
wills, a war of titanic superintellects that could
end only in madness or death.

Also by Louis Charbonneau

THE SENTINEL STARS

Published by Bantam Books

PSYCHEDELIC - 40
BY LOUIS CHARBONNEAU

BANTAM BOOKS
TORONTO · NEW YORK · LONDON

PSYCHEDELIC—40
A Bantam Book / published January 1965

Bantam Books are published by Bantam Books, Inc., a subsidiary of Grosset & Dunlap, Inc. Its trade-mark, consisting of the words "Bantam Books" and the portrayal of a bantam, is registered in the United States Patent Office and in other countries. Marca Registrada. Bantam Books, Inc., 271 Madison Avenue, New York 16, New York.

PRINTED IN THE UNITED STATES OF AMERICA

With love to
Carrene and Mike

Prologue: 1976

Kemp Johnson's father spoke gently, without looking up from the fishing reel he was repairing. "You won't forget to take your pills."

"Do I have to take them?" The boy was chagrined at letting his rebellious thoughts echo so clearly.

"Yes." The man's tone was heavier. "You have to."

Kemp Johnson did not argue. No whiner, he had learned early in life that, once his father had formally announced a decision, no storm of tears or wind of sighs would sway him. The boy, ten years old, had memories of his mother, whose instructions had been more softly made, less sternly enforced—whose resistance had often been short of impregnable. But these were dim, blurred by a fuzzy warmth of feeling.

"I wish . . ."

"What?" Powell Johnson, a tall, gaunt man made more bulky by hip-high rubber boots and a plush-lined mackintosh, glanced at his son.

"Oh, nothing."

Kemp's father grunted. His attention returned to the fishing reel. His hands, big but surprisingly sensitive of touch, were brown, wrinkled, roughened from the winter months in the high, wild country of northern Idaho. His face too was red-brown, weathered where the new beard did not cover it, and deeply seamed. It was hard for Kemp to recall what his father had looked like before, although the two had been alone together in this lonely, rugged land for no more than six months. He watched with intent curiosity as his father's fingers deftly unraveled the tangled line inside the covered reel. Kemp forgot his embarrassment.

"I wish we could fish together," he said abruptly.

The man did not reply. Kemp, long used to the extended silences into which his father would fall, waited patiently, neither angered nor dismayed. In their other

1

life Powell Johnson had been a lively, challenging talker. During the months in the wilderness he had grown more silent, more thoughtful, more brooding. But he always listened, and the boy knew he would have his answer.

Kemp's father sighed. "We are always together."

"Yes, I know, but . . ."

It wasn't the same, Kemp thought. Being able to make mental contact at will was better than being completely alone, of course, but not as good as being *really* close, where he could see his father expertly casting or entering with zest into the duel with a flashing trout, with all the clarity of sight rather than that strange, distant, inner vision of the mind. Even when the pills worked the magic Kemp had come to accept as quite natural, neither frightening nor very astonishing, there was always the knowledge of separation. It was like shouting to someone a long way off, hearing an answer carried on the wind— or looking at something through a telescope. The object in the glass could be as large and clear and vivid as life— but it never really *felt* close. You always knew how far away it was.

Kemp watched his father test and adjust the brake mechanism on the well-used reel which the boy had found balky the previous day. "I've told you why it has to be this way," Powell Johnson said. The seams in his face seemed to deepen. "If they should somehow trace me here and discover us together, they would try to harm you."

"We could fight them together!" the boy cried hotly.

"No!" His father's tone was harsh. "Promise me again —if anything happens, you will do exactly what we've said. You won't try to help me!"

Tears suddenly blurred Kemp's vision. He always had to make the same promise, and in his heart he denied the words he expressed.

"Promise me, Kemp!"

"I—I promise. But it isn't right, Dad!"

"Some day you'll have your chance to fight them. When you grow up. You may be the only one who can fight them." Powell Johnson handed his son the reel. "Try that now."

Half-heartedly Kemp tested the mechanism, seeing instantly that it worked freely. "It's fine. You always know how to fix things."

His father smiled faintly. "I am still of some use," he murmured.

An hour later they were ready to set off up the river. The ritual of precaution repeated each day was completed. In a loose plastic sack tied with a cord at the top Kemp carried his few clothes and the small hoard of mementoes he retained from the other life. In the log cabin which his father had built there remained no sign that Kemp had ever been there. They had come to its site by separate routes which Powell Johnson had carefully mapped out, so that no one had ever seen them together since they left the city far to the south. Kemp understood and accepted the reasons for all of this careful plotting, but as he started along the bank of the river, which ran wide and slow near the cabin, he glanced back over his shoulder at the lean, tall figure of his father with a tug of mingled pain and fear. Each day as they parted the boy felt cut adrift. Each night when he returned to the cabin on Powell Johnson's signal he had to renew, it seemed, his claim to the only life he wanted, the life they shared.

"Good catch!" The man called after the boy.

"Bet I land the biggest one!"

In the distance, soundlessly, Powell Johnson laughed.

Kemp continued upstream. Without looking back again, he knew when his father began to follow him, walking at a slower pace. They never fished near the cabin, and never within a mile of each other. In recent days, when his father had been more distracted than usual, the boy had noticed that the distance maintained between them lengthened a little more each time they went out. The greater separation didn't seem to make communication more difficult, but Kemp felt more alone, more cut off from his father.

It was surprising, though he seldom thought about it, how easy their private exchange of thoughts had become, even over considerable distances. There were few distracting influences, Powell Johnson had explained. In a crowded city it would be impossible to communicate clearly except at close range.

The morning was chill and invigorating, with the promise of bright sunshine to warm the day. The higher peaks were still wearing white capes, and there was deep snow in the more shadowed wooded areas. Little snow remained along the banks of the river. The ground was soft and often slippery underfoot. But the winter had toughened the boy and he walked with little difficulty and no trace of fatigue.

It was almost eight o'clock when he reached his appointed cove. Here the river made a sweeping bend. On the far side it ran fast, boiling over rocks, but where Kemp was to fish a kind of inlet cut into the bank on the outward extremity of the curve. Here the river was wider, the water calmer, and Kemp had no difficulty keeping his footing.

At eight he took his first pill of the day. The residual effects of the previous day's intake were invariably with him throughout the night, and he experienced none of the drastic reactions that commonly shook him when he had been off the drug for any considerable period.

He was in no hurry. In an hour he could catch more fish than they could eat, and his father could do the same. Hunting and fishing had enabled them to survive, supplementing their hoard of tablets with necessary fresh protein. They were now in a season of plenty. Fishing was a way of filling Kemp's days while his father worked in his cabin laboratory or brooded alone during long solitary walks.

Kemp sat on the riverbank watching the patterns of the water and listening to its endlessly varied roar. There was no dizziness or nausea now in the first half hour after taking one of the pills. In the beginning he had always had these unpleasant symptoms conflicting with the delightful early sensations. His father had been keenly disappointed those first few times when Kemp described his reactions, though he had tried not to show it. The pills had parted a curtain on a strange new world of bright, intense colors and shimmering beauty, of flowers pulsating with life Kemp had never seen in them before, of objects and faces that peeled off layers as he stared, revealing new aspects, of tears and laughter that had no meaning, and of fragmented visions of his own brief life imprisoned in pieces of colored glass. It was a world both fascinating and frightening which the boy had entered each time with a mixture of eagerness and apprehension.

Gradually the unpleasant reactions had faded, weakening with each new experience. Kemp's hopeful recounting of this had left his father unmoved, still frowning when he thought the boy would not notice. Then came the day

4

when Kemp answered one of Powell Johnson's questions in the middle of an experiment before the words were voiced. At first he was not aware what he had done. His father stared at him—and Kemp felt the leap of elation in the other's mind as clearly as if the emotion had been his own.

"You've done it!" Powell Johnson exclaimed aloud.

"Done what? What does it mean?"

"I couldn't be sure—I'd hoped the predisposition was inheritable, but you can never be sure. We don't even know if it's a dominant factor, but that doesn't matter now—you have it!"

"Dad!" the boy protested. "What do I have?"

"You're a Special!" Powell Johnson exulted. Suddenly he paused, perceiving the boy's bewilderment. "Try it again," he said more calmly. "I'll show you what it means. I'm going to stop talking. Concentrate—see if you know what I'm thinking."

There was a period of silence. Kemp could hear his father's breathing, excited and uneven. Then he saw lines of tension deepen into a frown. "Nothing?" Powell Johnson asked.

Kemp shook his head. "There—there's a kind of pressure, like a headache."

"You're blocking me. Wait—stop thinking about it. Don't think about anything. Make believe your mind is a— a clean blackboard. There's nothing written on it at all. It's just black and empty. Do you understand?"

"Y—yes."

"Now. *How many fingers am I holding out behind my back?*"

"Two."

"*Don't say it—think it! How many now?*"

"*Three.*"

"*Good! Now do you see?*"

Kemp stared. All of a sudden the meaning of what they were doing burst upon him. "Telepathy!" he cried aloud.

"*Yes. And that's only the beginning!*"

It was a beginning. In the days and weeks that followed the boy came to see how small a demonstration of his latent talent that initial success had been. There were daily practice sessions, broken periodically by intervals of several days or even a week when he was allowed only to fish and relax and enjoy himself. His father taught him how to block his thoughts so that the older man could not hear them, and how to project them with increasing strength. Sometimes he would seem to lose control of his power, and his mind would churn with confused impressions, sounds of the woods and his father's voice and the shadows of objects he was not looking at but had seen before. At first there was simply excitement tinged with awe as new areas of consciousness opened up to the boy. It was only when the thrill and the novelty began to wear off—and after a disturbing session when Powell Johnson had had Kemp mentally direct the activity of a field mouse in one of the laboratory cages, only to have the animal go berserk and tear at its own body with its tiny teeth—that the boy began to regard his unusual abilities with uneasiness.

Kemp learned there were drawbacks to being a Special. The world into which the pills led him could never be a normal one. There was always a feeling of strain and mental exhaustion after the experimental sessions with his father. Sometimes there were savage headaches, needle-sharp pain in his temples more intense than he had ever felt before. There were disappointments, too. His father, for instance, could cause small inanimate objects to move or fall over without touching them. Kemp failed at this. The natural world around the cabin was even more beautiful when he perceived it with his awakened consciousness, but other things, like hunting and fishing, lost all their zest. Gradually it was borne upon him that his special power was not a toy. Having it was more like holding a potentially dangerous pet in your hands, not quite tamed, squirming so that you were never sure you could hang onto it—and not sure if it would stay tame once you lost control of it.

Worst of all, his developing powers became the instrument which separated the boy from his father more and more. Powell Johnson was bluntly emphatic in stressing the necessity of these longer separations. One day, after having Kemp commit to memory two entire books on chemistry and one on physics, his father showed him a complicated formula he had written on a sheet of paper. While most of the symbols were familiar to Kemp from his recent reading, he could not understand the formula.

"Never mind," his father said. "Just make a mental copy of it and file it away. You'll understand it later."

"Why is it so important?" Kemp demanded.

"From this you can reproduce PSI-40," Powell Johnson said slowly. "That's the name given to these pills we've both been experimenting with." He lit a match and held it at a corner of the sheet of paper. They both watched as the sickle of brown spread over the page before the devouring flames. "I helped to develop this formula. But the group of men who knew about it, working with me, wanted to keep it to themselves. They wanted to be the only ones able to draw upon the powers PSI-40 makes possible. Now you have them—and you have the knowledge to reproduce the pills. They can't be sure of that, but they won't take any chances. Once they find me—"

"They won't find us here!"

Powell Johnson was slow to reply. "If they do, we can't let them catch us both together. Soon we'll have to separate completely. As soon as I'm sure you'll be safer alone than you are here."

A sudden terror seized Kemp. He fought back tears. "I don't want to leave you! Why can't they let us alone?"

It was after that conversation that he began to feel obscurely resentful of the special abilities awakened by the pills. He welcomed the breaks when he could return to normalcy, when trees and birds and eddying waters revealed no hidden depths, no pattern or color or intensity which the normal eye could not perceive, when time had a measurable importance and a battle with a fighting trout on the end of a line called forth all the prideful skill a boy could want. Then he was just a boy living with his father in the wilds—no one special.

The resentment was with him that morning as he sat idly on the bank of the river several miles upstream from the cabin and almost two miles from the point where his father was also relaxing by the river, reading a book. Kemp guessed two miles, although distance, like time, ceased to have its ordinary meaning when he was under the influence of PSI-40. The eight o'clock pill had already begun to take effect. The rush and tumble of the rapids above him had a sharp clarity of sound, and the water a peculiar luminescence. Such responses were common to most people who took the mind-expanding drug, Powell Johnson had told his son. The extrasensory powers which Kemp experienced were extremely rare.

Kemp wondered if he could ever be satisfied with a

more limited response to PSI-40. Instantly he realized that the speculation had no importance. Under the drug's influence he did not think things out in the usual way, reasoning to a solution, but rather perceived truths whole. What he saw now was that he was a Special, in much the same way that the turbulent river and the darting sparrow and a quivering leaf was each purely and beautifully and mysteriously itself. To wish that he was different had no value or significance whatever. He was—

The first stab of warning struck. It ripped like lightning across the sweep of his mind. Kemp jerked up from his prone position. In an instant he was standing without knowing how he had got to his feet. Again the alarm lashed him. He trembled. His father's crackling message did not come in words—there was no need, and to voice a cry would have betrayed Kemp's presence to any Special among the attackers. The warning was not a wordless shout or a scream, but a total response to the fact of danger. All Kemp's body juices and nerves and muscles reacted— there was no need on Powell Johnson's part to control them. Like an identical twin, Kemp felt everything his father felt. No other language was needed for Kemp to understand the urgent plea: *"They've come! Hide! Hurry!"*

Without conscious volition the boy picked up his rod and reel and hurled them out over the river. He was hardly aware of the tug of regret as the precious equipment sliced through the foaming water and disappeared. He scooped up the plastic sack containing all of his belongings and ran into the woods. He had already picked out a place to conceal the sack—a hollow where some burrowing animal's shallow tunnel had caved in. Kemp scooped dirt and leaves over the sack and dragged a large fallen branch over the area, letting it drop across the covered hole. Now he had only to hide himself.

The boy went still. Motionless, he let his mind open out, as receptive to impressions as parched earth is to drops of rain. He felt it again—pain like a blow. "No," he whispered half aloud. "Dad, I can't let them!" He was whimpering as if the pain were his own. "Dad!"

The scene he knew was taking place two miles downriver flashed through his mind. For a moment he was looking through his father's eyes. He bent over double in his fierce concentration, trying to blot out all other awareness. He seemed to be lying on the ground. The horizon tilted, and a leaning figure loomed over him. The face stabbed down like a hawk's, as if the knife-slash of a nose was a beak above a mouth ready to tear. *"Who else knows?"*

"No one."

"You're a fool, Johnson." Dark, hooded, unblinking eyes stared brightly. *"You could have been one of us."*

"And ruled the world?" Powell Johnson was smiling through his pain. His ribs felt crushed. *"Who is the fool?"*

"Someone always rules." The stranger's mouth curved into a cruel scissure. *"Where's the boy?"*

"I don't know!"

Kemp felt his father's smothered fear. And suddenly he knew that the other man, the stranger, felt it, too. He saw the triumph leak into the gray eyes.

"We'll find him," the stranger rasped. *"He has the talent, doesn't he? Did you think you could hide him when you can't even hide your thoughts from me? You've already told me—"*

A sudden darkness covered Kemp's mind. Reaching out with all his power, straining, he seemed only to plumb a void, like a searchlight blindly probing the dark of a starless night. The boy shivered. His father's mind had closed against him deliberately. He was cut off.

Then, tears blurring his vision, Kemp was running downstream, slipping and falling on the muddy ground, picking himself up, hurling himself on. Pain smashed into his chest, thudded around his face and arms like blows. His father had blocked off his thoughts and perceptions, but he could not contain all sensation against the boy's awareness. All Powell Johnson's urgent warnings, the promises repeated, meant nothing now. Kemp could not stay away, cowering in his hiding place, while his father suffered and fought alone. Suddenly the danger and the violence which had seemed remote, unreal, were as clear and present and scalding as a scream.

A scream.

Something burned Kemp's throat and stitched a fiery thread through his intestines. "Dad, don't!" he yelled. "Please! You can't . . ."

His headlong plunge slowed. He pulled up. The tears ran freely over his cheeks. His legs quivered, and after a moment he sank to his knees. In one moment, forcibly, at the age of ten, he grew up.

He felt his father's body marshal its forces against the poison freely swallowed, bulwarks hastily thrown up and speedily eaten away. It was a brief, hopeless struggle. As no grown man before him had ever known it, Kemp faced the image of death. And in the last few seconds of life, when Powell Johnson's control of his mind deserted him, Kemp knew his grief and pain and crushing burden of failure. Kemp's father died without hate.

That emotion was the boy's own.

There was no definite crossing of a line to tell him when Powell Johnson died. It was only when, for several moments, he had been sensing a different pulsation in his mind, strong and somehow angry, that he knew it was over. And simultaneously knew that the hunter's attention was turning from the dead man toward the live quarry.

He stumbled back along the bank of the river toward the cove where he had been fishing. His brain was not yet functioning clearly. He gave no thought to the muddy trail he was leaving. All along his father had known they were coming, Kemp thought. And he had used himself as bait so that Kemp would have a chance to escape. How long had he been carrying the poison, knowing he would use it at the last to prevent any betrayal of his son's presence?

For the first time anger sliced like a cutting wind through the boy's insulating coating of grief. And for the first time he reacted to the fact of his own danger. He had little time. The hunters, since they had managed to surprise his father, must have an air-boat capable of riding safely over the rapids on its cushion of air. That meant they would cover the two miles or so upriver in a few minutes. And they could move with equal ease overland.

Instinct helped him now, aided by the months of his father's careful coaching. Kemp turned abruptly away from the river, making his way rapidly through a scattering of trees and climbing toward a denser forest which would bar the passage of any land vehicle. He wore only a lightweight jump suit, amply warm without being cumbersome. He moved at a tireless jog, covering ground with deceptive speed.

The air-boat was almost silent in operation, its motor creating no warning whine or drum that could be heard at a distance. But when Kemp paused at the edge of a thick stand of pines, where the ground and the remaining snow showed a well used deer track, he could sense the nearness of his pursuers. They had found his trail at the point where he doubled back—where he had felt his father die. For a while they would be slowed down, but they would soon enough discover where he had cut away from the river.

The boy had a half-realized premonition of the sudden mental probe before it came. His schooling had been thorough, and the fleeting apprehension was enough. When the thrust came, his mind was effectively screened. He could not fully comprehend the nature of the assault, but even with his consciousness shielded he had some intimation of its strength and boldness. Awed rather than frightened, Kemp nevertheless had sense enough to realize that he could not resist such power for long. He bolted into the woods.

Kemp realized that, in failing to follow the plan of immediate flight at his father's first warning, he had sacrificed minutes that might now mean the difference between escape and capture. But he felt confident that he could evade the cumbersome air-boat and certainly outrun his pursuers. If they had had a plane or a helicopter, they might have spied him. Without it—

The boy's confidence evaporated suddenly. Of course they would have a plane of some kind! Secrecy and silence had been important to them when they needed to surprise Powell Johnson. It was no longer necessary. Their plane was simply waiting for a signal.

Kemp wondered almost immediately if he had sensed the plane's presence before hearing or seeing it—when his extrasensory powers were active he could not always be sure how he knew a particular fact—for a moment later he heard a distant engine's mutter.

He ran—through a stand of pines, stumbling and sliding down a long slope, angling along a pass between two hills. Now he could hear the flapping of a helicopter's big blade, slowly drawing nearer. The boy melted into the shadow of a tall pine, anxiously scanning the thickness of the needle screen overhead.

Then he realized that the helicopter pilot would not have to see *him*. His tracks alone, visible from the air, would guide his pursuers. Snow was a hunted quarry's worst enemy.

Luck favored Kemp on the plane's first swing near him. It droned on without pausing, moving slowly, no more than a hundred feet in the air. As it veered away, Kemp darted out of hiding and began to run again. A sense of futility nibbled at him. The occasional glimpses he threw over his shoulder told him the helicopter was searching the terrain in widening circles. If it didn't find him or his trail on the second pass, it would surely do so on the third.

Climbing a slope, keeping among trees wherever possible, the boy caught a view through a break in the woods of an open stretch leading down toward the river. It was still empty. But as he started to turn away a flicker of movement attracted his eye. He stared, squinting against the snow's glare. A big, clumsy but menacing air-boat streamed into sight.

Kemp stared fascinated. The vehicle seemed to be moving directly toward him, as if its driver could see him in the distance among the trees. And overhead, the helicopter was once again approaching in its ponderous circle.

In despair Kemp turned—and froze.

Thirty yards away, poised as if on the brink of flight, stood a huge, powerful buck deer. Frightened perhaps by the helicopter's noise, it had blundered close to Kemp without sensing his presence. The boy did not move. He felt that he could hardly breathe.

In that split second of suspended time, while the helicopter crawled against the blue sky and the air-boat crept over the snow and the deer hovered, quivering, Kemp remembered the experiments he had shared with his father —experiments first with mice, then with a squirrel, later with a fox. Never with any bigger animal. Never with a deer.

But the only failure had been with the mice.

A deer would leave no trail, the boy thought, excitement growing. There were so many deer tracks over these hills and gullies that one more set would have no meaning.

There was hardly time to think. In seconds, as the helicopter pounded closer, the deer would bolt. The boy stared at the big, handsome animal. A quick, soundless command went out from his brain to the similar, but less complex brain of the deer. The buck started, but he did not break. Kemp did not look up as the helicopter swept over them, hardly visible through the screen of trees.

The deer held his ground, though his heart pounded in panic. Kemp waited until the plane was well away from them. It was, he knew, about the last time he could hope to avoid detection.

Slowly, avoiding any sudden movement, he approached the motionless buck from behind. As if mental reins stretched out between them, the animal remained in check. He quivered when he felt a human hand seize one of his great antlers, but he did not bolt. Kemp sucked in a whistling breath and vaulted onto the deer's back.

Miles away from the river and his pursuers Kemp Johnson felt the big buck begin to labor.

He dismounted on high, broken, rocky terrain where he could move without leaving a trail that would be visible from the air. He released the deer. It stood in frightened confusion for a moment before taking a few tentative steps, scenting freedom, and racing away, stumbling a little with weariness. Kemp watched his strange mount flee, relieved to know that he had not seriously harmed the animal.

Kemp was in terrain familiar to him from his hunting expeditions. He also had a boy's natural cunning at games of hide-and-seek. With the margin of time he had gained, he knew that his pursuers would not find him. The pattern of his further flight, which would have to wait for darkness, had been charted for him by his father, worked out with several alternative routes. On each of them a place had been designated for a rendezvous between the two. Kemp knew now that these had been meant only to ease his fears. Powell Johnson had never believed in escape for himself.

Words echoed in the boy's mind. "They won't know what you look like. With your hair dyed, you'll look like any other boy. And I've destroyed all your records and photographs. You'll never be completely safe, but you'll have a chance."

A chance.

Tightening his lips, Kemp stared at the blue, empty sky. Tears filled his eyes and the air was cold against them. "They'll never catch me!" he whispered aloud, and the words were a kind of vow. "But they'll wish they had! I'll make them wish they had! You'll see!"

His eyes were clear and bright when at last he turned and started to climb the rugged promontory behind him. Soon he vanished among the rocky crags.

Chapter One

In that uncharted region of split seconds before awakening, reality and dream are curiously confused. In the dream Jon Rand lay upon a hospital table under a battery of haloed lights that turned everything into a dazzling whiteness. Electrodes were clamped to his temples and, like a current running between two poles, a humming noise in his head drove out all other sensation. Above him grotesque figures swam into view—white robes, white faces, pale lips forming unheard syllables. One face peered close, distorted by his upside-down view of it, but the aristocratic features—the thin, long, strongly bridged nose with its deeply cut and flaring nostrils, the hooded gray eyes, the sharp-edged curves of a sensual mouth, the deeply cleft chin—were unmistakable. It was the face of Loren Garrett.

The humming rose into a piercing whine of pain. Rand began to struggle, but he was bound to the thinly padded slab by invisible weights, pinned under the brilliant battery of lights. He tried to shout, but his throat was thick, his mouth stuffed with cotton. A voice said, "He's yours now." There was a sudden, intense pressure on his brain, and—

Jon Rand woke. His eyes opened slowly and blinked against the morning light slanting through a window that was not in the right place. And the bed was not his own. While not a slab, it still resembled a hospital bed. He felt a tug at his temples. There were electrodes, too. A light touch lifted the suction clamps free. But the face and figure which moved into view were not those of Loren Garrett. A pretty technician smiled as Rand propped himself carefully up on his elbow.

"You slept well," she said cheerfully.

Gingerly Rand moved his head, not in denial, but to test it. With relief he confirmed that his headache was gone. And he felt rested and strong. The hands of his telewatch pointed at 8:15 A.M. He had slept for fourteen minutes—the equivalent of more than eight hours of natural sleep.

The technician moved toward the door. "Do you want breakfast now?"

"Just coffee and a break-tab," Rand said.

He lay back when the door closed behind her. The room was soundproof, totally silent. Beyond the window, which was on the seventy-fourth floor of the headquarters complex of the Mental Freedom Syndicate, the New York skyline was penciled in gray against the silent white, splendor of a winter morning. January 20, 1993. The President would be inaugurated at noon today. Garth Taylor would be among the dignitaries the television cameras would glimpse in the background during the swearing-in ceremony. Rand wondered how the old man would take the cold.

Like a small cloud the hazy shape of his dream drifted across his mind. He wondered if Loren Garrett's presence in his dream had been induced, but quickly dismissed the question. The dream was obvious enough, except for that strange phrase—what was it?—"He's yours now." The words had an oddly familiar ring, as if in some way they bridged the gap between dream and reality.

With another abrupt shake of his head Rand swung out of bed, stood and stretched. Naked, he stepped into the adjoining bathroom and punched the cold shower spray. The water coursed down over the stocky, powerful body of a man in his mid-thirties. A deceptive roll around his middle suggested surplus weight but was in fact a hard band of muscle. His thighs were thick and his shoulders and upper arms were heavily muscled. His hair, close-shaven over his skull, was black, underscored by heavy black eyebrows. His face was broad and square and—perhaps because of the thick eyebrows and brown eyes— seemed to glower.

It was not a face or physique designed to suggest the mind of a Sensitive.

When Rand emerged, shaved and refreshed, from the bathroom, he found a pot of coffee and his break-tab waiting for him. He chewed the tablet slowly and washed it down with coffee. Then he carried a cup over to the window. The busy morning flow of traffic was visible above and below. There was still an hour before his flight time, and Rand felt no need of haste.

His relaxed mood was in sharp contrast to the urgency of his emergency briefing before the Syndicate's Board of Directors during the night. The midnight-till-dawn timing of that meeting had been unusual enough to lend importance to Rand's assignment. Garth Taylor's presence on the night before the inauguration had been extraordinary. And the nature of the briefing by the entire board on a matter of security—where Loren Garrett ordinarily exercised sole authority—had been even more remarkable. Perhaps, Rand mused, that accounted for the Security chief's rather testy manner during and after the briefing.

"A waste of time," Garrett had snapped as soon as the door panel to his private office had slid shut behind them. He had brought Rand there directly from the board room, ostensibly to clear up last minute details of procedure. "Sit down, Rand. We'll speak aloud here."

Rand nodded, taking a chair by the window with his back to the early morning light. When you dealt with someone like Garrett, you needed any advantage you could get, however small, and Rand preferred to have the light on the other man's face. Garrett's cryptic comment about speaking aloud had been voiced without emphasis, but it was a sharp command nevertheless, making it clear that Garrett regarded their discussion as of the highest security. Walls could be made soundproof to seal in the sound of voices, but they were not as foolproof in preventing thought transmission. Like Garrett, the other board members were Specials, and he didn't want them listening in. Vocalizing, oddly enough, tended to confuse and override thought waves.

Speaking aloud would also eliminate the awkwardness of communication between a Special and a Sensitive. Where Garrett could read complete thoughts clearly, Rand was capable of receiving only basic impulses—thought synthesized or fragmented, emotions, visual images.

"Well, what were your impressions of the briefing?" Garrett asked.

"If the board wanted to get across the idea that this case is top level, they succeeded," Rand commented. "Do you think this man in Baja is a Special?"

17

"It seems incredible, but—yes, I believe he is." Garrett stared past Rand through the window. The tips of his long, tapered fingers tapped his desk top. The hands were pale, attesting to long hours indoors. They were carefully manicured, the nails polished with a satin pearlized coating. Rand had no objections to the use of cosmetics by other men, though he shunned them himself, even nail polish. "You have a perceptive mind, Rand," Garrett said. "Be more explicit. I want all of your reactions. I want to know what you heard in there and what you guessed. Start at the top."

"Taylor?"

"Yes."

Surprised, Rand took a moment to marshal his impressions. He hadn't been wrong then—there was trouble on the board. You couldn't be in the same room with five minds as powerful as those of the Syndicate's directors—minds so responsive to the psychedelic drug PSI-40 that they developed the extrasensory powers fully realized only by Specials—you couldn't sit before these men through half a night of urgent, often heated debate without sensing a clash of wills. Ideas colliding, no less than atoms, could produce an explosion—a chain reaction, too. And you didn't have to have Rand's own exceptional sensitivity to thought currents, or his minute knowledge of the Mental Freedom Syndicate's organizational machinery, to guess that the trouble was an undeclared struggle for power.

Garth Taylor, Chairman of the Board for the phenomenal seventeen years of the Syndicate's existence, had ruled the swiftly growing organization with the sheer force of a ruthless intelligence aided by a remarkable metabolism. At seventy he had bulled his way through twenty-four-hour days of high-pressure work, causing younger assistants to be used in relays to combat exhaustion. Coupling a rare degree of organizational skill with deft political sense, he had used the talents of a Special to shape the intricate, self-protecting machinery of the Syndicate. More than any other man he had charted the course of its leap to power. He had colored its public image. He had held the conflicting elements within the Board of Directors in check, while coldly striking down the weakening voices of opposition outside the organization. To many outside—including an army of the politically and economically influential in the nation—Garth Taylor *was* the Syndicate. But—

"Taylor is dying," Rand said.

Garrett smiled. The expression was unreadable, and Rand made no futile effort to glimpse what lay behind it. It might have been approving, like the indulgent nod of a parent when a bright child gives an intelligent answer. It might have been disdainful or disapproving—the inverted image of a frown. The only thing Rand was sure of was that it was not amused.

"What makes you believe that?" Garrett asked.

"Oh, he's covered it up well," Rand said. "The makeup is good, and he looks as healthy and vigorous as ever. I'd heard the rumors, but for the first hour in there I was half convinced they were wrong. Then, when he had to handle Pierce about our tactics over those Anti demonstrations, I could see it."

"He handled Pierce."

"Only because Pierce isn't sure—yet. It wasn't the Garth Taylor in that room who whipped Pierce into line, it was the Taylor of five or ten years ago."

Garrett studied the manicured tips of his fingers, toying with an imaginary chip in the polish. "Do you think *you* could match wits with Taylor now?"

Irritated by the condescension in the question, Rand shook his head. "No," he snapped. "But you could."

Garrett leaned back. For a fleeting instant, arrogance rode unmasked on his face. It was gone so quickly that, had Rand not known his superior so well, he would have doubted his intuition. Though arrogance became Garrett's face as a natural guise, Rand had never seen the expression clearly exposed before. The security director always had himself completely under control. He inspired fear, but he did it with a silken manner and a smooth, quiet voice that was never raised above normal pitch. Rand had heard him deliver more than one death sentence in the tones of a man exchanging polite amenities. His gray eyes were agates, cold as glass, their true expression as effectively shielded as was the mind behind them. Rand had never seen him exhibit the frightening power of a Special for display alone, as many of the Sensitives did—those lesser tools of the Syndicate, like Rand, who possessed an inferior degree of extrasensory talent under the influence of PSI-40.

"Go on," Garrett murmured, the surface of his face once more unruffled.

"Taylor is old, he's sick, and he's losing control," Rand went on. "Even a year ago he wouldn't have let the discussion wallow around the way it did tonight. He'd have listened, but then he would have told the board what to do—and no one would have argued with him. Now he's not sure of himself. And he's worried."

"Worried? About the Antis?" Garrett voiced with contempt the name given to the despised group who decried the existence of the Syndicate and its monopoly over the more powerful consciousness-expanding drugs.

"Not so much about the Antis as about the Syndicate itself and what's going to happen to it. It means too much to him now that he feels himself losing it. He wants to control it from the grave, and he's not sure he can. He—" Rand checked himself, wondering if he was going too far. But Garrett merely smiled faintly and waited. It didn't matter, Rand thought. Garrett already knew what he was going to say. "He's afraid of you."

"Ah!" Rand thought there was approval now in his superior's eyes. Garrett asked, "Why should he be afraid of me?"

"Because he recognizes himself as he was ten years ago. And because he's changed now. I think he's got conservative. The cries of the Antis have begun to bother him. He's concerned about his place in history, perhaps, and about the future of a drug-ridden society." Rand paused. "No one wants to die believing that the chief work of his life has been the creation of a monster."

To Rand's surprise Garrett laughed. "A monster! I like that." He examined the notion with amusement. "You're right, of course—Taylor is fading fast. But he's still holding the reins of his monster." Garrett's smile became more remote. "Not for long, I think. What other guesses have you made, Rand?"

Instinctively Rand glanced around the room, studying the walls that made flimsy barriers against the mind of a Special beyond them who wanted to hear what was being said in Garrett's private offices. Something had disturbed him, something that was not really a sensation at all, but could only be described as a tickling of the mind. "Someone . . ." he said.

Garrett was already out of his chair. Rand hadn't seen

him touch any of the buttons on his desk but a concealed panel opened in one wall before Garrett got there, moving fast. Rand was only an instant behind Garrett in reaching the buffer corridor beyond the office wall. It was empty. A door opened to the outer ring of offices and a guard appeared. Garrett gave him no more than a flickering glance. Pushing past the guard, Garrett strode through the reception room and out to the main corridor. Close behind, Rand could sense the Security director's mind darting and probing, reaching out with mental feelers.

Rand's own reaction to the PSI-40 dose he had taken at midnight in preparation for the board meeting had not yet worn off, but the tickling awareness of a listener was no longer present in his mind. He left the probing to Garrett. On impulse Rand turned back to the buffer corridor. He ran toward the far end. At an emergency exit Rand held out his hand while an invisible light beam scanned his fingerprints. A second later Rand shoved through to a service corridor.

Twenty paces away the doors of a service elevator were closed. A finger of light overhead traced the descent of the elevator. It was already down to the sixty-second floor. There was no point in further pursuit. Rand stared at the elevator doors, wondering if there had been time for the descending box to make more than one stop. There had. Straining, Rand could sense the recent presence of someone in the corridor. His mind read the emptiness and detected the shadow of life, like an imprint left in space. But the shadow was already vague, blurring . . .

With sickening impact pain struck like a needle driven through his skull. Rand winced. Swaying, he put out a hand to brace himself against the wall. Sweat appeared on his forehead. Grimly he waited out the first violence of the attack. When the pain eased a little, he forced himself to walk, though every step gave the needle another jab.

Garrett was waiting for him in his office. The Security chief took one look at Rand and punched a button on his desk. He spoke briefly. Thirty seconds later one of Garrett's staff of trim, efficient secretaries entered. She carried a hypodermic needle and a small vial of pink fluid. Slumped in the chair by the window, Rand automatically rolled up his sleeve. He hated the spectacle he was making for Garrett's eyes, although the director knew all about Rand's headaches. They were the one side effect of PSI-40 which Rand had to suffer in return for the powers released by the drug. He never knew when a headache would strike. One hazard of his work was the chance that he would have an incapacitating attack at a moment of danger. Luckily this had never happened. Yet.

Five minutes after the pink fluid entered his blood-stream Rand was sitting up in his chair, his eyes clear. The pain was subsiding rapidly. For the first time he spoke. "He was in the service corridor. No chance to identify."

Garrett, who had waited patiently for Rand to recover, nodded. "It's beginning," he said. He seemed unperturbed by the incident. "If you're well enough, I'd like to continue our talk. We won't be disturbed again."

Rand took a deep breath. His mind was functioning again with almost normal clarity. He was not entirely convinced that it was safe to talk, but the point seemed irrelevant. He was already in too deep. As one of Garrett's key Security agents he would never be trusted by any of the other directors. "There's a power struggle going on," he said at last. "It's not out in the open yet, but it will be when Taylor dies—or drops the reins. Right now I'd guess it's between you and Pierce. Taylor slapped Pierce down today, but I think he wants him to win."

"Why Pierce rather than the others?"

The question was spoken lightly, the lips which shaped it were almost amused, but Rand took his time answering. He knew he was being tested, and he wanted to give his head every chance to recover. Methodically he flipped the names and faces of the directors over in his mind like cards in an I.D. file, recording and evaluating the pertinent facts. Garth Taylor, 75 years old; Chairman of the Board. Still in control of the manufacturing of PSI-40 and its derivatives, intimate of Presidents, Congressional leaders, chairmen of the board across the country, and until now perhaps the most powerful man in the United States. John Zimmerman, 65: Research and Development. White-haired, distinguished, deceptively mild in appearance, like the grandfather of a child's tale. Above all an intellectual. One weakness—vanity. Andrew Drummond, 56: Public Relations. Big and florid and handsome, with a predilection for high living and beautiful women. A mind that, for all its latent power, ran rather quick than deep. George Pierce, 44: Sales and Distribution. The youngest man on the board, four years Garrett's junior, and in some ways the most complex and brilliant of the lot. An opportunist, yes, but a man capable of larger vision, and more sensitive than the other directors to the real issues involved in the outcry being made by the Antis. There was little question that his more moderate views clashed violently with those of Garrett. Which brought Rand to the fifth man on the board, Garrett himself . . .

"Well?" Garrett prodded.

Rand plunged in. "Zimmerman and Drummond are out of it. I don't think Zimmerman has a taste for in-fighting. He probably considers himself above it, and his pride wouldn't let him scramble for any prize, however big. Drummond is a follower, not a leader. My guess is that he'd side with Pierce, Zimmerman with you. Taylor knows that, and that's why he's still in control—because the rest of you are split down the middle. But there's another reason why Zimmerman and Drummond won't take over for Taylor. Research could stop right now and the Syndicate wouldn't be hurt—not right away. There will be other discoveries, so research couldn't stop indefinitely, but there would be time. As for public relations, I've often wondered if that job wasn't created just to find a place for Drummond. The Mental Freedom Syndicate can live without it."

"It's useful," Garrett murmured.

"But not essential. The government could make the distribution and use of PSI-40 illegal tomorrow, and the people would still have to have it. They don't need to be sugar-pilled any more."

"That leaves Pierce."

"And you. Distribution and Security, the two branches the Syndicate can't live without. Each one needs the other, but each functions like an independent organization. You've built a service that's loyal to you first and the Syndicate second. If I'm any judge, Pierce has done the same. That was probably one of his men in the corridor."

When Rand had finished, Loren Garrett stared at him in silence for long minutes. "Impasse," he said at last, as if he were savoring the word. "Interesting. Indeed, an excellent analysis, Rand. I didn't underestimate you." He leaned forward, his whole manner subtly more alive, more urgent, like a polished bar of metal that begins to vibrate with invisible currents. "That is why you were picked for this assignment. You can see why a quick disposition is vital!"

Slowly Rand nodded. "How long will Taylor last?" he asked.

Garrett hesitated. "We don't know the answer to that."

"One thing surprises me," Rand said after a moment's silence. "I've never heard of an open case that stayed open so long. Seventeen years, Taylor said."

"If this Special is the man we think he is, it's been seventeen years."

"From the beginning."

"From the very beginning."

Rand frowned. "How has he remained free?"

"He's a magician," Garrett muttered, for the second time that morning letting his composure falter, revealing a baffled anger. "Every time we've closed a trap, he's been just around a corner! Once, seventeen years ago, he escaped on a—never mind. Just remember he's clever. I can't afford to have a Special make a fool of Security right now. Especially right now!"

Rand did not reply. No answer was necessary. Two agents sent on the trail of the mysterious Special had disappeared. Rand didn't know who they were—one of Garrett's powerful controls over his own agents was the fact that they remained anonymous, even to each other. But Rand could judge their caliber—and that of his adversary— by the simple fact that he was the third choice.

"You'll have more than this Special and the Antis to reckon with," Garrett warned. "There's also Pierce."

Rand said nothing, waiting.

"He wants me to fail," Garrett said coldly.

"He knows the Syndicate can't risk having an outlaw Special working with the Antis."

"He'll want the Special caught, but he wants *me* to fail. That's just the lever he needs to raise himself into the chairman's seat. Security is my responsibility. If I can't handle a single Special . . ." Garrett shrugged negligently. He was in complete control of himself once more. His thin smile was sardonic. "Careers, movements, sometimes the fate of nations turn upon one moment of failure— or one success. I don't intend to lose, Rand."

The threat was clear. Rand met it with his first smile of the interview. "Neither do I."

24

Later, standing by the window drinking his mid-morning coffee, Rand smiled again, somewhat grimly, at his boast. The smile faded as an unanswered puzzle recurred to him. The fact had brushed his mind as he stared at the service elevator down which the spy had escaped. The sudden headache had banished any further inquiry. Rand was not surprised by Garrett's casual treatment of the affair. He had no doubt that the Security chief had ordered an immediate investigation, with which neither he nor Rand needed to be concerned at the time. What teased Rand's investigator's mind was the fact that Garrett, a Special, had not known or guessed where the intruder was.

And Rand had.

Chapter Two

Blazing like a hot ember in the morning sunlight high above the earth's curve, the stratojet raced to meet the giant shadow still lying over the western plains. On the plane's second passenger level where Rand reclined in his chair by a window, it was cool, quiet, with no sense of speed or motion.

A stewardess twitched down the aisle, offering coffee and flavored biscuits. Rand declined, but the passenger on his left, who had been resting quietly, long-lashed lids half-dropped over blue eyes, accepted both. While she was busy adding powdered cream and a drop of sweetener to the coffee, Rand studied her. They had exchanged only brief smiles when she slipped into the seat beside him just before takeoff—the polite, quickly appraising smiles of strangers compelled to spend a couple of hours in close proximity.

Though complete in seconds, Rand's appraisal was methodical and thorough, a habit born of long training, and one which he made no attempt to curb. He confirmed his first impression of a strikingly attractive young woman— in her mid-twenties, he guessed. He wondered why he hadn't thought "beautiful." She was as tall as he, with honey-blonde hair piled on top to add to her height. Her features were rather bold, and it might have been that which made her striking rather than conventionally beautiful. A Scandinavian, he classified. Leggy—his eye approved the long, clean line of thigh outlined under a thin, white traveling dress—athletic, able to challenge a man in most sports. The blue eyes were as cool as the waters of a northern lake. And as deep? He smiled to himself. The well tanned, glowing skin suggested more than active sports. It was not an artificial tan. To maintain it through the winter cost money. As did the unobtrusively expert grooming which complemented her tanned good looks; the costly simplicity of the white dress; The expensive shoes and handbag; the small, Moroccan leather case she had carried onto the plane and placed on the ledge overhead.

There was a minor discordant detail. Her hands, slender and graceful, were not soft. But that might be explained in company with the firm flesh under the healthy skin. Fun and games. Rich girl racing sports cars in Italy, dabbling in bullfighting in Rio, sailing in Baja California. People could firm their muscles and toughen their hands with the diversions idleness made possible, where they turned soft under the indoor regimen of normal work.

With a shrug of dismissal Rand turned toward the window. But the girl's image lingered in the emptiness of space outside. Habits could be limiting, Rand mused. The features hovering before his vision were those the trained agent had discarded as irrelevant—but which any man noticed first. The strong planes of her face were lovely. Her mouth was wide and full; even carefully made up, it suggested the soft puffiness of lips which have just been kissed. Below the golden triangle of her throat, high, firmly molded breasts strained against containment . . .

Rand shifted restlessly. He had delayed long enough getting to work. A portfolio of minirecords had been delivered to him at the airport. There would be time to wade through half the file before the plane touched down at Baja. If he wanted to stare at girls playing tennis or frolicking on the beach, the resort centers would offer opportunity enough.

"Do you mind if I smoke?" The blonde was smiling at him.

Startled, Rand sat up. "Not at all."

He was too surprised to think of reaching for the lighter he carried, though he did not smoke himself. Watching the woman light her cigarette and inhale with obvious pleasure, Rand had the feeling that, as an MFS agent, he should be disapproving. "It's not a common vice any more," he commented.

She laughed, relaxing against the cushioned seat. "Maybe that's what I like about it."

"No health worries?"

"I don't smoke that much." She studied him through the rising smoke. "And at least I retain my perspective."

Rand felt a tingling of warning. The remark suggested Anti propaganda. Was she baiting him? "Are you anti-drug?" he asked abruptly.

The woman lifted one shoulder in a gesture of indifference. "I like to try new things. That doesn't mean I'm against the old ones."

The remark fitted the character Rand had drawn for her, but he was curious enough to pursue the subject. "But you're satisfied with ordinary insights?" For a Syndicate man, the question was heretical. The popular, diluted derivatives of PSI-40 had made available to everyone a pleasurable release and stimulation which had helped to banish smoking and alcoholism as major social diseases, and colored the whole fabric of life. "I would have thought you'd be impatient with the usual, Miss——?"

"Erickson." When Rand waited, she added, "Taina."

"Jon Rand."

"I wouldn't have expected you to be a drug salesman, Mr. Rand."

He laughed. "I find PSI-40 very beneficial," he admitted. "But I don't have to sell it. The experience does that."

Her answering smile was challenging. "I suppose one can hardly argue with statistics. What everyone loves must be lovable. But then everyone used to smoke cigarettes, didn't they?"

"There's a difference," Rand countered. "The mind-expanding drugs are not narcotics. You don't become addicted to them."

"You don't become addicted to sex, either," Taina Erickson replied coolly. "But—what was it you said?—the experience sells itself."

Rand's defensiveness relaxed in a grin. "Is that bad?"

He was pleased to note a stain of color in her cheeks. In that moment her blue eyes seemed warmer. "I think I chose a poor example," she said carefully.

"Depends on your point of view," Rand said cheerfully, enjoying himself.

"You haven't really answered me, you know. I don't say that PSI-40 isn't beneficial. It can heighten reality for some. But for most people it doesn't mean that at all—it's just another way to escape." She squashed her cigarette with rather unnecessary emphasis. "It makes people think that religion, for instance, is all a matter of how many rainbows can you see. Everyone agrees, everyone takes another pill, and pretty soon that's what religion is—a competition for more and better rainbows."

Rand frowned. "You're distorting things a little."

"I'm not distorting," the woman beside him declared with finality. "Your drugs do that."

Rand sensed that the conversation had become more serious than either he or Taina Erickson had intended, and he regretted the turn it had taken. Quite suddenly the talk seemed to run out of momentum. Rand changed the subject. He learned that Taina was in fact Swedish, and that she was going to Baja, America's winter playground, on vacation. Rand lamented the fact that he was going there on business. After a few more comments they both fell silent. Rand wondered if she now wished that she hadn't started the discussion—and if she really was an Anti. Unaccountably the possibility disturbed him more than he wanted to admit.

When Taina settled back into her reclining seat with an air of preparing to rest, Rand accepted the end of a casual interlude and tried to turn his attention to his mission—not the pursuit of rainbows, he thought with a trace of irritation, but of an enemy trying to destroy the Syndicate. His enemy.

Rand carried a small computer-recorder in the inside breastpocket of his coat. He adjusted the private earphone —the unit was wireless and unobtrusive—in his right ear, the one by the window. No one observing him as he sat relaxed, gazing out into the bright darkness of space, would have guessed that he was listening to a carefully prepared dossier on a man he was committed to find and capture—or kill.

The miniature computer-recorder was capable of receiving and interpreting questions, searching its bank of information, and converting the answer into the language of the question. Because, on the mechanical level of straight thought-wave transmission and reception, the mind of a Sensitive was a much better sender than receiver, the earphone Rand used was necessary to rapid and accurate exchange. But Rand was able to address his questions to the miniaturized electronic brain mentally.

Jon Rand was officially classified as a Sensitive. The fact had been discovered when he was still in college by a recruitment team of the Syndicate—then an obscure young organization of which he had heard only vague rumors. At that time testing one's response to PSI-40 had progressed far beyond the stage of college pranks and Hollywood fads, but it was still voluntary. The test did not become law until several years later, when the use of the drug had become so widespread that lobbyists for the Mental Freedom Syndicate were able to convince Congress that universal testing was necessary to the health and welfare of the nation. The law, which met little effective opposition, made the test at Syndicate clinics all across the country compulsory for every man, woman, and child over ten. The MFS was genuinely interested in analyzing the response of users to screen out the mentally disturbed or psychotics who could actually be harmed by use of the drug. A more significant function of the clinics, from the point of view of the Syndicate's directors, was to discover those whose untapped levels of consciousness were awakened to a high degree by PSI-40; Sensitives.

And, once in a very great while, a Special.

The difference between Sensitive and Special, Rand knew, was one of degree. But the difference between a trickle of water and the Mississippi was similarly a matter of degree. Rand was not vain enough to envy the Syndicate's directors—the only true Specials he had personally encountered, and he had some doubt that any others existed in spite of recurrent rumors. His more limited extrasensory powers as a Sensitive were still an unending source of wonder and challenge. The only real complaint he ever had about his reactions to PSI-40 concerned the violent headaches, which he had never quite been able to accept simply as an occupational hazard.

Rand had volunteered to take the recruiters' tests. Youth's natural curiosity wouldn't have let him pass the chance by. Like all users, he had found new vistas of sensory and mystical experience, though a minimum of the latter, perhaps because of his temperament. Unlike most, he had taken a vital step beyond. He was, the recruiters told him after completing the tests, a Sensitive. The Syndicate could use him.

It was said that the Syndicate had never failed to recruit a Sensitive it wanted—and it wanted them all. It was also said—rumors again, cropping up often in Anti propaganda—that the few who refused had a way of disappearing. Rand gave little credence to the rumors. The lures the Syndicate offered were irresistible: high bonuses, prestige, outlandish salaries and company benefits ranging from free luxury housing to extended paid vacations, and, most of all, the excitement of opening a new door to discovery and human achievement for which the Syndicate owned the only key.

Rand had started with the Security branch of the organization, headed then as now by Loren Garrett. He had moved up in rank and stature as the Syndicate grew into a giant. If he had one area of special pride, it was the fact that in his fifteen years as an agent he had never failed a Security assignment.

But he was aware, as he gazed pensively out of the stratojet's window and listened to a review of Anti activities in Baja and southern California in recent months, that those fifteen years counted as nothing against the challenge he now faced. Abruptly he cut off the recorder's recitation and began to ask questions.

"That boy in Idaho—what was his name?"

"Kemp Johnson."

"How did he escape?"

"Commandeered animal transportation."

"Animal? What kind?"

"Deer."

"Deer?" Rand felt both surprise and amused appreciation. The boy had been ten years old. *"Who were the agents who apprehended the father and let the boy escape?"*

There was a fractional delay in the computer's response. Then it said, "Regret information not included."

The computers, Rand reflected, always sounded somewhat pompous, except for the habitual omission of the article. For a moment Rand was silent, speculative. Could Loren Garrett have a personal motive, beyond the con-

30

flict among the directors, for wanting Kemp Johnson caught? Only Garrett could have had the names of the original agents on the case deleted from the record. If he had been leading the original attack force—which seemed more likely the longer Rand thought about it— he could be held double responsible for any damage the boy, now a young man, caused. If indeed the Special in Baja and Johnson were the same.

"What evidence links Johnson to the Special operating in Baja?"

"Direct evidence not on file."

"There must be reasons why the suspicion exists."

"Direct evidence not—"

"All right!" Direct evidence wasn't really needed, Rand supposed. Garrett had said the Johnson case was the only one currently "open" in Security files which involved a suspected Special. *"The other two agents must have filed preliminary reports of their investigations before they disappeared,"* he addressed the computer-recorder. *"I'd like to hear those reports."*

"Complete?"

"A summary will do. If I want specific information, I'll interrupt."

The machine complied. The first agent assigned to the case had taken the obvious tactic of trying to trace Kemp Johnson's movements over the years following his escape through a review of the early, fruitless search and the occasional items of information added to the file. The boy had been tracked across Oregon to the coast, where he disappeared completely. There was scant information about an incident in a small university town north of San Francisco four years later involving a red-headed boy of "about fifteen." Kemp Johnson was variously reported as having had red, black and blond hair. The youth had seemingly saved a swimmer, a student at the university, by mysteriously controlling an attacking shark. A parallel incident several years later, further down the California coastline in Monterey, had been witnessed by a Syndicate agent, a Sensitive stationed at the local MFS clinic. The agent had not been physically present, but he had been less than a mile away. His mental witnessing had made a prompt investigation possible.

"I'd like to hear the details on that one," Rand interrupted.

"Agent's report follows," the machine answered laconically, and there was a barely perceptible pause before the eye-witness's recorded account was pulled from the bank of information. "I was in my office when the first impulse reached me," the record of the account began in the agent's own words. "I'd taken PSI-40 just a few hours before, so I was in a particularly receptive state. Even so, I was astonished by the strength of the communication, especially since it wasn't directed at me. It was, at first, a blinding stab of alarm and shared fear, followed instantaneously by a vivid picture, as if viewed through a window directly overlooking a park. I recognized the scene at once—a public park not far from my office. A child, a little girl of four or five years of age—later established as four—had climbed through a wire fence separating the park from a VTOL pad, for vertical takeoff and landing craft and she was running across the cement strip directly under a descending VTOL. The pilot obviously could not see her directly under him, and the child froze in panic when she saw and heard the VTOL.

"All of this was immediately clear to me as if I had been physically present. The sender, in the concern he felt for the child, made no attempt to control or shield his reaction. His intervention was spontaneous and, in the circumstances, brilliant. He sent out a powerful signal—so strong that I was jolted by it almost a mile away—focused on the instrument panel of the VTOL. I later learned from the aircraft's pilot that standard red warning lights lit up all over his panel. He couldn't know the course, of course, but he automatically stopped the plane where it was and held it stationary in the air—about six feet above the landing strip. By this time the ground crew in the control building had seen the danger and were trying to signal him. Their signals were jammed by strong static and they never got through—until one mechanic had the sense to run across the pad and scoop up the girl. As soon as the child was safe, the interference with the plane's instrumentation ceased.

"I raced to the scene, arriving there less than three minutes after the incident occurred. A crowd had already gathered, and there was a great deal of excitement and confusion, which undoubtedly enabled the stranger to escape. I was able to initiate an immediate search, calling on my entire staff of agents, but without success. Extensive questioning called attention to a youth, a boy of seventeen or eighteen described only as slender and taller then average, with either brown or black hair cut short, who had been in the park near the scene. One woman testified with angry indignation that the youth had been closer to the child than anyone else when she ran onto the VTOL pad, but he had stood motionless, making no attempt to save her.

"It was the conclusion of our investigation that this boy had in fact saved the child's life by interfering with the aircraft's electrical system, that he had left the scene the moment the danger to the girl was over to avoid our investigation, and that he was unquestionably, to judge from the ingenuity and the power of his mind, a Special."

At the conclusion of the eye-witness account Rand was silent, thoughtfully analyzing what he had learned. He was intrigued by the fact that Kemp Johnson—if he was the strange Special in each instance—had managed to remain undetected all these years, betraying himself only on rare occasions when his unusual mental power was needed to save another's life. The knowledge was revealing—and potentially valuable.

"Was the first agent able to turn up any similar incidents?" he questioned the computer.

The answer was negative. The agent's report traced a youth who might have been Kemp Johnson to Santa Barbara, where he had lived briefly, and from there to Los Angeles, where he had taken a menial job as a hospital orderly on the campus of the University of California at Los Angeles.

"Where he had access to the university library and its laboratories," Rand mused.

"Information not available," the computer promptly replied.

With a smile Rand thought, *"Continue with the first agent's report."*

What followed was brief. The agent had lost the young man's trail in Los Angeles, and had then proceeded to Baja California for direct investigation of the more recent rumors of a Special working with the local Antis, masterminding a series of drug thefts and acts of sabotage, as well as an incendiary campaign of propaganda. After the agent had landed on the Gulf coast, he had never been seen or heard from again.

The last piece of information made Rand grunt aloud, and he sensed that the blonde in the seat beside him glanced his way. When he turned, her head was resting against the seat back, her eyes closed. Their lids were colored a delicate blue shade to complement her eyes. In repose her features seemed less bold, and her full mouth was no less inviting.

Rand turned back to the window. *"What about the second agent's report?"* he asked.

"Preliminary report filed one week after agent's arrival in Baja," the computer informed him. "Agent had made contact with local Anti organization and was preparing to join in its activities. Referred to important leader known only by name 'Killjoy.' No details available. Agent promised supplementary report within week. No report submitted."

"That was all?" Rand demanded.

"Investigation failed to reveal agent," the computer answered with objective indifference.

Slowly Rand removed the earplug and turned off the computer-recorder. He had enough to think about for now. While he had learned little about the second agent, the first one had been revealed as skilled, intelligent and thorough. It was hard to believe that such a man could have been caught by surprise. And Kemp Johnson —again the qualification had to be made about identity —had acted with disturbing swiftness once the agent reached Baja.

Killjoy. A trace of a smile touched Rand's lips. K-J for Kemp Johnson? It seemed like a good guess. And the name was aptly chosen for an enemy of the Mental Freedom Syndicate, the bringer of a new kind of joy to millions. Rand reflected that he was learning more about his quarry. Kemp Johnson, or Killjoy, was tall and slender; he had a highly developed humanitarian sense, which did not appear to extend to MFS agents; he had an agile, clever mind, quite apart from prodigious extrasensory powers, and he had a sense of humor.

And to all these facts must be added another quite stunning in its implications. Johnson had twice used the powers of a Special at times when he could not have anticipated them. Unless Rand assumed that Johnson was almost always under the influence of PSI-40—which seemed only remotely possible—or, even more unlikely, unless Rand accepted the coincidence that on these two occasions Johnson had just happened to have taken his drug, then the extraordinary possibility existed that he retained the expanded consciousness awakened by PSI-40 for long periods of time. Or, indeed, was in effect always an active Special.

Rand himself was aware of residual effects of the drug even when he had been off it for days or even weeks. Even without its chemical stimulus, his mind was now capable of insights beyond the sensory—the result, he supposed, of years during which the brain's dormant potential had been tapped, until the exceptional had, in small ways at least, become normal. But the full powers of a Sensitive or a Special invariably declined without recourse to the drug. And the responses Kemp Johnson had demonstrated were far from rudimentary.

Deliberately Rand tucked this and the other information he had absorbed away in his mind, where his subconscious could work it over for any important detail he might have overlooked or conclusion he might have failed to draw. He stood, stretched, and carefully stepped around his sleeping fellow passenger into the aisle. Taina Erickson did not stir.

The lounge was crowded. Rand stepped into a restroom and locked the door. He extracted one tiny pill from the container hidden behind his belt buckle and washed it down with a half cup of water. The break-tab he had eaten in New York would have little or no effect on the action of PSI-40. By the time the plane landed in Baja, Rand would be ready.

He lingered awhile in the lounge, watching the rainbow-hued cloud formations far below with absorbed interest, as if he had not a care in the world. When he returned to his seat the stratojet had begun the long descent which would bring it down at Baja. Taina Erickson was sitting up, her cool blue eyes showing no hint of sleepiness. Rand grinned at her.

"Friends again?"

"Of course."

"Can I sell you any drugs from my sample case?"

She smiled back. "I wonder what it is you really have in your sample case, Mr. Rand."

Rand shook his head, still grinning, wondering again if there was more to her than met the eye—although what he could see was certainly worth investigating in itself.

"I'll never tell. Then I'd cease to be a fascinating enigma."

Taina Erickson laughed outright. "Whatever it is you do, Mr. Rand, I imagine you're rather good at it."

Her blue eyes were warm and alive, her full lips parted, her tawny throat an inviting gateway. She was flirting with him, Rand thought. The perception made him wary. Attractive women did not generally find him that attractive. He was too roughly hewn from the block for that. Perhaps the challenge of their earlier verbal duel had piqued her interest. Perhaps it was only the spoiled playgirl's interest in anything new. But it was worth remembering that she had deliberately chosen the seat beside his at the beginning of the flight. . . .

The plane plunged into clouds, seemed momentarily lost suspended in a world drifting without moorings, then burst into the glittering sunlight of the denser atmosphere below. To the south, flat like a painting, were the china-blue waters of the gulf. Ahead, on a descending line along which the plane raced like a toy hurtling down a wire, were the lush green playgrounds of Baja, America's Riviera.

"We're both going to be in Baja for a while," Rand said. "If I'm as good at my business as you say, maybe we'll have time to tilt sailboats."

"And you'll open your sample case?"

"Why not?"

The woman regarded him steadily. "I'll be in La Luz. I've a cottage at the Del Pacifico," she said. "If you'll promise to rescue me from chasing rainbows, Mr. Rand, you might find me there."

"You can count on it," Rand promised.

For some reason, just then, he remembered his adversary's chosen alias: Killjoy.

Chapter Three

It was not until the mid-1980's that the dream of large-scale and relatively low-cost conversion of salt water became a reality. Though complex installations were required, the cost per ton of water was very low. Valuable years of development were lost during the scare times before and after the war-that-didn't-happen, the aborted move of the Eastern powers against ARFGA, that "strange bedfellow" alliance of Anglo-Russo-Franco-German-American forces. And in the years that followed the big salt-water conversion projects gradually were afflicted by the same peculiar national lethargy which consistently slowed, delayed and put off the moon-base and Mars landing projects. Anti propagandists were quick to blame the Mental Freedom Syndicate and what they liked to call the "moral sabotage" involved in the widespread dependence on PSI-40, although in fact there were always practical reasons for the delays.

Whatever the reason, or reasons, the only real showcase for salt-water conversion in the Americas in 1993 was Baja California. Here a combined Mexican-American project had resulted in the Rivera Pump. That single installation in less than a decade had converted almost a hundred miles of mountainous coastal desert into a lush resort paradise. Contained by the inland range of lava mountains, the resort development stretched along the Gulf of California coastline from Santa Rosalia in the north, about halfway down the peninsula, almost to the coastal plain of Loreto, where the huge air terminal had been built. The center of this vast complex was Mulege, twenty-five miles north of the airport, and only a five-hour drive from San Diego along the Autocon, the glistening new superhighway with its automatic controls, which sliced across the arid peninsula to Santa Rosalia at the northern perimeter of the green oasis.

Aside from the deep blue of the gulf and the irrigation rivers, contrasting with the brilliant greenery of forests of fan and date palms, the arresting feature of the Baja development from the air, as Jon Rand's stratojet swung in a wide circle for a landing, was the shining newness of everything, from the huge private villas along the waterfront of Conception Bay to the towering aluminum cubes of hotels to the multi-colored checkerboard of lower-income housing farther inland.

American genius, Rand reflected, was demonstrated in the great hotels, models of pure efficiency. But it was the Mexican genius to turn the whole Baja development into a vast and colorful mural.

He had a final word with Taina Erickson when he lifted

her small Moroccan leather bag from the rack above their seats and offered to carry it off the plane.

"I can manage, thank you," she said. "It's not heavy."

"Women," Rand suggested, "are becoming too independent."

She stared at him with an odd intensity, as if she were trying to understand something that puzzled her. Then she smiled. "We only act that way. Like you, Mr. Rand, we're not really all we seem."

"A lot of people aren't."

"You look like a—a boxer, or a football player."

"I've done a little of both."

"You talk like an intellectual—"

"I read a lot."

"—and you have the manners of a diplomat."

"There you've got me." Rand laughed. "I've never been called diplomatic before."

Passengers had been pushing along the aisle toward the exit, and at last the way was clear. Stepping into the aisle, the blonde glanced back once more. "You'll remember where to find me? Or do you record everything on that little machine of yours?"

Startled, Rand managed to mask his reaction. "Business I record," he said. "Pleasure I remember."

Her blue eyes were amused as she turned away. Following the lithe figure down the aisle, Rand reflected that he hadn't been very prudent. His own questions to the computer-recorder had been too low-pitched, he was sure, for even a powerful Sensitive to catch them. But even at low intensity the machine's answers might have been audible to an acute listener.

Here was a factor he hadn't really faced before. In all his work Rand had encountered only one Sensitive outside the Mental Freedom Syndicate's organization—and that man had been a defector. Moreover, he had been identified, so there hadn't been any problem of dealing with unknown talents. Now a different situation existed—one which Loren Garrett and the Board of Directors hadn't emphasized. Kemp Johnson knew how to reproduce PSI-40. He didn't need black-market or stolen drugs, neither of which were very easily obtained under the Syndicate's tight security. Seventeen years had passed since the boy first escaped with his secret knowledge. In those years how many others might he have tested with his own drugs, searching for an ally? And how many might he have found with the responsiveness of a Sensitive—or even a Special?

Not that Taina Erickson was likely to be one of them. She had probably noticed Rand's use of the earphone, or seen him reach into his breastpocket to start the recorder. But he had been careless. His two predecessors must have made similar mistakes—perhaps only one small slip, one moment's lack of caution. And they had disappeared.

Near the exit Rand was briefly delayed by a passenger who, with heavy hand and voice, was trying to cajole the stewardess into meeting him in town. By the time Rand squeezed past, Taina Erickson had already caught one of the chair cars which moved on a continuous belt from the landing strips to the main terminal building. Rand hopped onto the next car.

He felt the sudden harsh impact of the white tropical sun, the stimulation of warm air stirring against his face, the assault upon all his senses of the naked sights and sounds and smells. The car's retractable top was open. During the month between assignments, living in the Syndicate's New York headquarters, Rand had been aware of winter's cold and snow only as pictures framed in assorted windows. It was never necessary to leave the vast complex of connected buildings for any need. If the desire had been there, the city's network of tunnels and covered esplanades allowed one to move almost anywhere coatless and protected in a sterile atmosphere of constant temperature. So there was something raw and strangely exhilarating about the abrupt plunge onto Baja's warm, pulsing reality, an effect enhanced by the powerful chemical Rand had swallowed.

When he reached the terminal, his blonde seat companion had already disappeared among the crowds of incoming and outgoing tourists swarming through the domed lobby. Rand checked in at the baggage counter, feeding his ticket and the number of his hotel in Mulege to the computer to insure automatic delivery of his one suitcase. Then he stepped into a telephone booth and dialed the unlisted number of the local MFS Security headquarters —which masqueraded as a boat rental to facilitate the easy importation of drugs. Rand depressed the button which prevented transmission of his picture over the circuit. Except in extreme emergency, his standing orders were not to reveal his personal identity even to fellow Security officers.

"02-107," he identified himself to the automatic answering service. "Proceeding from the airport to Mulege. Will report arrival at hotel and subsequent moves at six-hour intervals."

He hung up without waiting for a reply. The frequent reports would be a nuisance, but Garrett had been emphatic. "We have to follow you every step of the way," he had said. "If anything does happen, we've got to know when and where, and any circumstances that might indicate how."

There was a brief delay while Rand's visa and papers were checked by Mexican customs officials. The inspection was cursory, accompanied by the smiling suggestion that these formalities were not important among friends, especially an important American businessman like Mr. Jon Rand, and would he please forgive any inconvenience. The important American businessman was affably unconcerned, and asked, as one friend to another, what was the most efficient means of transport to his hotel in Mulege. The officer, a Lieutenant Juan Huerara, drew his new friend aside and hinted darkly about the safety of the ancient helicopters commuting from the air terminal to the resort centers. On the other hand, he had a nephew, an excellent driver, who could take Mr. Rand safely to his hotel in a manually operated automobile, traveling with great speed and comfort, or, if desired, with a highly diverting tour along the way of Baja's most interesting attractions. In keeping with the leisurely pace of the Baja development, and its unique character, manual vehicles only were allowed on the roads.

Such anachronisms, the lieutenant suggested, had a certain antique charm which he was sure Mr. Rand would appreciate. Mr. Rand did, and moments later he was sitting beside the driver of a front-engined 1976 model Ford, gasoline-powered and driver-controlled. He had not been in a nonautomatic car for at least five years, and he entered it with some misgivings, but it was sometimes useful in a strange territory to establish a friendly relationship with a law-enforcement officer possessed of a large family.

"I am Miguel Huerara," Rand's youthful driver announced with a touch of pride. "But you are American, so you will call me Mike."

With a grin Rand agreed that he would. Mike was as slim and graceful as a whippet. Scarcely twenty, he had a child's dark eyes in a thin brown face. There was pride in his manner, in the pencil-thin line of his moustache, in the quick flash of his smile, in the casual ease with which he steered his automobile through the maze of the parking area to the main gates. The quality, Rand thought, sat well on the youth's thin shoulders.

The car shot toward the exit across the glaring pavement and skidded to a stop with a vigorous slamming of brakes. "You see, there is no worry," Mike said. "The brakes are very good."

"I'm glad of that," Rand muttered.

There were several exit gates but only two were open— ground traffic leaving the terminal was not heavy, most travelers appearing to prefer the cumbersome-looking helicopters. Rand had seen no VTOL's anywhere, and he guessed that these modern aircraft were considered out of keeping with the Baja development's old-fashioned charm. After a brief delay a guard appeared from the nearest office.

"Salud!" Miguel Huerara called. "Where is my good friend Corporal Gonzalez?"

"He is not well."

"But I saw him when I came!" Mike protested. "That was but an hour ago!"

"He had to leave." The guard's tone was impatient. He was standing close to the car on the driver's side, and Rand could not see his face. "You have your operator's license?"

"Surely that is not needed," Mike argued. "I am Miguel Huerara, and I come this way—"

"Your license, please!"

The dark eyes rolled comically as Mike showed Rand his opinion of overly official guards. But he produced his driver's license and vehicle authorization with a flourish. The guard grunted and fumbled them back to him. Then he insisted on seeing Rand's visa. Rand handed it across, and Miguel Huerara displayed it proudly, as if he shared with Rand this legal triumph over the obstructive authorities. Waving them on, the guard showed his back as Mike accelerated with a defiant roar.

The old car shot like a catapult across the hot, flat plain of pavement surrounding the air terminal. Rand had glimpses of brown, barren hills to the west and a wink of sunlit water from the blue gulf to the east. Ahead, as sharply defined as a hedge, though a mile or two away, a wall of tall date palms fringed the southerly end of the huge green oasis fed by the Rivera Pump. Moments later the road dipped through a hole in this wall into a sparkling fretwork of sunlight and shadow.

"You have not been to Baja before, Mr. Rand?" Mike asked.

"Never had time."

"Then you must let me show it to you. It is beautiful thing, Mr. Rand, to see what a little water will do."

"And a little money."

"But of course! In my country, water and money are very close cousins. It is not only the *turistas* who bring money to Baja. It is also the things that grow where there is good water."

Rand settled back in his seat. In spite of the car's reckless speed, he felt no misgivings. Mike's hands caressed the wheel with the light, sure touch of an expert lover. The automobile was surely compliant to his whims. And Rand guessed that the youth knew a great deal of what went on in his beloved Baja. A scenic tour might prove valuable.

The road Mike followed left the main highway and wound up among the foothills on the inland side of the Baja development. As the road climbed, broader vistas opened up. Near the gulf's edge and along the shores of the inland waterways were the concrete and aluminum shells of the popular resorts. The green belt, contained by the hills and the bleak, flat-topped lava mountains to the west, sometimes narrowed to a strip only a few miles wide, then opened into broad fertile valleys reaching twenty or thirty miles inland. Here in the valleys were the new fields ripe with date palms, bananas, and mangoes, and the citrus forests. As the car sped north there were the multicolored housing developments, laid out neatly like a ceramic design, and, closer to the resort complex at Mulege, the great waterfront estates and the larger hotels. In the wash of sunlight it was all color and quiet and beauty. But at a distance, Rand thought, so was a jungle.

"Is it not beautiful?" Mike Huerara asked.

"It's beautiful," Rand agreed. Then, with a grin, "Don't you have anything ugly to show me at all? No troubles?"

Mike shrugged. "Where there are many people, there are many troubles."

"What about these Anti demonstrations—I've heard about them down here."

Mike threw up both his hands, and for a moment the ancient car raced along on its own. The quick brown hands caught the wheel just at the beginning of a steep curve near the crest of a hill. "They do not like the drug," Mike said with disgust. "Who can understand such people?"

"You have used PSI-40?"

"Ah! The things that I have seen—you would not believe them, Mr. Rand. But maybe you know. To be against it is like being blind to the sunrise, or ready to spit on a beautiful woman. You understand, I do not take the drug all the time, only when I do not work."

"Why?"

The youth seemed surprised. "One does not work when he has taken the drug, Mr. Rand. One does not wish to work—it is such a beautiful thing."

Rand chewed the comment thoughtfully. It was easy to forget that he was unlike others in his response to PSI-40, which stimulated his activity. The stultifying effect of the drug was a favorite argument of the Antis, who claimed that the overuse of PSI-40 sapped moral fiber, weakened the will, destroyed ambition.

"Have you heard anything about a strange man among the Antis here in Baja—a man of unusual power?"

There was no answer. Rand glanced at Miguel Huerara. The youth was staring ahead fixedly, his hands gripping the wheel so tightly that the muscles corded along his forearms. Rand shot a quick glance ahead. The car sped along a winding stretch of road well up in the hills with precipitous drops on the right toward a carpet of citrus trees far below. The road demanded a skilled driver to maneuver it at the old Ford's speed, but Mike had been handling similar terrain with careless ease. Rand turned—

A vivid image exploded in his mind. Indistinguishable from the reality his eyes recorded, the mental picture was a glimpse of the Ford in mid-air, turning end over end in a long roll, easily, as if in slow motion, then plummeting downward, racing to meet the ground . . .

"Mr. Rand!"

"What's wrong?"

Mike's throat muscles worked. "Mr. Rand—"

The car's tires squealed as Mike fought it around a curve. Rand sensed that their speed had sharply increased. "Take it easy, Mike—slow down!"

Drops of sweat quivered on the youth's forehead, and now Rand saw the tension of pain compressing Mike's drawn lips and knotting his jaw. Hard, tight fists bunched on the steering wheel. The car lurched through another curve, leaning far over, tires howling. As Rand grabbed at the wheel and the car wobbled back to the center of the highway, he saw the blur of another vehicle briefly visible at the top of a rise ahead. It vanished, like frames cut from a film. The old Ford raced toward a closer hump of the land, drifting inexorably toward the wrong side of the road. Mike's whole body was as rigid as steel. He had been drugged. And Rand knew that no physical force would break that frozen grip on the wheel or wrench the locked foot free of the accelerator.

With a quick, almost reflex action Rand probed the youth's mind. There was a sense of confusion and terror, but that was all. If Mike had been paralyzed by fear, Rand might have been able to counteract it. But the poison in Miguel Huerara's blood stream was immune to any command.

With harsh authority Rand used hypnosis to knock the young driver out. The rigid hold on the wheel did not break. Rand's hand stabbed out at the ignition key. As the engine died there was a sudden, breathless hush, broken by the buffeting wind and screaming tires. Rand threw the whole weight of his body against the wheel. It yielded an inch. The car leaned farther to the left, edging close to the wrong side of the road. There was no time to try to bring it back to the right. The Ford seemed to bound over a rise. In that moment Rand glimpsed an approaching car plunging toward him, while trees and bushes and a brown shoulder of land hurtled past the windows. Then the Ford's left front wheel hit dirt at the road's edge. Gravel spat off the car's undercarriage. The black shape of the other car shot past on the right. The impact of air from its passage just inches away struck the Ford a physical blow. The car drifted through a suspended moment, slammed into something solid, and entered a long slow skid as it went completely off the road.

Suddenly nothing was visible through the windshield but a flying branch and a broad sheet of blue sky. The car left the ground as a wide ditch opened out beneath it. The nose dipped and the rear end began to climb. Slowly, like a dancer in a classic patterned movement, the car turned end over end in a graceful, floating somersault.

In that breathless, terrible moment of free fall, duplicating the clairvoyant image which had warned Rand, as two tons of metal and glass and plastic plunged toward destruction, there was time for him to feel surprise that an unknown enemy could strike so quickly and successfully, time to feel pity for the innocent behind the wheel, time even for the beginning of self-disgust and anger at being trapped so easily in a situation where his mental powers were useless. He felt blows against his chest and belly, and knew that the automatic safety braces had been activated, pinning him in his seat. At the same time jets of foam sprayed windshield and instrument panel and doors and ceiling with a thin but precious cushion. At the last second Rand willed himself to go completely limp.

The collision came—a violent impact of yielding metal and unyielding earth, a concussion that seemed to drive Rand's bones into each other, that rattled his brain and loosened his teeth. He felt like a doll made of separate fragile parts, all held loosely together by elastic string. And here and there the elastic seemed to snap . . .

But, incredibly, the Ford had rolled in a full circle, landing like a cat on all fours, flattening out like a cat to cushion the shock, instantly springing up again in another leap. With that second jump much of its force had been spent, and the illusion of a living thing changed. Cumbersome and out of control, with tires burst and springs broken and rods snapped like twigs, the clumsy weight slammed against the side of the ditch and bounced into a sideways roll. The roof crumpled at a glancing blow. A door exploded off its hinges, and one wheel shot free to skitter along the bottom of the ditch.

Abruptly it was over. The car lay on its side, rocked feebly, twitched once, and was still. Dust and leaves and debris filtered down upon it. The air smelled of oil and gasoline and burnt rubber. The sudden crash of silence somehow gave a frightening emphasis to the rending, tearing violence which had come and gone so quickly.

Inside the car Jon Rand lay pinned against the door on

the bottom side, stunned and battered and aching, half smothered by Miguel Huerara's body which sprawled on top of him, and dazedly astonished to find himself still alive. On the last roll the separate motor controlling the safety devices had been smashed. The clouds of foam had provided some protection, but both Rand and the young Mexican had been thrown about brutally.

"Mike?" Rand's voice was a kind of croak. Thickening silence answered him. More sharply Rand repeated, "Mike? You all right?"

But even as he spoke he knew there would be no answer. There was no filter of panic to screen the youth's mind against Rand's sensitive probing. Miguel Huerara's brain was a cavern of darkness deeper than sleep. There were no lights winking in even the remotest corners.

Rand tested his free arm. There was a sharp pain in his shoulder, but he could move it. His hand fumbled over the boy's crumpled form and ripped open his shirt. But even as he felt for a heartbeat, Rand knew the futility of the gesture.

He lay back. With an effort of concentration he seemed to become detached from his own body, able to hover over the demolished car, looking down upon the tangled bodies at the bottom of the wreckage. At the same time another part of his mind checked and tested the intricate labyrinth of nerves in his body for evidence of damage. He was whole. Nothing broken. Bruises, muscle strains, a cut in his right shoulder. The safety braces and the layer of foam had saved him. They should have saved Mike Huerara, too, but Rand had a hunch the youth had been killed by whatever drug it was that had paralyzed him at the wheel.

His assessment completed, Rand edged from under the boy's inert weight, taking a gentle care with the body. The car rocked on its side as Rand hauled himself free. It seemed like an hour since he had first seen Mike's panic, though in fact it had been no more than two or three minutes. Rand sensed the return of the other car even before the sound of its engine broke the unnatural silence. By that time Rand was climbing through the opening where the left door had been. He lowered himself to the ground and, on trembling legs, scuttled up an incline and dropped behind some bushes. On the road the returning car pulled up and a door slammed. As Rand crawled away, impervious to the pain in his battered body, excited voices broke out. "The crazy fool!" one cried. "He almost got us, too!"

Awed, another voice declared, "Nobody could have come out of that alive!"

Grimly Jon Rand crawled on, moving away from the voices. It must have looked like a good bet, he thought. But you could never be sure about murder by accident. Too many things could go wrong. Whoever had drugged Miguel Huerara had made *his* first mistake.

Chapter Four

Except for one long bank of windows on the waterfront side, overlooking the dark blue midnight mirror of Conception Bay, the huge house was dark. Rand had not been sure that Garth Taylor would be there, although he had guessed that the old man would not linger in Washington for the celebrations after the inauguration ceremony. A sick or wounded man, like any other animal, took himself home as soon as he could. The early evening news telecast had confirmed Rand's hunch, carrying brief footage of Taylor's arrival at the airport in Loreto.

Rand waited for darkness, but he gave no serious consideration to trying to scale the high fence protecting the land boundaries of the estate. It would be electrified, for one thing, and the grounds beyond would be too well patrolled. The old man would just have to ask him in, whether he liked it or not.

There was an electronic sentry at the main gate. Rand allowed his fingerprints to be scanned. Within seconds a voice grated from a speaker built into one of the gate pillars. "State your business, Mr. Rand."

"I have to see Mr. Taylor."

"Mr. Taylor is not receiving visitors at this hour."

"It isn't a social call."

"I'm sorry—"

"Don't be!" Rand snapped. "Just tell Taylor I have to see him."

"How do you know he's here?" the voice demanded testily.

"You wouldn't be wasting your time if he weren't. Just give him my message. If you don't, he'll hear about it from New York within half an hour."

The threat was a bluff. If Rand had been willing to call New York for help, he wouldn't have been coming to Taylor at all. But the guard couldn't know that.

"Wait there," the voice over the speaker said curtly.

Rand waited. He didn't have much choice. Either Taylor helped him or his usefulness as a Syndicate agent in Baja was at best badly curtailed. The same evening telecast which Rand had picked up on his wrist-screen, confirming Taylor's arrival from Washington, had carried another local story. Authorities were investigating unusual circumstances in the death of one Miguel Huerara in an automobile accident that morning. Rand knew what the unusual circumstances meant. An autopsy had revealed the presence of a poison, perhaps confirming it as the killer. A search was being conducted for an American believed to have been a passenger in the car at the time of the accident.

"Mr. Rand?"

"I'm still here."

"Mr. Taylor will see you."

The voice over the speaker wasn't any friendlier, but there was more respect in it. A lock clicked open and the gate swung inward. Rand walked through it and along a winding path beneath a canopy of palms. He heard a low growl and stopped short, cool fingers caressing the nape of his neck. But there was a guard at the end of the leash restraining a big snarling Dane. Rand walked on.

A butler opened the front door while Rand was crossing the wide veranda. An unhappy-looking male secretary with a hastily donned coat was waiting near the foot of the escalator in the foyer, along with a surly guard. Rand ignored the guard. "Where's Mr. Taylor?" he asked the secretary.

"He will see you in his sitting room. Really, Mr. Rand, this is most unusual. You must realize that Mr. Taylor is quite fatigued from his journey today—"

"I understand," Rand said. "We're all tired. It isn't every day a President gets inaugurated. Suppose you just take me to him."

The secretary stiffened visibly, and the guard looked angrier than ever. Rand knew he was being peevish and bullying, and there was no excuse for it, but the day had done little to sweeten his temper.

"If you'll follow me . . ." The secretary's voice squeaked a little.

They rode up the escalator and followed a wide balcony which overlooked the two-story entrance hall. At the far end double doors opened into a wood-paneled room with a desk and sofa and a pair of oversized wing chairs. It was a big, warm, comfortable room, one wall lined with books, another dominated by a massive stone fireplace. A second pair of doors led into a bedroom facing the bay. Garth Taylor was sitting in one of the wing chairs by the fireplace, although there was no fire.

"Will you be needing me, Mr. Taylor?" the secretary asked doubtfully.

Taylor caught Rand's signal without looking at him. "No," he said. He waited for the doors to close before he pointed toward the other tall chair flanking the fireplace. "Sit down, Rand. It hasn't taken you long to get into trouble here."

"You've heard?"

"I've heard nothing. I returned from Washington only a few hours ago. But you wouldn't be here if you weren't in trouble."

Rand settled against the high back of the chair and studied the gaunt, white-maned old lion facing him. The room was lit by two oblong light panels, one set in the wall to the right of the desk, the other running the length of the ceiling. Both were set at low. In that softened illumination Taylor looked ten years younger than his seventy-five. The harsh lines and commanding aspect of his features were smoothed out, and even the grim mantrap of a jaw seemed less immovably set. Rand wondered if the effect was all illusion.

"Well?" The authoritative rumble of Taylor's voice had not changed.

"I want the local police pulled off my back," Rand demanded bluntly.

"You don't need me for that. You're Security—you have representatives here. Garrett can throw his weight—"

"I can't go through channels," Rand broke in. Taylor jerked forward in his chair, his eyes flashing. The old man wasn't used to being interrupted. Calmly Rand went on, "I have reason to suspect a Security leak."

Taylor eased back with a grunt of interest. "I think we'd better save some time. I can read you."

Rand nodded. He allowed his mind to open. He thought about the plane ride briefly, although for some reason he diverted his attention from Taina Erickson. He reviewed in detail his arrival, the suggestion by Lieutenant Huerara that he take a car into Mulege, the ride, Mike's drug-induced paralysis and the accident. The full account streamed through Rand's consciousness in a matter of seconds.

"Why did you leave the scene of the accident?" Taylor asked.

"I didn't want to be boxed in. And I didn't want to answer too many questions. It's part of my job not to be noticed. The police are looking for me now, but at least they don't have my picture on the evening newscast. And my Syndicate connection."

Rand knew that, even more than he, Taylor was concerned about unfavorable publicity for the MFS, especially anything that would give credence to Anti charges about the Syndicate's ruthless tactics.

"Your disappearance made the accident seem suspicious—"

"The police are not stupid," Rand said. "They were sure to order an autopsy. As soon as that happened, there was no accident any more—it was murder."

Taylor grunted again. His gaze hardened. "What makes you think there was a Security leak?"

"Mr. Taylor, only five men besides myself knew—or were supposed to know—who I was and why I was coming to Baja. But minutes after I landed I was directed to a car whose driver was drugged before that car left the airport. Someone knew I was coming, and had time to plan the accident. There had to be a leak." Rand leaned forward. His tone was flat. "Either that or one of the five men at that meeting wants me dead."

Taylor scowled. It was a formidable expression, and it was meant to intimidate. "That's a dangerous accusation, Rand."

"Right now it's a speculation, but I can't ignore it. That's why I had to come directly to you for help instead of asking New York." Rand paused reflectively. "The more likely answer is that Johnson has someone planted in the Syndicate—someone close to one of the directors. It could be an assistant in a position to know about last night's meeting, a bodyguard, any number of people. If they guessed why that meeting was held, I suppose it would have been simple enough to follow me to the airport and confirm it." Even to plant someone on the plane, he thought.

"It's Security's job to screen out spies, Rand—your branch's job!"

"We don't exactly get full cooperation from the other branches," Rand retorted. "You must be aware of the rivalry."

"I am. You don't have to couch it in euphemistic terms, either. I'm also aware that your suspicion could be a deliberate attempt to implicate one of the other directors to Garrett's benefit."

Rand shrugged. "You read my thoughts. I don't think you seriously believe I would try to deceive you."

Garth Taylor continued to stare at him. Thoughtfully Rand let his mind go blank. In effect the action erected a mental screen to block his thoughts. Taylor smiled. "I begin to see why you were chosen for this assignment, Mr. Rand. Even though you've bungled it up to now."

"I haven't really got started, Mr. Taylor."

"What do you want of me?"

"Freedom to do my job, that's all—without being hauled in by the police."

"You want immunity."

"I didn't kill Huerara. I want the chance to find out who did."

"That's not your assignment."

"It's connected," Rand said shortly.

"We don't like doing this—interfering with the local authorities. You're supposed to avoid——" Taylor broke off abruptly. A sudden hacking cough made him lean forward in his chair. The coughing spell ended in a dry wheeze. Taylor remained hunched over, as if he were staring at something on the carpet. Rand felt a stab of alarm and started out of his chair.

"Rand!"

The unspoken word—it was not a word as such, but a subtly altered image of himself—exploded in Rand's mind, urgent and forceful. His response was instinctively mental. *"What is it?"*

"Pills—bedroom—table! Act!"

The sharp, successive telepathic images came like cracks of a whip, goading Rand into motion. He raced into the big bedroom. His glance, ignoring the night glitter framed by the window wall, caught the glint of a glass bottle on a nightstand. The table was not the same as the image which had jumped into Rand's mind as Taylor communicated, nor was the bottle the same one he had pictured. Rand tended to receive primary images, which he automatically interpreted in terms of his own memories and thought associations. He strode toward the table. *"Yes!"* Garth Taylor communicated a simple, strong affirmation, and Rand knew that the exact bottle's image in his own mind had been seen by Taylor. Another idea struck. *"Water!"*

There was a decanter of water and a glass on the nightstand. Rand spilled water into the glass and carried it with the pills into the adjoining room. Taylor, bent double, looked up as he approached. Prepared as he was, Rand was shocked by the transformation in the old man's face. His skin was white, drawn like thin paper over the strong bones. Drops of sweat quivered on the high forehead.

Rand poured pills into his palm. Taylor's long, big-knuckled fingers shook as they fumbled for a pill and thrust it into his mouth. Rand had to hold the glass steady while the old man drank. Water dribbled down Taylor's chin. In that moment he was old and pathetic and sick. Conscious of the strength of the telepathic commands which had sent him into the bedroom, Rand found it hard to reconcile that mental vigor and force with the pale, shaken figure in the chair. He felt a kind of awe for what Garth Taylor once had been.

The old man sat more erect and fell against the back of his chair, his hands clutching the arms. The lids were closed over his eyes, reminding Rand of a death mask.

"Hardly a flattering picture," Taylor murmured, his eyes still closed.

Rand started. It was unnerving to have his thoughts read when he made no attempt to project them.

Taylor opened his eyes to stare at Rand. "Difference between you and me," he said, his voice weak but clear, "is Sensitives are good telepaths, but not nearly as perceptive. You had better remember that if you're going to deal with a Special."

"I'll get you some help," Rand said.

"No need. Couldn't do anything for me you haven't done."

"A doctor—?"

Taylor snorted. "They can do nothing! Tried to tell me I had to stop taking PSI-40. That was the best the whole lot of specialists could offer. Might as well kill me and be done with it."

"There's a life without the drug," Rand said slowly.

Taylor's eyes burned in the bony skull. "Not for me! You're not a Special, Rand. And you didn't build the Syndicate from nothing—from just an idea!" His voice trembled with emotion, and the long fingers dug into the arms of the chair. "How long do you think I'd remain in control if I stopped being a Special—if the drug were cut off? I'd lose it all! I'd be nothing, Rand!"

Rand had no answer. It was enough to think of Loren Garrett's reaction.

"Yes, Garrett," Taylor muttered. "The others, too. But that's no business of yours. Your business is Kemp Johnson."

"It can wait."

"No—it can't wait." The old man was silent. He seemed to have regained some of his strength. There was a hint of color in his face. But for a moment his mental control slipped, and Rand had a brief impression of old wounds, painful memories, anger grown cold. "I knew his father," Taylor said. "No matter. He must be stopped, and soon. We can't afford the luxury of being generous right now."

The words seemed to cost Taylor something in effort. Rand said, "You need rest, sir."

Taylor shrugged impatiently. "Don't *you* try to coddle me, Rand! I'll do what you ask—you needn't worry about the police. They won't bother you."

"I need something else . . ."

"What is it?"

"An address."

"You will have it. But after this you're on your own. You understand that?"

"That's fair enough."

"And there's something else." There was a keen, inquisitive alertness in Taylor's eyes as he peered at Rand. He recovered quickly, Rand thought, a sign that he might hang onto his throne longer than Loren Garrett hoped. The old man said: "I won't be involved in any fight between Garrett and Pierce. Unless one of them tries to act while I'm still in command." The deep voice rumbled with warning, like the defiant challenge of an old lion. "Whoever doubts that will find I'm not yet buried!"

"I'm not here to play politics," Rand said mildly.

"See that you don't," Taylor growled. Then he added slowly, "You don't have any doubts, do you?" Not really expecting an answer, he said, "It's all simple for you. The Syndicate pays you well, and you do your job accordingly."

"I'm not sure that I know what—"

"Kemp Johnson and the Antis are on the other side, so you do what you have to. That's the way I've always played it, Rand. I never saw any other way. You start looking at two sides, and you don't fight as hard. That's the thing you'll notice about men at the top. They never pull their punches, and they don't worry about the consequences. They don't let the issue get all fogged up with academic questions about hurt feelings or the social customs we call morality." The old man was not really talking to be heard, but rather listening to himself. Rand stirred uneasily, but Taylor continued, "You'll find Kemp Johnson. I can see that. And you can beat him, too. He's a Special, from all I hear, just like his father. He has powers you don't have, Rand, but you can still beat him. He's like his father in other ways. He won't fight with everything he has . . ."

"Two of our agents have disappeared," Rand murmured.

Taylor tossed his white mane impatiently. "We don't know what happened to them."

"I know what happened to Mike Huerara," Rand pointed out dryly. "I've heard about this Johnson's compassion for his fellow man—his saving a couple of lives at the risk of exposure. But maybe he just did that to test his own powers, to see if he could do it. That Mexican boy was nothing to Johnson. Whoever drugged him didn't care very much about wasting an innocent life to get at me."

Garth Taylor stared at him. "You're right, of course. You wouldn't be worth much in your work if you thought otherwise. I would have picked you myself, Rand, ten

54

years ago. You're the kind we wanted in the Syndicate —the kind we had to have." He sighed. "Perhaps we still do."

The old man slumped wearily in his chair. Parchment lids closed over his eyes, and one bony hand waved. "You have your assignment, Mr. Rand."

It was a dismissal. Rand turned away, frowning. As he did so Taylor called out, "My secretary will get that address for you. Send him in here."

Rand left the room with the disturbed feeling that something important had skirted close to him and slipped away. He almost bumped into the male secretary hovering in the hallway just outside the double doors. Suspecting that the man had heard Taylor's last comment, Rand brushed past the secretary with a curt comment. "I'll wait downstairs."

Scowling, Rand shook himself angrily, trying to dispel a vague feeling of depression. Taylor's belated attack of conscience was no concern of his. The only significant point was that contained in Taylor's simple dismissal. "You have your assignment . . ."

As he started down the stairs, Rand felt the first warning twinge of one of his severe headaches.

Chapter Five

Morning in the Baja development brought a dazzling brightness which made Rand's eyes ache and quickly revived the stabbing pains in his head. The day was already warm when he emerged from the small, drab room he had rented in the waterfront warehouse section south of Mulege, well removed from the plush resorts. He felt lethargic, heavy-limbed, a penalty to be paid for the brief sleep he had gained by taking both sleeping and pain-killing pills the night before. At a busy workmen's cafe near the docks he drank strong black coffee, ignoring curious stares, and stared listlessly at the view through a dirt-streaked window. A strong wind, buffeting down from the inland hills, whipped a scattering of paper and minor debris through the streets, and sprinkled a frosting of white over the blue of the bay. High, disk-shaped clouds scudded across the brilliant sky. The wind ruffled Rand's temper, and his eyes squinted protectively against the glaring beauty outside.

He could save himself both discomfort and valuable time by going to the Syndicate's headquarters in Mulege, where electronically induced quick-sleep would refresh him in minutes and the normal treatment would be given for his headache. But as long as the pain remained endurable, Rand was on his own. Loren Garrett would already be angered by his agent's failure to report regularly as ordered, but Rand had no alternative. The normal channels of communication, even within Security, could no longer be trusted.

Rand did not believe that the man who called himself Killjoy could have built up an extensive national organization so quickly, but, having allied himself with the Antis, Johnson—if he was Killjoy—had their older and well developed organization to call upon. It was naive to think that the Antis would have failed to infiltrate the Syndicate over the years.

Reluctantly Rand forced himself to face the harsh sunlight. Leaving the cafe, he followed a narrow side street leading toward the center of Mulege. The streets were already busy with manually controlled automobiles, a sight which Rand viewed with an uneasy distrust that had little to do with his narrow escape in the accident. Letting human hands and feet and reflexes be solely responsible for the direction, speed and stopping of a speeding vehicle simply left too much to chance for comfort.

With a grimace of acceptance Rand hailed a taxi at the first main thoroughfare he reached. He gave the driver the address Garth Taylor had obtained for him and settled back in the rear seat, closing his eyes. A familiar rainbow-hued canvas was painted against the closed lids. He had taken a PSI-40 pill on arising. From now until the assignment was resolved, one way or another, Rand would be actively a Sensitive.

The route along which he was driven followed the valley of the Rio Mulege inland, leaving the crowded resort and business centers behind. The road wound through newly spawned residential communities which were speedily encroaching on the sprawling date and citrus ranches made fruitful by the converted water brought into the valley from the Rivera Pump. It was ironic, Rand mused, peering at the green valley through half-closed eyelids. For the first time in history there was enough water to grow what this land could produce in abundance. But, loud and clamorous as the demand was for the fruit of the land, the cry for living space in this new paradise was even louder. Housing tracts were cutting into the ranches where palms waved and swayed now in the strong winds. More homes were clambering up the hills. As fast as the water came to make the valleys fertile, the people followed to rip up the shallow-rooted palms with their own destructive gale of needs.

Shifting restlessly in his seat, Rand dismissed the problem. He had his own to deal with, and humanity's contradictory impulses were not his concern. He tried to relax, turning his thoughts inward, but the play of light and shade through the car's moved windows had served to intensify his headache. The blunt, square set of his jaw and the firm line of his mouth showed stubborn determination. He was going to have to live with the pain for a while—he always did when he was on assignment and taking regular dosages of PSI-40, and this time he was deliberately cutting himself off from relief—so he might as well accept it.

The house before which the taxi at last drew up was in a development of small, modest dwellings too new for even the swiftly growing tropical trees and plants to erase the impression of raw, bare, unprotected streets and yards. Rand told the taxi driver to wait. He went up the walk slowly toward the pink stucco house, his eye arrested by the wreath on the front door. It was a house in mourning.

A young, pretty, brown-skinned girl opened the door. Her dark eyes had a faraway look, and Rand had the feeling that he was only something unrecognizable in the foreground. "I'm looking for Lieutenant Juan Huerara," Rand said.

"Come in." The girl invited him with a small impersonal smile. She was in her late teens, close to Miguel Huerara's age. Rand wondered if she was a cousin, a sister, even a girl friend. But there seemed to be no grief in the eyes watching some distant horizon of their own.

"I thought he might not be working today," Rand said. "Or that I might catch him before he left."

"He is inside," the girl murmured.

With a start Rand realized that she was under the influence of one of PSI-40's commercial derivatives. He had been prepared for antagonism, grief, suspicion, anger, but not for this blissful indifference. As he followed the girl down a short hallway, he felt an uncomfortable qualm at what he was about to find.

The body lay in an elaborate, pink-lined coffin at the far end of a small living room, placed just in front of the stone fireplace and almost surrounded by masses of brilliantly colored tropical flowers. Scattered about the room, or moving slowly to and from connecting areas, were roughly a dozen members of what was obviously the Huerara family, ranging in age from a slender boy of twelve or so to an ancient, silver-haired woman in black, who clutched a string of beads in withered hands and smiled serenely as her fingers fluttered from bead to bead and her lips moved soundlessly. One women of middle age cried softly and without cessation. It was a moment before Rand understood that the disturbing element in her sobs was the fact that they were without passion, as remote from normal sorrow as a drug-induced laughing jag is divorced from joy. Both crying and laughing spasms were common reactions to moderate quantities of the psychedelic drugs.

"Isn't he beautiful?" The young girl was still at Rand's side.

Rand stared at the coffin. He found nothing beautiful in Miguel Huerara's stiff, lifeless body. Modern mortuary techniques managed to arrest death's immediate decay, but they could not recapture the aura of youth's vitality, render the mobility of mirth on lips forever fixed in a meaningless curve, nor find the lost pride which had been expressed in Mike Huerara's fingers caressing the steering wheel of his fine automobile. It had not occurred to Rand that the boy might have lived with his uncle, and that he would be intruding on this strangely macabre wake.

"He was your—brother?" Rand asked.

The girl smiled. Her eyes shone with the joy and beauty of her private vision, in which, Rand thought, there would be neither measured time nor constricted space to give death its sharp-edged reality, and the lovely breathing flowers would divert the eye and mind from the unbreathing body in the coffin. "We were betrothed," she murmured.

"I'm sorry."

The girl nodded, but as if she had not heard. She drifted slowly away, still smiling. Rand turned uncomfortably toward the other occupants of the room, arranged in a quiet tableau like other, brown-faced flowers of sorrow. As Rand turned, his eyes met those of Lieutenant Huerara, who rose from a chair before some glass doors in one wall which faced the cool shade of a roofed lanai. The lieutenant stood stiffly erect, confronting Rand with an impassive dignity of bearing which somehow managed to surmount the splendor of his dress uniform.

"You are the American businessman," Huerara said tonelessly.

"Yes. I didn't expect to find your nephew here."

"He lived with us."

"Yes, I see." Rand frowned. He glanced again at the assortment of dark, oddly incurious faces. Few were watching him. They were all under the drug, he thought, wondering at the disturbance this knowledge brought. "Lieutenant, it might be better if we spoke outside."

Huerara's face was unreadable. He had undoubtedly taken the drug himself, but there was no way of gauging its effect on him. With a stiff, brief bow of assent he said, "As you wish."

Rand followed him out onto the shaded lanai. Here the morning's gusty winds slapped at some loose, slatted blinds, and the tropical sun framed the dim, cool rectangle under roof with walls of brilliant light. Rand breathed more easily than in the unnatural calm of the house, even though the brightness sharpened his headache.

"You have powerful friends, Mr. Rand," Huerara said. "The police are no longer searching for you."

"I'm not responsible for Miguel's death, Lieutenant. He didn't die from the crash—I'm sure he was drugged."

Huerara nodded disinterestedly. "An examination was made."

"Then you must have learned how the drug was given," Rand said with quick interest.

"There was a small prick in one finger."

"You can see I didn't do that! Lieutenant—there was a guard when we left the airport. Miguel was expecting someone else at the gate. Wouldn't he have known all the regular guards?"

Lieutenant Huerara frowned. One hand brushed vaguely at his forehead, as if he found it hard to concentrate. "That would seem probable . . ."

"But you can check on that guard! Miguel must have been poisoned then, when they were sure I was in that car—it's the only time anyone came close enough to Miguel to touch him!"

"Perhaps . . ." The problem seemed too difficult for Huerara to cope with.

Rand's impatience threatened to erupt into anger. He knew that Huerara and his family were of a people given to quick, hot passions, in their normal way as volatile in wrath as they were exuberant in celebrating happiness. The lieutenant, in spite of his composure and polite deference, would have made a dangerous adversary. But there was no sign of the bitterness Rand had been ready to meet. An infinitesimal amount of a man-made chemical, upon which the entire structure of the Mental Freedom Syndicate had been built, had thinned and cooled the hot blood of sorrow and rage. For all his allegiance to the Syndicate—and for all his knowledge that he was fortunately different in being one of the few for whom PSI-40 simply tapped the total effective power of the mind—Rand felt frustration and disgust.

"I liked Miguel, Lieutenant," Rand said coldly. "But he was your nephew! He's dead—murdered! Doesn't that mean anything to you?"

Huerara seemed to shrug almost imperceptibly. "You are of the Syndicate, Mr. Rand—I am not a fool. It is to you we owe our release from grief." He smiled—the faint, aloof, reflective smile of one who has escaped the smell and taste and touch of ordinary life into a new world of heightened senses and altered perspectives. "What are life and death, Mr. Rand?" he murmured. "And who is alive? Miguel is in another dimension, laughing at us. Is the sun dead, Mr. Rand, because it sets, and we do not see its fire or feel its warmth?"

Rand groaned aloud. Huerara was one of the philosophical ones, those for whom PSI-40 revealed eternal answers to life's baffling mysteries—answers eternal until the drug wore off. He would be grimly realistic enough in a day, or two days, or whenever he returned to normal.

"Try to remember that guard," Rand insisted. "It probably won't do any good—I'm sure they've covered themselves already. But they must have set up other——"

It was no use. Lieutenant Huerara's attention had been caught by the architecture of light made by the flapping slats of the blinds. Inside the house someone began to laugh, steadily and uncontrollably. A gray-haired woman continued to weep without tears. A girl who had lost her betrothed drifted through the living room, smiling gently at the drooping flowers—were they still breathing for her, pulsating with a strange inner vitality, above the lifeless form of her beloved?

With sudden impatience Jon Rand concentrated sharply on the uniformed man standing with him in the shady lanai. He let his mind open, receptive to the faintest spark of thought. The images which came to him were faint. Bars. A pattern of lines converging upon infinity. Prisms of light. A giant flower, pink petals unfolding, layer upon layer, and in the center a still, crumpled human form. Black bars again, slanting across the idealized pink coffin, which floated in a room without walls. The bars expanded, beating the light into thin slivers. *Those damned blinds!* Rand thought.

He tried to break through the surface layer of Huerara's consciousness. He assembled his own thoughts, the ones he wanted, in their simplest form. Motion, activity always got through most clearly. The first image was of a human finger and a needle plunging into it, pricking the skin, raising a tiny droplet of blood. The second was of a speeding car, a youth laughing at the wheel. The third was the picture he had borrowed from Huerara's own mind—the crumpled, lifeless form of Miguel Huerara. The final thought was only a word: Killjoy! Scowling with effort Rand projected the basic images at Huerara like successive blows.

Huerara's head snapped around. His black eyes narrowed in what might have been pain. His body jerked to military attention. For a moment his drug-induced serenity was shattered. "What does this mean? How can you be sure Miguel died so?"

"I was there!" Rand snapped aloud. "And they were after me, not Miguel. Does that name mean anything to you?"

"What—?"

"Killjoy!"

"I have heard it . . ." Lieutenant Huerara's hand passed feebly across his forehead. The alertness was fading from his eyes. His shoulders slumped. "I do not know."

A quick probe of Huerara's mind revealed only confused images, in which the dazzling structures of light and shade and color opened by PSI-40 were rapidly submerging the harsher thoughts which Rand had projected.

Huerara's eyes stared through Rand. "Death is an illusion," he said, his composure once more undisturbed. "There is only oneness . . ."

Rand's mouth tightened with resignation. His head throbbed painfully. The effort had had little hope of success. Huerara probably knew little of value to Rand beyond what he had already revealed. But at least he would remember later the images Rand had planted in his mind. These might awaken more useful knowledge after Huerara's consciousness was free of the effects of PSI-40.

"I'll be in touch again, Lieutenant," Rand said.

He sought a way to avoid going back through the house. He found a cement walk leading past the side of the building to the street. It was a kind of relief to step from the protected lanai into the harsh reality of sunlight, to feel the heat like a burden across his shoulders, even to accept the reality of pain stabbing through his temples, narrowing his eyes to slits.

It was not the way to face death, he thought sourly, dreaming it away, drowning it in illusion—

Rand faltered. When he walked on again, more slowly and with the scowl deepening on his face, toward the waiting taxi, he was thoughtfully examining an unfamiliar feeling of guilt.

Chapter Six

"Where to, Mister?"

Rand, brooding in silence in the back seat of the taxi with his eyes closed, was a little surprised when the driver spoke. He was a stocky swarthy man with rounded shoulders and a short neck. His long black hair was carefully pomaded, and his fingernails bright with blue lacquer. Without conscious effort Rand had previously recorded the information on the license mounted in a frame on the dashboard, including such details as height and weight— "5 ft. 9 in., 186 lbs.," the card read—as well as color of hair, eyes and complexion. The latter was noted as "Fair," although it would have seemed so only to a darker-skinned Mexican official. His name was Max Gordon.

"Where do you suggest, Max?" Rand asked.

"You a tourist?"

"Yes."

Max shrugged, his neck completely disappearing. "Maybe you wanta see the Pump. Everybody does."

"Not this trip, Max."

Rand saw the quick brown eyes watching him in the rear-view mirror. The eyes flicked away. "You wanta see the sights, maybe you'd like to make a deposit. I mean, if I'm gonna tie my cab up—"

"How much for the day?"

Max had a brief debate with himself. "Thirty bucks."

"Fair enough."

"Plus mileage," Max added quickly.

Rand grinned. "Where are you from, Max?"

The swarthy face in the mirror creased in an answering grin. "You theenk I am from Mexico, senor?"

"New York, I'd guess."

"No less," Max said proudly. "The capital of the U.S. of A."

"It's not the capital."

"Well, in a manner of speaking it is. That's where the Syndicate has its HQ, don't it?"

"What does that have to do with it?" Rand said easily.

"Lissen, who you kiddin', Mister—?"

"Rand."

"Yeah. Well, lemme tell you, Mr. Rand, if them Chinks dropped a bomb on Washington, it wouldn't mean half as much to most people as it would if they bombed them Syndicate buildings in New York. And you know it!"

"Even down here, Max? With all this sunlight and the beaches and sailing and the rest?"

"Huh!" Max snorted. "You think that's what people come down here for? Maybe that's what it was supposed to be, and maybe that's what it was in the beginning, but that ain't what it is now!"

Rand studied the back of the thick, short neck, resisting the temptation to make a quick probe. "How do you feel about it, Max?" he asked.

"What? Lissen, I take the pills—they're the greatest! Who don't?"

"What about the Antis—aren't they active down here?"

The driver spat through the open window. "You Anti, mister?" His tone was markedly less friendly.

"What I am is my business."

For a moment Max was silent. "You're not Anti," he said with finality. "You don't look the type."

"What do they look like?"

"They're kooks. Look, Mister Rand, I can size up a fare. That's my business. Like you—if you don't look like a right guy, a guy who don't wrinkle his nose at a little fun, I keep my mouth shut. I take you where you wanta go and that's it. But you don't look like no bluenose to me."

"Bluenose?"

"Anti. It's an expression."

Rand nodded absently, more in confirmation of a question in his own mind about the general reaction to Anti propaganda than in response to Max's words. The taxi was cruising slowly back toward Mulege, without specific direction. Rand himself had no concrete plan of operation. The assignment did not present itself in any neat pattern. He knew too little of Kemp Johnson, too little of the terrain on which they must meet. But he had learned from experience that a hunted man usually had less patience than the hunter. If you kept probing, searching for soft spots of information, adding up facts, sooner or later the man you were after would make a move. At the moment Rand doubted that Killjoy or anyone else knew where he was or what he was up to. He might as well take advantage of the lull to survey the battleground.

"You know this territory as well as you knew New York, Max?" he asked the driver.

"Better! I went to L.A. right after they outlawed driver cabs in New York. Then they banned us on the Coast, too. When this place opened up, and I heard they was gonna use the bit about keepin' the taxis to make it like the old days, well, I got here fast. Anybody could see it was gonna be a sweet setup for a cabbie. I've watched this place grow, Mister Rand. I know it like my backyard."

"Then suppose you start showing me the garden."

Max grinned. "The works?"

"The works, Max—including the Antis."

Max's eyes flicked at Rand through the rear-view mirror. "You some kinda Federal cop?"

"No."

"Just nosin' around, huh?"

"Like I said, that's my business, Max."

"Sure, Mister Rand—sure." Max paused. "Look, uh, where we're gonna be some of the time, you need any pills? I could maybe swing it for a price."

Rand settled back in his seat. "I'm already up there, Max. Couldn't you tell?"

Rand was vaguely disappointed when the taxi pulled up, shortly after noon, before the entry gates of a high-walled park. A discreet black and gold sign identified the "Baja Sun Club." Max left the cab and huddled with a uniformed attendant at the gate. The taxi driver came back with a triumphant grin.

"Sun worshipers?" Rand inquired dubiously.

"It's one of the most exclusive clubs in Baja!" Max protested, offended. "I didn't have some juice with the guard, you couldn't get in! Look, it's worth a quick go-round, Mr. Rand—take it from me. I even go for it myself sometimes. You don't like it, we go on to the next stop."

Wearily Rand climbed out of the taxi. The persistent throbbing in his head had given him second thoughts about the value of an escorted tour of Baja, but he told himself somewhat grimly that he had asked for it.

The attendant at the gate ushered him in rather hastily. "You can leave your clothes in one of those booths, sir." He pointed at a row of green plastic cubicles set under the protective canopy of a cocoanut grove. The prevailing wind off the inland hills was still brisk, setting the palm fronds overhead into a persistent clatter and rustle oddly reminiscent of the babble of a cocktail party somewhere in the treeless concrete forest of the Syndicate's headquarters in New York.

Rand glanced back at Max through the gate. "You're not coming in?"

Max shook his head. "I gotta drive. So I can't take

no pills. And without pills, it's a good idea I don't minglin' with all them naked women."

He grinned at Rand's expression and turned back the cab with an airy wave. For a moment Rand hesitate The gate attendant was eyeing him anxiously, with occasional glance along a brick path leading into park. With a resigned shrug Rand went into one of green plastic booths.

He regretted the decision almost as soon as he emerg The wind, cool before, prickled his bare skin, and shivered. He hurried out of the shade toward a pa of open lawn and welcome sun. It was a choice betw submitting to the glare that made the waves of p in his head dance more actively, or enduring the cl It was only when he was out on the green lawn in warmth of the sun that he became suddenly consci of his nudity—and of the throngs of equally nude and women scattered across the broad, grassy clear strolling among the stands of date and cocoanut pal or relaxing on a wide terrace spanning what appea to be a clubhouse and administration building.

Rand grunted, aware of his heavily muscular b with its curly mats of black hair, and his skin, ex for his hands and face, a pallid white, marked by old scar along his right thigh, and by fresh, dark, plish bruises on his legs, hips and upper arms—meme of the accident the day before. Discomfited, he f a small patch of sunlight half-screened on three by low, flowering bushes. He eased down on the and surveyed the strange scene before him.

Back to nature. The fad had been champione isolated individuals and groups for a century or n ever since people started moving in droves from farms to the industrialized cities, which grew bigger uglier and progressively more divorced from the na landscape. A Thoreau went back to find serenity to rediscover truths about himself, man and societ mid-twentieth-century nudist colony exalted the wo working benefits of the sun.

But the members of the Baja Sun Club were philosophers, Rand thought, nor sun worshipers, d their nudity. The presence or absence of clothes little difference, and Rand's self-consciousness was pletely his own. Few of the strollers in the shaded g or the others sprawled across the grassy areas, were even aware of each other. There was a stillness about the entire park which gave it an eerie, unnatural atmosphere of waiting.

Rand's arrival had gone unnoticed. He studied a man who sat nearby in rapt contemplation of the sleek, thinly engraved trunk of a palm tree. The bark would not be smooth to his eyes, Rand thought, but an infinitely complex design, with layer upon layer subtly overlaid. He remembered his own first experiences with PSI-40, and the intense beauty he had discovered in ordinary objects. The phase with him had been short-lived, as the remarkable chemical quickly plumbed deeper reservoirs of his mind.

Most of those in the park were North Americans, and there seemed to be more women than men. One Latin beauty, olive-skinned and sloe-eyed, with small brown breasts and boyishly narrow hips, reminded Rand of Miguel Huerara's girl. She even moved with the same dreamlike quality, the same ethereal smile, remote and untroubled.

Untroubled. That was the key.

Rand was not sure why the spectacle of the sun club disturbed him. The existence of such groups—and of many others with special orientation, banded together because of a mutual response to PSI-40—was hardly a surprise. But it struck Rand that his life for many years had been in a real sense artificial. He lived, worked, thought, acted within the lines defined for him by his commitment to the Mental Freedom Syndicate. Between assignments he stayed in the huge headquarters complex in New York, where everything from the finest restaurants to the most exotic entertainment was readily at hand. Occasionally, on vacation, he took advantage of the Syndicate's own resorts maintained in different parts of the globe. Here again, he was a Syndicate man, using Syndicate facilities—never an ordinary citizen. And when he was on a job, Rand tended to have a one-track mind. Generally he was aware of the milieu in which he moved only as it directly affected his purpose.

He was, Rand thought wryly, out of touch with the way people lived outside of the Syndicate. And it had happened without his being aware of it—damaging admission for a trained Security agent. The existence of nature camps had been a fact recorded in his mind, but making little more impression than a set of statistics on mean average income or the ratio of divorces to marriages. The widespread impact of PSI-40's commercial derivatives upon the whole population, their growing dependence on it, was another matter of fact, around which Rand's life had been woven—but the fact had remained impersonal. He had viewed PSI-40 primarily in terms of his own response to it—a Sensitive reaching out for the mind's full potential, seeking a true enlargement of consciousness. He hadn't thought of it simply as a kind of escape.

It had not meant a young girl smiling over her lover's corpse.

A brief, vivid image darted across his mind. Rand sat up, every sense alert, his mind alive to every current. What had the impression meant? An elongated shape, vaguely phallic, like a spire. More important, who had communicated it?

Casually Rand studied the naturists around him. The blond, bony-chested man was still admiring the texture of a tree trunk. The slender little Mexican girl had drifted across the lawn. Rand could see her black hair, caught at the nape of her neck, trailing down her spine like an exclamation mark. Within sight there were at least thirty people, and a more careful search among the palm groves and scattered bushes would reveal another twenty. All close enough to communicate.

Slowly, easily, in the way an athlete or a yogi relaxes the body's muscles, Rand let his mind relax. The action lowered his mind's natural, built-in defense mechanism, the protective screen which shielded it from a bewildering onslaught of impressions. Rand was immediately aware of the minds all around him. He could not read their thoughts, or detect more than a blurred orchestra of images, in a way analogous to the ear's ability to hear the muttering and restless movement of a large audience, without hearing any specific word or voice. For a long moment there was nothing else. Rand waited patiently. Then another impression slid into his conscious mind— clear, sharp, individual.

Rand had an exceptional directional sense. The fact was noted on his top-secret Security classification. He had verified it the morning of his conversation with

Loren Garrett over this assignment—Rand had known where the intruder was and Garrett, a Special, had not. Now, with convincing certainty, he located the origin of the telepathic communication. There were two people lounging in plastic cocoons at the far end of the veranda. One was a portly, sunburned man wearing only slippers and a hat—a comic effect with his pink, naked body. But the impression Rand had received had indicated a feminine viewpoint. And it had been starkly sexual.

The woman might have been thirty-five or forty. She made a half-defensive gesture at covering her body with her hands when she saw Rand approaching. In the process she dropped something from her lap—a drawing pad, Rand saw as the woman tried to pick it up, along with a piece of charcoal. He had a glimpse of the drawing. It was a crude, simple approximation of a spire—the image Rand had caught. Yet he must have received the conception in her mind rather than the drawing itself, which was inept and childlike. When he saw her trying to retrieve the charcoal, he understood why. Many people suffered a disruption in the ability to perform simple tasks while under the influence of PSI-40. What was remarkable was the coupling of this disorientation with an ability to communicate.

Rand had already discarded any notion that he was dealing with a rival agent—either of Killjoy or someone else. The woman's communication had been unconscious, he was sure. Her evident confusion now, as she at last straightened up, her face flushed, after retrieving the charcoal on the sixth try, confirmed his hunch.

Casually sitting on the top step leading to the veranda, trying to stay in the sunlight rather than moving into the cool shade of the veranda itself, Rand said, "Hello. You're new."

"Y-yes."

"Thought so." Rand smiled. "It shows."

"What—what do you mean?"

"I know what you're thinking."

The woman's cheeks flamed. "You can't possibly!" The drawing pad slipped from her hands onto the tile floor. She stared at it in horror, as if it were the object of her shame. Rand seized the moment's weakness—angrily thrusting down a feeling of compassion for her and revulsion for what he had to do—for a quick mental probe. The emotional content of her mind came to him with surprising ease, though wrapped in symbols. He felt her fear and the burning sensation of shame, mixed with an awareness of him as a man, a longing and a fear.

He withdrew. Without the drug she must be a very inhibited woman indeed, he thought. Even PSI-40 didn't entirely release the deeply rooted restraints. The ability of the chemical to let down normal, subconscious bars in some subjects was well known. But the woman's general reaction was unusual. Rand felt sure he knew why. She was—what was the term for it?—a latent Sensitive.

Aloud he said, "Well, if it's that bad, I wish I did!"

She had retrieved the pad, and at his words her relief was transparent. "You—you shouldn't say things like that."

"I apologize, Miss—?"

"Mrs. Deere."

Rand raised an eyebrow. He glanced at the sunburned man in the chaise nearby, but the comic figure was unnaturally still, its expression vacant and self-absorbed. Another common response to PSI-40. His consciousness totally turned inward, the portly man was oblivious of Rand and his partner.

"Is there a Mr. Deere?" Rand asked.

"N-no. He's d-dead."

Stuttering, too, Rand thought. Hers was a complex response to the drug. An incomplete release of repressions. Sexual stimulation. A partial, weak telepathic sensitivity, as if the door to the mind's potential under PSI-40 had been opened only a crack. A lowering of defenses— she showed no resentment of Rand's intrusion, rather an immediate willingness to talk. And with all that, physical disorientation. She needed therapeutic help— or she shouldn't be taking the drug.

"You're alone then?" he asked with genuine sympathy.

She hesitated. Without effort he sensed her pain. "Yes. I have a son. They t-took him away from me."

"They?"

"That—that S-Syndicate."

Momentarily Rand was startled. Then he understood. "Your son is a Sensitive."

"Y-yes."

Of course, Rand thought. What she could only partially realize was fully developed in her child. The factor was hereditary. The man Rand was after, Kemp Johnson, was a classic proof.

"But that's fine!" Rand said. "Mrs. Deere, there's nothing terrible about that. Your son has a special talent. He'll get the chance to develop and use it."

"J-Johnny d-didn't want to go. He's only t-thirteen!" she burst out. "They had no right to take him away!"

"Take him away? You had to sign a contract, Mrs. Deere," Rand said gently. The law was clear on the point, and the Syndicate had always been scrupulously careful to observe it. Rand had been older when the tests had proved him Sensitive, but he had been wooed by Syndicate investigators more eagerly than any star athlete by a football coach. The bonus Rand had received had enabled his parents to look forward to a life of comfort, free of worries.

The woman's attention had strayed and she did not reply. When she became aware of his quiet scrutiny, she averted her gaze quickly, her cheeks and neck as pink as the sunburned skin of the fat man in the next plastic cocoon. Rand wished that he had kept his clothes on.

"I'm sure Johnny is getting along fine," Rand assured her.

The woman caught the thread of thought once more. "I wouldn't l-let him go," she said bitterly. "I refused. B-but I lost my job. They s-said they didn't have anything to do with that, b-but they did it! S-so I wouldn't b-be able to keep Johnny!"

Rand was frowning. The expression made his dark, solid face glower as if in anger. "I'm sure that was a coincidence."

"They m-made him ashamed," she whispered. "So he'd go with them."

The bitterness faded from her voice, and once again her attention began to stray, as if she could not sustain it for long. Rand groped for a way to escape, wishing he had never intercepted her stray communication or felt the need to investigate it. "You must be very proud of him," he said. "And you must have received a handsome bonus." For some reason the remark sounded hollow.

"They s-sent me here," the woman said listlessly.

Rand was suddenly wary. "They? The Syndicate?"

She made no reply, but Rand needed none. He pushed quickly to his feet, but the warning had come too late. Without looking he was aware of two men striding purposefully along the veranda toward him. As he started back across the stretch of open lawn he glimpsed the pair, one in a business suit, middle-aged, handsome and graying, the very model of a sun club director, and the other a burly figure with shaven head and powerful arms, wearing a guard's uniform that looked a size too small.

Rand had taken no more than a dozen steps before the sharp command rapped out behind him. "Just a minute—you!"

Slowly Rand turned to face them, his expression conveying only passive disinterest. The exit gate was too far. And there was the matter of his clothes.

His manner caused the distinguished-appearing director to hesitate. "I don't believe I know you," the man said smoothly. "I thought I knew all our members."

The truth, Rand thought quickly, was the most plausible and the most innocent explanation he could possibly give. But he answered distractedly, playing his role as long as there was any possibility it might be convincing. "It's cold," he mumbled. "Everything is strange—floating."

Rand saw the quick exchange of glances between the directorial type and the husky guard. The latter appraised Rand suspiciously, and Rand wondered if he held his job because of talent other than his powerful hands and shoulders. How else could they have got onto him? Most of the time he had simply opened his mind to receive impressions, but there had been one quick probe of Mrs. Deere's consciousness—a probe that any Sensitive nearby could have felt, even if its meaning remained blurred.

Rand glanced once more around the park. The sun was still bright overhead, the wind still brisk, causing the palm trees to converse loudly. There must be other guards, he thought, mingling with the naturists, though he had detected none.

"What is your name?" The director broke into Rand's thoughts. When Rand appeared to stare right through him, showing no reaction, the director's tone sharpened irritably as he repeated, "Your name! Where is your club membership card?"

Rand affected a visible effort to focus his attention on the man and the question. "Card?" His gaze, bemused, went down to his nudity. "With my clothes. Over there where the trees are. It's like green water," he said in apparent surprise. "With trees floating upright. Noisy trees."

The director appeared less sure of himself, but the husky man in uniform said, "He could be acting," in a tone too low for Rand to be meant to hear.

The director nodded. "The woman won't give any trouble, but you'd better take him to get his clothes and check his membership card, just to be sure. He could be . . . "

"Yeah," the guard agreed.

Rand didn't need to hear the unspoken word to know what it was: "Anti."

Rand allowed himself to be led across the lawn toward the front gates and the plastic booth where he had undressed. The pressure of the guard's blunt fingers on his bicep was unnecessarily heavy, biting into his flesh, but Rand remained tractable.

When they reached the row of booths the guard growled, "Which one?"

Rand stared at the identical green cubicles, as if the problem of singling out any one was immensely complex. Under cover of this confusion he verified that the front gates—and their attendant—were out of the line of vision from the correct booth, whose number and location he placed without difficulty. A pair of naturists drifted among the palms some distance away, but their backs were toward Rand. Momentarily no one was in a position to notice Rand and his guard.

The fingers tightened on Rand's arm. "Which is it, friend?"

Rand controlled his anger. He pointed. "I think that is it."

He was dragged over to the booth. When the guard jerked open the door and turned to him for confirmation, Rand nodded. "Those are mine," he said in a normal tone. "And take your hand off me."

The guard was surprised, and in that instant the pressure of his fingers eased. Rand pulled free. But the guard was well trained. He recovered quickly, and there was a fleeting mockery in his eyes. But he telegraphed his mental blow, like a clumsy boxer, betraying the massive assault which was meant to leave Rand dumb and paralyzed. He was, as Rand had guessed, a Sensitive. The Baja Sun Club was Syndicate controlled and operated. But the job of chief bouncer or strongarm guard in such a place was not an assignment given to a topflight agent. Rand's calculated risk paid off. He was able to deflect the guard's hypnotic command. The burly figure was moving in fast with his fists, ostensibly on a paralyzed, helpless subject, and Rand felt a quick disgust at this brutal abuse of a Sensitive's power. At the last second, as the guard swung, Rand planted his weight solidly and put it all behind a straight, chopping left hook. The blow caught the heavy guard moving in, landing solidly on the side of his jaw and cheekbone. He seemed to fall without a break in his forward motion, pitching onto his face. Rand stared down at him in brief satisfaction.

He dressed quickly. One wandering member of the sun club walked near, but his gaze was fixed upon the marvelous structure of his bare feet as they flexed and pushed. He paid no attention to Rand or the prostrate guard.

Rand hoped that Max was awake and waiting with his taxi. The guard groaned and tried to roll over as Rand pulled the last zipper closed. Fully dressed, he stepped around the stirring body on the ground. He rejected the impulse to deliver a mental probe of his own. As matters stood, the guard knew only that Rand had somehow failed to succumb to hypnotic command. He couldn't be sure that he had met another Sensitive of stronger mind than his. Thoughtfully Rand allowed the guard to lift his chin clear of the ground as he struggled to rise. Then Rand tapped the exposed chin just hard enough with his foot. The guard sagged softly.

At the gate the attendant showed relief rather than alarm at Rand's departure. Max was waiting, dozing behind the wheel. Rand slapped the driver's shoulder as he climbed in. "Let's go," he snapped.

Max shook himself awake. Catching the urgency in Rand's tone, he had the sense not to ask questions. The old-fashioned turbine engine fired immediately, and the taxi's wheels spun as the car shot away from the gates.

It was easy to underestimate the Syndicate, Rand thought, slumped in his seat. Even when you belonged to it.

Chapter Seven

It was late in the afternoon when the taxi nosed into a narrow street in midtown Mulege, north of the entertainment district. By then Rand was almost beyond caring where he went or what he saw. His headache had intensified through the long afternoon. Now the top of his skull felt like a thing apart, separate and sensitive. Cold air blew in upon his brain where the tender upper half of his skull had been severed from the lower. When he tried to move too quickly or turn his head, the pain sliced across this plane like a cleaver.

If it didn't let up soon, or if it got worse, he would have to go in, Rand admitted to himself. He couldn't function this way. The temptation to seek the relief he could get at a Syndicate station was so strong Rand imagined himself leaning forward to tap Max on the shoulder and give the dock area address of the Security cover operation. This daydream was as vivid as a mirage, and for a moment Rand was not completely sure whether or not he had actually spoken.

"Listen, you okay?" the driver asked.

"Yeah. A headache, that's all."'

"Well, believe me, Mr. Rand, in a couple minutes you're gonna forget all about your aches and pains. I've been savin' the best part for last. Anyways, these clubs don't really get goin' until it's getting on toward dark."

The smirk on the strip of face in the rear-view mirror, the leer in Max's voice, failed to excite any curiosity in Rand. The stocky little driver complained, "Ain't you gonna ask me which clubs?"

"I think I get the idea," Rand said wearily. "But you picked the wrong night—"

"Wait! Now wait! Don't say a thing, Mr. Rand. Just promise me this, before you say a single thing. Promise me you'll go in and have a look-see. That's all. Just look around. Have a drink, look around. You still wanta leave, I take you straight to your hotel. Hey! You never told me where you're stayin'!"

"No, I didn't, did I?"

"You need a drink, Mr. Rand—you need to relax. I can see that. We're there right now. I'll park the car and come in. You wanta leave, you just let Max know. Right?"

An attendant, appearing unobtrusively from the deepening shadows of the narrow street, was opening the door of the taxi, waiting expectantly. Rand stared at him, aware also of Max swiveling around to face him anxiously. It seemed that the cost of effort to resist was more than Rand could pay. It would be easier to go along. Maybe a drink would help. And he had come this far, he might as well finish the grand tour of Baja.

"Fine, Mr. Rand!" Max enthused, with more relief than Rand's capitulation seemed to warrant. He must get a cut on the customers he brings, Rand thought.

Rand stepped very carefully out of the cab. The street was quiet, almost empty except for Rand, Max and the attendant. No door in the white plastered wall was evident. There was one gaily colored poster—

Someone walked out through the wall. In the instant the body passed through the solid-appearing curtain, brassy music was thinly audible. In spite of his headache, Rand smiled at himself for being startled. The wall-photograph, thrown against a sound-insulating air curtain, was remarkably realistic. Even now, in the pale light of dusk, Rand could not detect where solid wall ended and photograph began. But the noise of the band made him regret giving in. He swung back toward the street. Max and the taxi had already moved away.

With a shrug of resignation Rand walked through the curtain wall, wryly amused at the instinctive tendency to flinch. Noise, smoke, smells burst upon him. He was on the entry landing, at bar level, of an exotic club. The bar and spectator tables were arranged in a huge horseshoe overlooking a dance floor on the lower level. Shadowed areas, impenetrable now, lay under the great horseshoe, circumscribing the dance floor. A dance band in romantically inaccurate Mexican costumes played on a platform at the far end of the polished dance floor. The blare of a trumpet and the steady slap of a drum made Rand wince.

"Your mask, sir?"

A tall girl with heavy bare breasts that swayed slightly as she moved, and with incredibly long legs encased in black mesh tights, winked at Rand through one of the holes in an Oriental face mask. The face of the mask was a cool green, remote and serene in contemplative aspect. But the long-lashed green eyes visible through twin holes in the mask were hot, avid with interest. Drugged, Rand thought.

It appeared that he had no choice of mask. The one she held out to him was hardly any improvement on his own face, though the matter was probably debatable, Rand thought. It was a copy of an ancient Aztec mask —probably a death mask. Rand was not superstitious, and he fitted the square, thick-lipped, big-eyed image over his own features without hesitation. The tall girl moved closer, her eyes bold on his. She allowed one full breast to melt against his arm with a soft pressure.

"Would you like to go downstairs, sir?" she inquired huskily. "No," Rand said prudently. "I just want to sit down and have a drink."

"Yes, sir. But if you change your mind . . ." She swayed this way and that, winked again and pivoted away from Rand toward a counter behind which were rows of varied face masks.

Rand retreated to the bar. From a stool it was possible to survey the dance floor below, or most of it, and one whole wall of the darkness flanking the polished floor, which was at the moment empty. And he could easily see Max when the taxi driver came in from the street. Rand didn't intend to stay long.

There were key clubs, private dance clubs, so-called entertainment clubs catering to almost any wish, in every American city of any size. It was hardly surprising to find one here in Mulege, which was quickly becoming a specialized resort for Americans and wealthy Latins. An erotic response to PSI-40, usually coupled with a stripping away of inhibitions and restraints, occurred in perhaps one case out of six or seven. Just as the nature clubs and the religious temples sprang up for those who enjoyed a mystical experience under the chemical's influence, so the sex clubs provided places where those who shared this specialized reaction could meet.

Under American law, however—because of pressure by the Mental Freedom Syndicate itself—the drug could never be used to provide public entertainments. By which the lawmakers had meant pornographic exhibitions. It appeared, if Rand's guess about the darkened sections adjoining the dance floor was correct, that the law was considerably more lax in Baja, a fact which was sure to give free ammunition for Anti broadsides.

Rand ordered a whiskey and water. When the bartender brought his drink, it was accompanied by a small white envelope containing a specified twenty-four micrograms of PSI-40 in the form of two pills. Rand paid for the pills and slipped the envelope into his pocket. There was always the chance that he would run short if he continued to stay away from Syndicate offices.

He was beginning to feel uncomfortably warm, a condition which he attributed to the face mask, a popular form of evening wear, especially in less respectable clubs, which Rand almost never affected. In fact, he owned neither a tuxedo nor a mask. He downed the iced drink more rapidly than he had intended.

He had ordered and paid for a second drink, and was just beginning to wonder where Max was, when a golden-bodied woman in a daringly brief dress paused on her way toward a table. Her escort, seeing her stare at Rand, took an aggressive step toward the bar, but a smooth, golden arm stopped him. Rand returned her stare blankly. His head was aching fiercely in spite of his drink and an excess dosage of pain-killing tablets. His face felt flushed under the mask, and his eyes were hot and hard to focus.

"Don't you recognize me, Mr. Rand? But of course— the mask."

She wore an Egyptian mask, complete with golden headdress. The mask had been gilded. Through the eyeholes a pair of cool blue eyes studied Rand with amusement.

"It was easier for you." Rand pulled himself together with an effort. "My mask isn't much of a change. But I should have known the rest of you couldn't be duplicated."

Taina Erickson laughed. "How nice—you see, you are a diplomat, Mr. Rand."

"No." Rand bowed. "Just a man."

Her escort, a tall athlete with a youthful, powerful body, lean of hip and broad of shoulder was growing restive, glaring at Rand through an African mask that was too small for him, giving him a pin-headed effect. "Come on, Taina," he complained. "The show's about to start and we haven't had our pills."

"There's time," Taina murmured, still measuring Rand. To him she said, "I wouldn't have thought you were a drinking man."

"And I wouldn't have expected to find you *here*," Rand retorted.

He thought she stiffened slightly, but with the mask her reaction was unreadable. Hers was a lovelier body than that of the mask-girl who had flirted with him when he entered the club, Rand mused, though he couldn't have said exactly why. Cleaner, somehow. Purer of line. Firmer, better cared for, less used, though too well controlled to be entirely innocent. Great Syndicate! Was he beginning to get erotic under PSI-40?

"Are you through?" Taina Erickson's blue eyes were ice cubes rayed with frost.

"We haven't begun yet."

"I see why you like PSI-40, Mr. Rand."

"It gets me into exclusive circles."

"It's going to get you into a lot of trouble, friend," Taina Erickson's muscular escort growled. She continued to block his half-hearted move to push past her.

"Friend? We haven't even been introduced," Rand snorted.

"You're drunk." Taina's statement was flat, contemptuous.

"Hardly." Rand paused. He *felt* drunk. It was impossible, but the symptoms were there. A reckless feeling kept pushing him into words he regretted. He was like a man unable to stop punishing himself with repeated blows. His head throbbed, his vision was blurred his face was hot under the ancient death mask. And he was inexplicably angry. "Take your playmate off in a corner, Taina, before he scares somebody to death. Or were you planning to take him downstairs?"

Her Egyptian mask seemed to quiver with indignation,

borrowing emotion from the sun-gold body in its white sheath. Rand grinned hollowly, forgetting that his smile, hollow or not, was hidden. "I'm not up on the latest social games," Rand said. What did it matter to him who she went with, where she went, what she did? "Have to get up to see you there in La Luz," he went on, unable to stop the flow of words. "Haven't finished my business yet. Soon. It was La Luz, wasn't it?"

"I'm sorry we had to meet like this, Mr. Rand," Taina said crisply.

"Don't be." Rand waved a hand airily. "Happens to the best of friends."

She was already moving away among the tables. The athlete glared balefully at Rand over a broad shoulder as he followed her. The smooth supple line of her retreating back somehow managed to express an angry withdrawal with moving eloquence, before the man's body came between her and Rand, shutting him off.

He could no longer see her among the crowd—wait, there she was! Sitting at a ringside table next to the railing overlooking the dance floor. The band was blaring again, and couples were drifting out of the shadows below to fit their movements to the rhythms of the music. In the distance Taina was a stranger—a glowing shoulder, a still Egyptian mask. Yet something of the woman had lingered behind her. Rand could sense it, feel it. Perfume? No, there were too many stronger scents saturating the place. It was an elusive imprint, like the afterglow of a woman's caress, the flesh still tingling after the touch has been withdrawn.

But it was Rand's mind which tingled.

In sudden anger he brushed the impression away. Foolishness! He liked her—yes, wanted her. And he was jealous, that's all. Male animal pawing the ground, snorting. The drug had affected him strangely. Or the drink, or his pain, or the combination of all of these. Something was definitely wrong. The room seemed to vibrate with the sensuous beat of the music. And where in hell was Max?

He pushed off his stool and began to weave among the tables. He had made no conscious choice of direction. Suddenly she was there, her head thrown back in laughter. Her broad-shouldered escort leaned across the table eagerly, possessively. Rand reached their table and stood over them, swaying.

The two masks turned up, concealing everything except their eyes. The man's snapped with anger. Hers—no, not disgust. A frown beginning, a question—?

Below them, the dance floor was crowded with couples. The music was low, subtle, underscoring the whispers of clothing being discarded, the occasional mutter or giggle. Warm lights played over the scene, heightening flesh tones. Around the bar and at the tables crowding the horseshoe balcony, conversation began to die out, movement ceased. The slow rhythmic shuffle of feet on the polished floor was clearly audible as the couples reacted to the music and the drug which enflamed them —and, perhaps, to the knowledge of being watched, of inciting other passions, of feeding and extending the flames. Their bodies were glued together as they swayed. And suddenly one couple stumbled off the floor to fall into the surrounding shadows. Like a curtain being raised, the darkness receded. Light glowed on nests of brightly colored pillows . . .

"Get away from her!" The athlete stood, towering over Rand, hissing at him. "Go take a pill!"

Slowly, as if the movement had been thoughtfully planned and rehearsed, Rand reached out to touch Taina Erickson's face mask, to examine it with his fingers, and then, with a spasmodic jerk, rip it away.

She gasped. Beneath the mask her face was white, frozen, her eyes wide and worried. "Mr. Rand—"

"Sorry," he muttered. "Don't know why . . ."

He sensed the first blow before it came. Even through the cloudiness which enveloped his mind he caught the naked emotion, the sharply telegraphed command of aggression from mind to muscles. But he couldn't seem to move out of its way. The angry athlete's fist smashed into Rand's mouth and knocked him back a full step. Solidly built and tough, Rand was hard to put down. It was no contest, he thought in a befuddled way. He could always sense a punch before it came and slip under or around it to deliver his own blow.

But this time he failed. He knew when the big fists were coming at him, where they would strike, how easy it would be to beat them—but his muscular coordination was gone. His arms were leaden, his feet clamped to the floor. He saw the round, pained, "Oh!" of Taina Erickson's mouth as another blow sent him stumbling back into an adjoining table.

Then, suddenly, other figures materialized, coming between Rand and the athlete, pushing the latter firmly into his chair, efficiently hustling Rand among the tables. There were at least three—no, four of them. Masks swam across Rand's vision as he let himself be half-pushed, half-carried away. Curtains seemed to part. Seconds later he felt a partition dropping between him and the smells, sights, sounds of the club. He was in a corridor, staring up at the ceiling light panel.

"You can—put me down now," he mumbled.

But the hands tightened on his arms, shoving him forward. A door opened, a gray-walled room was visible. From behind Rand someone, something, approached swiftly. An arm swung in a swift arc toward his head.

For a brief time alarm cleared the vapors from Rand's brain. He ducked the blow from behind. A heavy object grazed his cheek and slammed into his shoulder. His knees sagged, but he didn't drop. They were leaping at him then, four masked figures with hands groping, clutching. One man had fingers at Rand's throat. Rand struck with vicious mental force. The attacker, hypnotically helpless, fell back paralyzed. Swiftly Rand stabbed a second command, a third—

Pain burst open the back of his head. Blackness rushed in through the gaping hole. Rand felt his brain going soft, shapeless, turning liquid, oozing through the opening, draining away, until his skull was a black, infinitely cold emptiness.

Chapter Eight

Rand's first awareness was of cold weights on his ankles and wrists. He was stretched out, arms pulled high over his head, like a man on a rack. His arms, legs, back muscles arched from the unnatural tension and rigidity. Beneath him, softness. Thin foam padding. A cot of some kind. And the cold weights?

He waited for full consciousness to return without making any effort to open his eyes. There was a pillow under his head, but even with that cushion his skull felt soft and spongy. Pain darted like the rays in splintered glass when he tried to move. Yet, oddly, the older, more familiar headache was almost completely gone. This new pain was specific, localized, bearable. Strike your head and it will hurt for a while.

Carefully Rand tested the cold manacles on his wrists and ankles. Chains, he thought. A smile played behind his impassive features, under his closed eyelids. Killjoy was taking no chances.

Rand opened his eyes. He lay in a gray, windowless room with a single air vent in the center of the ceiling. He could hear the low murmur of a circulating fan. The wall opposite him, softly lit, reflected a dim image in its glass panels. He could see himself stretched out on a low plastic cot which had been extended by the addition of a crude wooden box, a shipping crate of some kind, at the foot, where his legs overlapped the cot. Thin metal chains, wrapped around his wrists and attached to the top corners of the cot, immobilized his arms. Separate chains bound his ankles, cutting harshly into his flesh, pulled taut over the shipping crate, then down and under it to fasten to the legs of the cot at its foot. Small locks secured each length of chain.

In the windowless room with its artificial light, there was neither night nor day. Wondering how long he had been unconscious, Rand felt the telewatch on his wrist. Twisting his head around, he tried to read the dial. There was enough play in the chain to bend his wrist. 5:25. Morning? It must be. He could hardly have been unconscious through a whole night and day. It surprised him that he would even have slept through an entire night from the blow he had received.

Not just the blow, or blows, Rand thought. His head still swam when he moved it. His vision still played tricks, not the special intensity or perceptual dimension that PSI-40 brought, but simple distortions and blurring, double images. He hadn't drunk enough to have so severe a hangover.

He was being watched. The sensation was unmistakable. Rand had not had a PSI-40 dosage since he'd left his room almost twenty-four hours before, and much of the effect of that pill ↑ ↗ become diluted. But not all. Some-one was watching him.

The light-wall, he thought. One panel of it was a one-way viewer. Turning his gaze away from the wall, letting part of his mind dwell idly upon the structure of the ventilating fan in the ceiling, he sent out an oblique mental probe, like a sidelong glance, a delicate feeler which sought—and found—another complex small mass of activity identifiable as a human brain. He could not have explained exactly how he knew the thing behind the light-panel was another mind, for he had read no thoughts. Telepathic awareness was not always trans-latable into conventional terms. It was simply that no other substance had the precise mental feel of an active human mind.

One other thing Rand knew: the watcher behind the wall was neither Sensitive nor Special. Such minds could erect barriers to balk invasion, but even in so doing they revealed their nature to another Sensitive mind. The ordinary mind might be a vague set of impulses, a chaotic potpourri of thoughts and emotions and their symbolic disguises, but it could not raise a shield at will that blocked off any attempt to intrude. Rand's telepathic powers were not as acute as they had been twelve hours before, but they were sharp enough to tell him that his invisible guard had quite normal mental activity.

Rand would need another pill soon. He raised his head—too quickly—and had to set his teeth against the pain. More carefully he tried again. He had been stripped to the waist, no doubt in course of searching. His pants belt had been removed. Since his shoes were still on, Rand guessed that the searchers had quit once they found the cache of PSI-40 pills concealed inside the belt buckle. An emergency supply was sewn inside the arches of his shoes, difficult to detect within a layer of foam—shoe heels had long before been abandoned as too obvious a place of concealment—but there was no way for Rand to get at the shoes, much less open them.

By the end of the day—certainly before another night had passed—Rand would be, to all intents and purposes, nearly normal again. Residual effects of PSI-40 lingered, but Rand needed daily dosages to be sure of reliable command of his Sensitive powers. After two days without a pill, he would have trouble detecting the watcher behind the light-wall, to say nothing of reading his mind. The ability to hypnotize lasted, but Rand's captors would undoubtedly be wary of that threat.

A memory teased him, slipped away, hovered just over the lip of his awareness. Deliberately Rand turned his thoughts away from the elusive memory, allowing it to come naturally. Ah! Yes, the pills in the little envelope he'd paid for at the bar. In his coat pocket, a place so obvious his captors might have overlooked it.

But his coat was hanging over the back of a straight chair, the only piece of furniture in the room other than the cot and its box extension. And the chair was a good six feet away.

Something to file away then, a remote chance at best. He—

The room's only door opened. Three men filed in, each wearing an evening mask. In the gray room's clear soft light, in the waiting silence, the masks seemed ludicrous, part of a child's game. Rand wondered what had happened to his own, the ancient native death mask. He preferred it to the white clown mask on one of the trio silently watching him, to the haughty Roman mask on the tallest of the three men, to the lacquered Japanese Kabuki face worn by the third.

"You are Jon Rand?" the tall Roman asked.

Rand shrugged. At least that was what he tried to do, until he realized that in his position no one could appreciate the gesture but himself. "You might as well answer." The Roman nose seemed to sniff. "We already know who you are and why you are here, Mr. Rand."

"Then why ask?"

"It will be in your interest to cooperate."

Rand smiled. There was no way of reading the expressions of his three captors. The masks had that useful function, which raised his opinion of the three men slightly. Not that they could conceal their reactions completely. He could sense the fear behind the clown's white mask, the uncertainty of the Kabuki dancer, the determination of the noble Roman. He knew something else: none of these men was Kemp Johnson. There were no —vibrations.

"I might feel more like cooperating if I weren't trussed up like this," Rand said aloud.

Kabuki-face—a squat man whose stocky body complemented his round Japanese mask—snorted derisively. But it was the tall Roman who answered. The other two took up stations near the door.

"That's hardly possible, is it?" Roman-nose said, in a tone that indicated he was ready to be friendly, but not to be taken for a fool. "There's no point in trying your hypnotic tricks, Mr. Rand. None of us has the key to those locks, so we couldn't let you loose if we wanted to. And even if you managed to put us to sleep and somehow free yourself, you couldn't crawl out through the vent, I'm sure—and that door won't be opened until the room has been monitored from outside through the glass wall. I suppose you know it's one-way glass." He paused. "And you don't walk through walls, do you, Mr. Rand?"

Rand said nothing. He wanted Roman-nose to keep on talking. A man who liked to tell you how clever he was often said too much.

"We've gone to a lot of trouble," the tall man continued, "and we're not about to take any chances. You're a dangerous man, Mr. Rand. Even after inhaling gas for three-quarters of an hour, you were able to knock two of our men—"

"Gas!" Rand repeated.

"You didn't know?" Roman-nose seemed surprised. "In your face mask, of course. The foam was impregnated with an odorless gas. Enough to put most men to sleep in half the time you wore your mask, Mr. Rand. But it worked. The effects are almost the same as intoxication, but without the hangover. You needn't worry about after effects—they're quite minor."

Rand stirred restlessly. His chains rubbed and chinked under the new pressures. An element was missing, he thought. They had been prepared for him in advance. The girl in black mesh tights had spotted him instantly. She had had the impregnated mask ready. Which didn't make sense at all, since he hadn't known himself where he would be that evening.

It made sense only if he had carefully been led into the trap. Rand grunted. He had certainly been a co-operative victim so far!

"Sorry about those," Roman-nose said, misreading Rand's expression. "We can loosen the chains in a day or two, when we're sure you've returned to normal—or whenever you're ready to do business."

"Business?" Rand felt the first tug of puzzlement. Kemp Johnson hadn't been concerned about dealing with the previous agents sent after him. Or had he? Those agents had simply disappeared. Their deaths had been assumed, but it was amateurish to assume anything, even after the apparent corroboration of the attempt on Rand's own life.

Had Garrett blundered, too? Hardly. He had simply allowed Rand to make any mistakes he would. He had given Rand only as much information as he wanted, letting matters then take their course. The fate of a particular agent meant nothing to him, Rand reflected, taking a direct, clear look at the fact. Garrett used agents as a boxer employer blows—for a feint here, a probe at a suspected weakness there, a quick strike elsewhere to draw a counterattack, to force a commitment. All right, Rand thought grimly. That was Garrett's job. And Rand had his.

"I'll talk business with Killjoy. No one else."

"Killjoy?" A sense of confusion, thoughts darting, suspicion, vague apprehension. Rand could not read the thoughts behind the Roman mask, but he sensed the main currents of thought and feeling. The expressionless Roman face exchanged glances with the Japanese, with the Comic-Tragic. Then the tall man snapped, "Who do you think we are?"

"Looks like I had it wrong," Rand said slowly.

"You've got it wrong!" Roman-nose sounded angry. "What do you think—that we're amateurs? Anti do-gooders? What kind of a Sensitive are you, Rand?"

"Maybe we got *him* wrong," the nervous, fidgety clown suggested, almost hopefully. "Maybe he is not the one."

"He is the one," the Kabuki dancer insisted, also in unmistakably Spanish-accented English.

"You know who I am and why I'm here," Rand said, addressing the tall man with the Roman mask, the obvious leader of the trio. "Suppose you tell me."

"If you're trying to stall for time," Roman-nose replied, "we have plenty of time. More than you, Mr. Rand. So I will tell you what we already know. You are Jon Rand, and you are an agent of the Mental Freedom Syndicate. Your Syndicate controls what everyone wants, Mr. Rand. You are a Sensitive—you proved that last night when you tried to fight, though, fortunately for us, you acted too late. Your Syndicate would not send you here unless it was something very important." He took a step closer to the cot, though he did not venture too near. Instinctive fear of the Sensitive, Rand thought, noting that the clown and the Kabuki mask stayed near the door, as far from Rand as possible. As if a few feet made any difference when mind reached out to mind! Roman-nose said: "A big shipment, Mr. Rand! We know it is coming! And we are ready to do business with you!"

Rand almost laughed outright. Only the knowledge that this might anger his captors and defeat his own purpose of obtaining as much information as possible checked the impulse.

Shaking his head, Rand said, "I don't know where you got your information, but you've blundered. I'm here to find Killjoy."

Roman-nose stiffened. "I told you we are not fools, Rand! They would not send you here to find a preacher! An unimportant Anti dupe!"

"More important than you think."

"Oh, I've heard the stories. But you and I know they are only propaganda, Mr. Rand. If this Killjoy were a Sensitive, your Syndicate would not have permitted him to run around loose for so many years. This Killjoy I have heard of is a grown man."

"He's the one I'm after," Rand said.

"And you were looking for him in a sun club?" The derision in Roman-nose's voice turned to impatience. "You are a Security agent, Rand—here in advance of a big shipment of PSI-40. That's why you were at the Baja Sun Club. That's why you will visit all of the Syndicate's outlets to prepare the way and to investigate security. You are clever—you visit many places which are not owned by the Syndicate. A good trick—but we are not amateurs, Mr. Rand. We have been waiting for this shipment for a long time. We know all of your outlets in Baja. There is just one thing we don't know —the time and place of arrival for the shipment."

"I see you're thorough," Rand said. The irony of the

situation continued to amuse him, though he matched gravity of manner to that of the tall Roman.

"We are. You can't escape, Mr. Rand. We have radio transmitters surrounding this building to prevent your sending any telepathic messages. In any event, that wouldn't help you, since you don't know where you are."

Rand said nothing to disillusion his captor. The radio interference would not have screened out telepathic communication, and an effective listener outside could have located the approximate area of origin of the message. What played into Roman-nose's plans was Rand's reluctance to contact the local Syndicate headquarters.

"We're ready to do business with you, Mr. Rand. You will admit we are in a bargaining position."

"So it would seem," Rand agreed.

"On the one hand, a shipment of drugs which can mean very little to you personally—I do not question your loyalty, Mr. Rand; I merely state a fact—drugs the Syndicate will not really miss. But you can refuse to cooperate, and at the cost of your life you can deny the drugs to us. Perhaps. On the other hand, your freedom, Mr. Rand, and your life. We are also prepared to sweeten the bargain. Do business with us, and we will make you a very rich man."

"The black market in PSI-40 must be good."

"Enough to make us all rich."

"Being rich doesn't matter if you're dead. The Syndicate counts treason a major crime."

"The Syndicate doesn't have to know you've helped us. At least you have a chance to live."

"You don't propose much in the way of alternatives."

"Think it over, Mr. Rand. We have time." Roman-nose backed away. "I don't expect you to agree until you see there is no other way."

"How do I know you'll keep your bargain?"

"I'm sure we can work out mutually satisfactory guarantees. Once we get the drugs, we will have nothing to gain by killing you. You will not be able to betray us without admitting collusion."

Rand stared at him during a prolonged silence. He was a pompous man, too sure of himself. His haughty Roman mask might have seemed impressive at night; in this calm, gray light it remained ridiculous. But there was never anything really comic about the threat of death. And the one who found himself chained in a ridiculous position was Rand.

He said, "I'll have to think it over."

"Of course." Roman-nose glanced toward the opaque glass wall. He must have made some signal, for the door opened seconds later. The nervous clown was the first to slip out. Perhaps his evident fright could be used, though Rand didn't immediately see how. Kabukiface, lacquered serenity hiding fearful belligerence, followed. At the door the tall leader of the trio said, "As I told you, there is time. But we do not wish to play games, Mr. Rand. You will give us your decision by tonight."

He bowed out. The door shut, and the gray room was once more an empty, silent prison, breathed upon by the circulating fan overhead, watched by invisible eyes behind the glass wall. Jon Rand lay stretched over his padded rack, conscious of a growing ache between his shoulder blades, and of an exasperated frustration.

Chapter Nine

Rand waited patiently. The room's silence, the complete absence of distractions, enabled him to concentrate with even greater clarity than usual. He was able to sense the activity of the watching guard's mind. The glass wall was no barrier.

The guard had to be put to sleep. But that would accomplish nothing if a relief came along a few minutes later and gave an alarm. Rand waited. At eight o'clock the guard was replaced. Rand could detect his gratitude, his weariness. The same man had been on duty when Rand awoke more than two and a half hours earlier. The shift was at least three hours, probably more.

The new watcher, left alone, stared through the one-way glass at Rand. Rand could sense the action without seeing it. The man was afraid, he thought. Fear always came across strongly. Sweat of the mind. Animals could smell it.

Housing the fear was the short, plump figure of the man who had worn a lacquered Japanese mask, but whose accent had been Spanish. His fear identified him.

Rand relaxed. It was essential to know there would be no interruption. He needed some time. Would they bring him food? Unlikely. They would have brought some long before if they intended to. He was aware of the guard's fear ebbing slowly as the man settled down to his vigil. Panic was a mental barrier, but it also offered an advantage. The guard would be concentrating completely on Rand when the time came to act. It was easier to invade a mind totally oriented to him.

A half hour later Rand acted. He made an obvious effort to stare intently at the glass wall, shifting his body slightly in the same direction, as far as his chains allowed. The movement drew his guard's attention instantly and awakened the sleeping fear. Rand peered at the wall for several seconds, unblinking. Then he tried to reach out with the whole strength of his mind.

"Open the door," he commanded.

Nothing happened. The result was half-expected. As confusion surged up in his subject's mind, Rand erased the command. It was impossible for the guard to obey him. Alone on duty, he must have no key. Rand's captors didn't know how much he was capable of, but they were covering every escape hole they could imagine.

"Sleep," Rand thought.

Quiet settled over his guard's mind. His fear drained away.

Rand bent all his attention to the problem of freeing himself. There was a small amount of play in the chains wrapped around his wrists and ankles. At the head the bed frame had a cross bar. The chains here encircled the two corner posts below the bar. They could not be slipped off.

The foot of the bed proved more hopeful. With Rand's legs and feet extending over the packing crate which lengthened the bed, the chains had been drawn tight over the box, then looped back under it to be secured to the cot's legs near the floor. These might slip free if the legs could be raised.

Rand wished he had that much control over physical objects. He scowled in concentration. After a moment he stretched his body out to its full length. His head rolled back and his feet pronated, lifting his rigid frame clear of the cot. It was an old conjurer's trick with a hypnotized subject, used to fake levitation. Rand's body, stiff and straight, was in fact carried by the points of his heels and the back of his head. With all his awareness turned inward, he was able to achieve a degree of muscular control impossible in a non-Sensitive. A slight shift let his weight move onto his right heel, freeing the left. His body, stretched taut, was a couple of inches longer than in the relaxed state of unconsciousness when he had been trussed in chains. That was translated into two or three inches of play in the chains around his ankles.

Rand worked patiently at the chains on his left leg, flipping them toward the edge of the crate. On the third try the metal cascaded over the side and chinked to the floor.

Now he had five feet of free play for his left leg—the length of chain required to encircle the packing crate. He repeated the maneuver with his right leg. When it was released, he set both feet against the wooden box and shoved, at the same time jerking his knees toward his chest. The crate rocked and skidded over the chains.

Rand lay limp on the cot, grateful for the easing of pressure upon his wrists. His back, shoulder and arm muscles ached without relief. A cautious probe told him his guard slept undisturbed on the other side of the glass wall, but Rand did not rest for long.

There was enough loose chain to enable him to swing both legs over one side of the cot. A little experimenting taught him the trick of lifting the bottom of the cot by hooking one leg under it and shoving with the other. He was perspiring with effort when one loop of dangling chain finally came loose. The second was quick to follow.

The increasing agony behind his shoulder blades goaded Rand on. With his legs free, he found that he could flop the lightweight cot away from the walls into the center of the room. He considered doing a somersault over the head of the cot to gain his feet, then discovered he could achieve the same effect by sliding off the bed and twisting his body around.

At last he stood facing the head of the bed and the round corner posts to which his wrists were still chained. The position, once he'd gained it, seemed hardly less ridiculous than the previous one, but it was a lot more comfortable. And it left him more mobile.

He hauled the cot to the chair over which his coat had been thrown. The small white envelope was still in the side pocket of the coat, unnoticed by his captors. Rand swallowed each of the two PSI-40 pills, easing them down with saliva. The dosage—12 mcg. in each pill—was less than his optimum amount, but he would still remain Sensitive for a while.

There were small locks holding the chains secure where they were wrapped around wrists and ankles. One circle remained large enough to squeeze over his foot. The remaining ankle loop, and both of those around his wrists, were too tight. Rand turned his inquiry toward the cot.

The cot's front panel and a matching full-length brace at the back were joined to the headposts by simple metal hooks fitting into slots. Though stiff, they were readily disconnected, leaving Rand tied only to the frame which had formed the head of the cot. This was not a one-piece unit. The cross bar was bolted into the side pieces. With tools and a free hand, Rand could have removed the bar in a minute. He had neither, and he was left carrying the frame like an anchor.

Rand was staring in frustrated contemplation at the metal appendage when a voice spoke. "If you're through now, Mr. Rand, perhaps you'd like some help in putting the bed back together."

A quick sidelong probe told Rand that his guard was still under hypnosis, sleeping soundly, his brain's activity muted in a way that came only with sleep.

"You underestimate us," the voice spoke again. It came from above. Rand stared toward the vent fan in the ceiling. "Yes, Mr. Rand. A small television camera and microphone. But surely that is an obvious precaution."

Rand grunted. In a spasm of anger he lifted the metal frame shoulder high, gauging the height of the ceiling and the offending miniature camera hidden in the ventilator.

"That will accomplish nothing," the voice warned sharply. It was Roman-nose, Rand noted, his tone smugger and more self-satisfied than before. "You merely cause us to take further steps, Mr. Rand. I was quite sure you would make an attempt to escape, no matter how difficult it seemed. I thought it necessary to permit you that one try, just to prove that you are not dealing wtih amateurs."

"A professional wouldn't keep insisting," Rand muttered.

"Aren't you ready to admit that amateurs could make a fool of you, Rand?" Roman-nose chuckled. "We have, you know. But no one need hear of that—no one need ever know anything about our business relationship . . ."

Rand hefted the metal headboard of the cot and swung it over his head in a chopping arc. One leg smashed into the ventilator overhead. A crackle of static erupted from the area of the vent. Over the static Roman-nose shouted, "That was foolish, Rand! You can't escape!"

Another blow from the cot's frame silenced even the static, leaving the ventilator assembly crumpled. Rand started toward the glass wall behind which his guard lay asleep. He heard a hissing noise, but the sound carried no immediate significance. He swung the metal frame into the glass. The smooth surface exploded outward from the point of impact in a thousand rays of light, but the shattered glass panel did not yield. The hissing increased, penetrating Rand's haze of anger. He paused, the awkward headboard poised for another blow.

Gas, he thought. His captors seemed fond of it. Already there was a heaviness in his arms and legs, balanced against the lightness of his head. He swung the metal frame against the glass wall. More shards of glass appeared, and he felt the bite of small slivers spraying out at him. Was the wall yielding? It seemed to have sunk a little. Another blow or two would cave it in. He tried to heft the H-shaped club. It weighed a thousand pounds. The splintered glass wall seemed to recede, dwindling into a pair of brilliant searchlights turned upon him. The room's floor began to tilt absurdly, like a ship foundering at sea. Rand's weighted legs sank into the soft tilting floor. The bedframe clattered, and the hissing grew louder, louder, filling his head like a crowd's hysterical roar . . .

"Where are you?"

He was dreaming, Jon Rand thought, surprised that the dream should announce itself, and not come disguised as reality.

"Rand?" Image of himself; square face, glowering, heavy brows, an unfinished bust by an amateur sculptor. World full of amateurs, Rand thought.

"Unclear."

He tried to catch the inflection of the communicated

thought. He was only a fair receiver, as Garth Taylor had said. But he could sense the personality shaping an image in the way an expert telegrapher could identify the touch on a key a hundred miles away. The tone of this thought was strange, but the mind behind it was familiar.

All right, Rand thought. It's only a dream.

He pictured the room in which he had been held prisoner. There was little to show. Somehow the ventilator seemed important. He concentrated on it.

"*Affirmative.*" The reply came, Rand thought, without the proper enthusiasm. He knew that he had shaped a perfectly good image of a ventilator. But it had been broken, of course. That *was* important. Happily he projected a picture of the smashed ventilator unit.

After a brief pause a question probed at him. He tried to make it out. It was vague, indistinct. Then he realized the sender was attempting to convey the sense of someone —Rand himself—becoming invisible, disappearing. Resultant concern, perplexity, inquiry. But who cared that much?

Rand shaped an answer: impression of violence, human shapes tumbling together, a mask over his face (death mask!), sharp blow at the back of his head, brilliance like a falling star racing toward—blackness.

The sender's reply was another cryptic question: "*Who?*" Image of a faceless man.

Rand imposed features upon the blank face. "*Roman-nose.*" He seemed to be gathering strength. His mind was functioning more clearly, more effectively. He followed the image of Roman-nose with those of his other two captors—the two he had seen wearing Japanese and clown faces.

"*Masks?*"

"*Affirmative.*"

"*Are you trapped?*" Rand received a clear, fully realized impression of a rat in a wire cage frantically scurrying about, bumping into the bars, endlessly darting up passages which led nowhere. It was hardly a flattering or encouraging picture. Funny, he thought, what your mind conjures up in dreams.

"*Affirmative,*" he thought. "*And who are you?*"

Flicker of amusement, sense of withdrawal, figure lurking around a corner just out of sight. Teasing, Rand thought. What a fantasy of wish fulfillment! Was he so desperate, his resources so exhausted that he had to dream up a kindred spirit, Sensitive or Special, coming to his rescue? And a woman at that! Who? Indistinct figure moving from shadows toward light, only a step away—

"He's coming around," a voice said aloud.

"It's about time." Roman-nose sounded both worried and petulant.

Of course it would be her, Rand thought, ignoring the voices intruding upon his reverie. Who else would it be?

"Mr. Rand!"

Rand felt annoyance mixed with regret at the abrupt return to reality. He opened his eyes, stared at the impervious Roman mask and sensed the impatient displeasure behind it, and was at the same instant aware of being flat on his back and entangled in a web of blankets. He looked down at himself. More precisely, he was in a strait-jacket. Simple, direct and effective, a treatment borrowed from the experience of dealing with another kind of lunacy, used to render Rand's special madness ineffectual.

But the two pills he had swallowed before his escape attempt was aborted had had time to take effect. Rand felt acutely Sensitive. He was able to effect detachment, that peculiar sense of being apart from his own body, able to look down upon himself and the others in the gray-walled room, to watch and to listen. The unhappy clown was stationed by the door; Kabuki-face was missing. Rand noticed without emotion the smashed glass on one wall. He supposed that a watcher on the other side could still look through into the room, though he would get a highly distorted view.

"You're not listening to me!" Roman-nose was irritated.

"You're still ready to do business," Rand said without interest, his awareness no longer separated.

Roman-nose checked an angry retort. He needs me, Rand thought, and he knows it. That's the fundamental weakness of his position. And he can't use truth serum on me because the chemical reaction of PSI-40 to the other drug was totally unpredictable and unreliable. As for physical torture, he knows I'd put him or his torturer to sleep.

"It must be clear to you now, Mr. Rand, that you will not escape."

"It looks that way."

"But perhaps I did not make clear just exactly what it is I am offering."

"I think you got through."

"Did I mention a million dollars?"

Rand allowed surprise to show on his face. "Not by name."

"Twenty percent," Roman-nose said, "of a five-million-dollar shipment of PSI-40. Maybe more if we can cut the stuff—"

"It's not heroin," Rand protested. "There's only an infinitesimal fraction of the chemical in any pill."

Behind his mask Roman-nose smiled. "The shipment is in undiluted form. Smaller, easier to ship. There's a chemical laboratory here which makes up the pills. You see, we do know your Syndicate's operation here in Baja, Mr. Rand."

"Evidently."

Roman-nose knew more about the Syndicate's Baja business than Rand did, although that was hardly surprising. Security agents were specialists, of necessity lone wolves. There were agents assigned to police the distribution of PSI-40, and Rand had no doubt that Roman-nose and his group would be quickly caught if they managed to pull off a major theft. But that particular area of operation was not Rand's. His specialty was pursuit. He was a hunter.

"At least a million dollars," Roman-nose repeated, dwelling upon the figure. "Your share, Mr. Rand, for doing nothing but supply a little information."

But little time in which to enjoy that million, Rand thought. Roman-nose and his friends would hardly let him survive once he had given them the information they needed. A crooked mind tended to be dishonest even when it wasn't necessary, instinctively hedging and cheating—the real value of the shipment on the black market was probably several times what Roman-nose had quoted.

He caught the quality of greed from the clown-face near the door—greed discolored by fear. Of course! Rand thought. The five million figure would be the one Roman-nose had given to his troops.

Aloud Rand murmured, "A million would buy a nice funeral."

"Don't be absurd!" Roman-nose snapped. "You haven't even heard the specifics of my plan."

"I'd like to."

"After you have agreed to cooperate, and given some proof of your intentions."

"I see."

"I will tell you this much, Mr. Rand. Your Syndicate has become too sure that no one would dare steal from them. They have grown fat and careless."

"They'll have a Sensitive guarding that shipment, if there is a shipment."

"*You* are a Sensitive, Mr. Rand," Roman-nose said with an air of triumph, "and you were easily caught!"

Rand refrained from saying that his violent headache had had as much to do with his being captured as any trick or maneuver on the part of his captors. The headaches, left untreated, had dulled his awareness, slowed his reactions, screened the warning symptoms of the gas. Surprisingly, the headache had subsided to little more than a minor irritant during this day of captivity.

"You said I could have time to think," Rand protested.

"I said until tonight."

"It's not night yet."

"In an hour it will be dark."

Rand nodded slowly, having obtained an answer he wanted. His watch was lost under the constricting folds of the straitjacket. "I've been out most of the day from that gas you doused me with. That didn't leave me much time to think."

"That was your own doing." Roman-nose spoke tartly —and with a hint of satisfaction. He was, Rand thought, beginning to act insufferable.

"I still need more time. And I haven't had anything to eat or drink. A man thinks better on a full stomach."

Roman-nose hesitated. "If this is another trick, Mr. Rand, it will be as futile as before. And I'm running out of patience."

Rand shrugged. "You brought me here. It wasn't my idea. Suppose we call the whole deal off."

"We can hardly do that now. All right, Mr. Rand, I will send someone in to feed you. Naturally you will not be released from that jacket. In two hours we will talk. Not generalities, Mr. Rand—facts."

"Like those specifics you mentioned about your plans."

"Like those—and the specifics you have *not* mentioned. Two hours, Mr. Rand."

Left to himself, Rand lay quietly on his cot. The straitjacket firmly encased his torso, immobilizing his arms, but his legs were not tied and he was free to walk about the room. Instead he stared thoughtfully at the ceiling. The vent fan was not working, the room stuffy. They hadn't had time to fix it, he thought. Which meant the television camera had probably not been repaired either.

He had not been dreaming.

The conviction was without rational foundation, without buttressing arguments, without any sign of proof. He simply knew. And, knowing, he was bemused by the unexpected turn of events.

His reverie was interrupted by the arrival of food and drink—and a familiar figure. The girl's figure was as recognizable as the delicately featured Oriental mask she had also worn when Rand first saw her. She was wearing the same black mesh tights, though her showgirl's bosom was now partly supported by a brief halter. She wobbled a little on her high heels, as if the problem of carrying herself and a tray at the same time was new to her.

"I've brought you something to eat," the girl said brightly.

"Does it have poison in it?"

Rand sensed her wince. "That's not my fault, about the mask," she protested plaintively. "There's a meat pill, and two kinds of veg-tabs—"

"Never mind. I'm not hungry."

"But they said—"

"It's all right. Did they also say you should stay here with me if I wanted?"

The girl took a tentative step toward the cot. There was subtle, indefinable change in her. "Yes."

"Uh-huh. What's your name."

"Lori."

"Your real name."

"That's it!"

"No, it isn't. It's Loretta."

"You—you're reading my mind!" The girl fell back, shocked and frightened and a little indignant.

"Not really—at least not very much of it. Some things get through, especially things you feel strongly about."

"Oh? Uh—everything like that?"

"Uh-huh."

She set the tray carefully on the chair which remained in the room. Somehow, without moving, she seemed to yearn toward the cot where Rand lay. Her eyes behind the

Oriental mask were warm and bold. "That's not fair," she murmured.

"Why do you work for them?" Rand asked.

"They give me the pills."

"You can get them directly from the Syndicate."

"They watch you too closely. And you never get enough."

She was approaching the cot now. As if she had suddenly remembered, she reached behind her back briefly, tugged at something, and drew the halter away. It dropped to the floor beside the cot.

Rand stared up at her. "You've had your pill for tonight?"

"Yes. I always take it early."

"You know why they sent you in here, don't you?"

"They want you to work for them." She eased down on the cot next to him. "It's not so bad if you play it straight with them."

"They don't play it straight with you."

She shrugged, setting up an intriguing rippling motion of flesh. "Let's not talk."

"They could be watching us," Rand said. "Through that glass."

She drew back, glancing over her shoulder with a trace of apprehension. "I—I don't care. They can't see much with the mirror broken."

"Well, I do care," Rand said. "Why don't you cover the glass."

She seemed uncertain. "What—how could I cover it?"

"Use the sheet from this cot." Rand paused. "We don't need it."

Behind the Oriental mask the girl brightened. "You'll have to get up."

Feeling his attempt to move, the girl stood. Rand swung his legs over the side of the cot. "I can't very well help you like this." He indicated the straitjacket with a nod.

"I can manage."

A giggle escaped her as she whisked the sheet off the cot, getting into the spirit of the game Rand had suggested. It took her a while to figure out a way to hang the sheet over the expanse of glass on the far wall. She found a narrow gap at the top into which the cloth could be wedged. The gap disappeared on the left side of the glass wall, but Lori shoved the chair into that corner and draped the end of the sheet over the chair back. Only one angle of glass at the upper left remained exposed. The girl glanced inquiringly at Rand.

"That's fine," he said.

Only one section of the wall, he had guessed, was a one-way mirror. The watcher had been on the right side behind that section. He was there now, startled, ready to give an alarm. There wasn't much time.

"It isn't going to be much fun with me tied up like this."

"I—I don't dare."

"They can't see us now. They don't have to know."

She hesitated. Rand studied her, making sure that the warm lick of her eyes over him was clearly indicative of her feelings. He didn't want any resistance under hypnosis. That would mean delay, perhaps defeat. But the girl was transparent. PSI-40 brought out one dominant response in her.

"Sleep," Rand thought, invading her mind with all the persuasion he could muster. She was instantly asleep on her feet. Aloud he said, "You can open your eyes now. Untie this jacket."

The alarm had been given, he knew. The guard was afraid to enter the room—fortunately it was the frightened one with the clown mask.

"Wait a minute," Rand ordered. "Put that chair under the knob of the door. Don't worry about the sheet. No one can see us."

The girl obeyed silently, dragging the chair over to the door and sliding the back under the knob.

"Now hurry!" Rand commanded. "They might try to interrupt us."

The girl's fingers fumbled at the ties of his straitjacket. He felt the folds loosen. He struggled out of the jacket. Lori stared at him. "Lie down," Rand said gently. "And sleep."

She was asleep, and Rand was busy rubbing circulation into his arms and taking the stiffness out of his muscles, when a weight slammed against the door. The chair under the knob held.

All right, Rand thought. If it wasn't a dream, now is the time.

"Rand!"

He glanced up at the broken vent fan in the ceiling. At first he could see nothing. Then he sensed a—presence.

A sudden picture of someone kneeling on a roof appeared in his mind. So the vent was direct, leading to the roof.

"Hurry!" he cried aloud. Something smashed against the door, a muffled voice shouted.

The ventilating unit moved. There was a scraping noise. Metal banged on metal. But at the doorway wood ripped, and part of the door yielded. Rand turned toward the door. He caught the configuration of Roman-nose's mind aflame with frustration and rage. Grimly Rand concentrated on that mind. With sudden, vicious force he projected the sense of pain—blind, tearing pain. From behind the door there was a scream.

"Urgent!"

Rand looked up. There was a round hole in the ceiling where the ventilator had been. A pale face stared down at him from the darkness beyond. A rope slid down through the hole and fell at Rand's feet. He tugged at it. The other end was solidly moored.

Hand over hand he climbed up the rope and hoisted himself through the opening, which was just large enough to allow his shoulders to squeeze through. When he was on the roof, the tall female figure in the darkness stooped to slide the ventilator unit back into place.

"Never mind that," Rand said brusquely. "We'd better go."

"Yes."

She was taller than he was, Rand thought. By maybe an inch. Ridiculous male vanity.

"I didn't think you were going to make it on time," he said.

Taina Erickson smiled. "I didn't know whether or not you wanted to be interrupted. She is attractive, isn't she?"

Rand laughed aloud. He found her hand and took it in his own. Together they started across the graveled roof.

Chapter Ten

"Does the Del Pacifico approve of your having overnight guests?" Rand asked idly.

"Baja is a pleasure colony, Mr. Rand."

He didn't ask whether she had tested the hotel's tolerant policy before. "La Luz seems different," he said. "Different from most of Baja I've seen."

"They've tried to keep it the way it was down here before the Pump went in."

"How did you find it?"

"It was recommended to me by—a friend."

"An old friend?"

"A temporary one."

"I see."

"No, you don't, Mr. Rand."

After a moment's silence he said, "My name is Jon. Though nobody ever seems to call me that."

"Then I'd like to."

"Some people are last-name types," he mused.

"That's because you're a Sensitive."

He glanced at her in surprise. Maybe the observation was true, though he had never really thought of his Sensitivity as making him aloof, someone normal people could not get close to.

It was almost midnight. They had talked little since their escape from the rooftop of the exotic club where Rand had been held prisoner. No one had tried to stop them—Rand's last minute terrorizing of the man he called Roman-nose had proved effective. Taina Erickson had her own car, a small, sporty two-seater with a gasoline-powered rear engine. Rand had enjoyed the wild ride, in spite of— or rather, because of—Taina's personal control of the vehicle. He liked watching her quick reactions, her smiling absorption with the task of driving. In her communion with the car, her pleasure in it, she was like Miguel Huerara.

An hour later the staccato drumming of the little engine had subsided to a growl as the car nosed into a quiet resort town north of Mulege on the road to Santa Rosalia. La Luz had a carefully preserved Mexican atmosphere, reflected in the adobe-walled, tile-roofed resort hotel where Taina Erickson was staying. In addition to the main building, there were, scattered over the huge palm-shaded grounds and overlooking the blue gulf, a series of private cottages, also red-tile-roofed, with brick lanais across the front. Taina had one of these.

She had insisted on preparing a meal herself, humming as she worked in the tiny kitchen. Rand relished the solid meal. Afterward they carried coffee out onto the patio. There, in comfortable silence, they had listened to the rhythmic roll and slap of waves, the night calls of birds, the clatter of palm fronds rustling in the wind.

Without Rand's noticing, the night had turned cooler. Taina saw him shiver. "We'd better go inside," she said. "You've been through more than you realize."

"Don't make it sound heroic."

"You've been gassed, tied up, slugged on the head, seduced—"

"Not seduced," Rand objected. "Not yet, anyway."

Rand followed her into the thick-walled cottage, his mind still filled with the image of her sitting close to him on the patio in the semi-darkness, her full mouth warmly inviting—yet remote. They dropped into native chairs, baskets of plastic leather hung in wooden frames, and looked smilingly at each other.

Rand wondered if it was time to talk. They had not even discussed her fortuitous intervention to aid his escape, and her revelation of herself as at least a Sensitive on a level equal to Rand's. It was if each of them had been willing to postpone that confrontation, to accept the quiet evening for itself as a selfish interlude.

"What made you contact me?" Rand asked finally.

"You were in trouble."

"How did you know where I was being held?"

"You forget I was in the club when they jumped you. You put up an audible fight—"

"Audible to you," Rand murmured.

"Yes. And you put up a very poor one with Kit."

"Kit? The one with shoulders?"

"Yes."

"A temporary friend?"

"Jon—"

"All right. I put up a very poor fight."

"That's how I knew there was something wrong with you—that and the strange way you acted. You were more than just drunk."

"There was a gas impregnating the mask."

She nodded. The game was not new to her, Rand thought. She said, "I didn't think you would want me to interfere then."

"I was glad enough when you did."

"I'd made some inquiries," she admitted. "And learned

something about the club and the people running it. The tall man, the one you call Roman-nose—"

"Did I say that?"

"You thought it."

"Oh—yes."

"His real name is Ortiz. He deals in the black market."

"He'd like to deal in a bigger way," Rand said. "He thought I was a Syndicate agent who could tip him off on a big shipment of PSI-40. But I don't think he'll be so anxious to tangle with Sensitives for a while."

"Could you have helped him?"

"No."

"But you are with the Syndicate. You are a drug salesman, after all."

"In a way." For some reason the admission made Rand less comfortable.

"Do you still believe in what you're selling, after what you've seen in Baja?"

"You use PSI-40," Rand said quietly.

"That's not the same."

"How is it different? Because you have a specific response to it? Everyone does. You and I are no better than anyone else."

"Not better, perhaps—but different!" Taina spoke intensely. "We're not withdrawing from—from *life!* That's what PSI-40 does to most people, Jon. And that's wrong! There must be another way to use it."

"That's not for me to decide."

"Why not? At least you have to decide whether you want to be a part of what's happening—part of a sickness that's infected the whole world, especially America, because we started it, and we're the wealthiest people. We can *afford* to run away from life—to create an artificial love, an artificial religion, an artificial happiness!"

An artificial death, too, Rand thought—a funeral without tears. But aloud he said, "That's Anti propaganda."

"What does it matter, Jon, who says it—if it's true?"

"You're oversimplifying," he evaded. "Nothing's that black-and-white."

Even you, he thought. Who had sent her? Killjoy? Or was she voicing Anti sentiments to test him? Was she one of Pierce's agents (though it seemed unlikely that she would then have acted to help him escape from a ticklish situation potentially embarrassing to Loren Garrett)? Or was she one of Garrett's team, a backup agent sent to help him where necessary?

"We always seem to end up arguing," he said.

"Yes." Taina smiled. "We weren't going to do that."

Her features weren't too large at all, Rand thought. The mouth was just right, and the rest of her face was simply in fine proportion. And her eyes . . .

"Which side are you on?" he asked, smiling back at her.

"Do we have to talk about it now?"

"I've been through a lot," he admitted.

"You need to relax."

"Rest," he agreed.

"Yes."

"We can talk in the morning."

"Yes, Jon." Her blue eyes were full upon him. He read the warmth and understanding there, the honest acceptance of the mutual impulses which had guided them to this moment, and he could not help contrasting what he saw with the hot, avid, mindless hunger he had seen in the eyes of the girl who called herself Lori. He did not pretend to himself that what he read in Taina's steady gaze was love—but it was not a drug-induced imitation.

Rand climbed out of the deep pocket of his sling chair. Taina made no move as he approached. The chair cradled her so that her head was tilted back, her long legs lifted provocatively by the high front edge, tanned calves and slender ankles dangling.

"What I like," Rand declared, "is a woman who knows when to talk." He bent over her. His mouth found hers, and he murmured against her soft lips, "And when not to . . ."

Waking slowly in the strange bed, Rand was conscious of the darkness still pressing against the window of the cottage's small bedroom—and of Taina Erickson beside him, a warm, unfamiliar presence. He was strongly aware of their differences—an old television comedian's joke made particular: his heavy muscles, solid frame, squarely built body against her supple, slender, smoothly muscled length; his hair black, tight, stiff as wire, hers blonde and silken, sun-paled; his roughly chisled features beside the finely modeled artistry of her clean high forehead, straight nose, high cheekbones.

He turned his head toward her, and felt a twinge of pain in his temples.

"Feeling better?" Her smile in the darkness was a light glowing behind a curtain.

"I felt pretty good before."

"No headache?"

"No," he lied. There was no point in telling her. Rand had been a little surprised to go so long without the familiar pain.

"You slept well."

"I should have." He grinned. "I was exhausted. You're a demanding wench, wench."

"Why, Mr. Rand!" Taina pretended shock.

"Don't you ever get tired?"

She smiled. "I get content. Not very often, but with you—very definitely." She stretched, catlike, beside him. The long, warm thigh brushed against his. "Does that flatter you?"

"Very."

He felt a slow, stirring response to the nearness of her, the knowledge of her, the memory of her that would be forever part of him. She was not a woman he would easily forget.

"You look vulnerable sleeping," she murmured. "Different."

"I look vulnerable when I'm awake sometimes. Especially when I'm trussed up in a straitjacket."

Taina Erickson shook her head, pursuing her own line of thought. "Awake you're so—competent. And hard."

"It's my eyebrows. They're deceptive."

She laughed. "They're ferocious."

After a moment's silence he muttered ruefully, "I haven't been very competent since I came to Baja."

"We weren't going to talk about that."

"No, we weren't." He spoke half-reluctantly, trying to read her expression. In the dimness her blue eyes were jewels under water. "But we'll have to, sooner or later. No night lasts forever."

"Not now, Jon."

Her voice was sad. Suddenly, without other preliminary, he was pulling her toward him. The talk, the waiting, the deliberate holding off of his response while he remained aware of it, the flirting touch of warm flesh upon warm flesh—all had been preliminary.

"Jon, Jon!"

The delayed, contained, impatient desire became urgent. His world quickly compressed to the microcosm of one man holding one woman, no longer aware of the night or the slow crash of the surf outside, nor of the thick, silent walls, nor the strange bed, but only of a heady perfume and the wine of sorrowing lips, and a sense of oneness never realized before, of identities fusing as rough and smooth, dark and light, heavy and slender, hard and soft became one and seemingly inseparable. Jon Rand felt as if his very self were slipping away. At the same time he was riding a long, slow wave of passion, contained within the deep hollow of the wave, as a surfer seeks and finds and rides the perfect hollow of the rolling wave. And in that moment of giving, wanting, holding, that final intensity of helplessness, he felt—

A probe!

Mind abandoned, passion and sensation trampling down all barriers, Rand felt the invasion of his mind. And for stormy seconds was helpless to resist. The wave crashed over him. Anguish came, anger, loss, torment. He emerged from drowning, his brain clearing quickly, his body cooler as the wash receded from him. He looked into Taina Erickson's eyes and saw an answering anguish, a quick protest of denial. His mind closed against her with the cold force of steel doors clashing shut.

"No," she breathed.

"You had to do it!" His tone was harsh.

"Jon, you're wrong!"

"I was wrong, all right! How wrong!" He was pushing away from her, almost in revulsion. "What a time to choose!"

She stared at him, shaking her head in small jerks, her lips moving soundlessly, shaping the single word: "No, no, no, no, no, no!" Her eyes were like windows washed with rain. Anger lashed Rand. What a perfect pantomime of innocent grief!

Laughter seized and shook him. It brought shock into her face. "Who are you working for? Pierce? Johnson? Tell him, whichever it is, that you succeeded! You did what you were supposed to. Then tell him it wasn't good enough!" Rand laughed, the sound as hard and cruel as a slap. "It wasn't even a very good idea after all. A man isn't thinking very much at a time like that, except maybe about the woman. So there wasn't all that much to learn, was there? Not for a Sensitive, not even for a Special! You can't read what isn't being thought, in a book or a brain!"

"Stop it!"

She huddled on the bed, digging her hands against her ears as if she might blot out the angry words and the bitter laughter, her mind frozen into blankness (he sensed this numbing of her mind, but found no meaning in the fact). Rand backed away from the bed, from her, from the sick emptiness that threatened to sap his rage.

"Was the black-market proposition part of the trick? No, that's too elaborate. And you didn't need anything that obvious, did you? Just be in the right place and make sure he gets a good look at you—those were all the instructions you needed." His voice turned dull, flat. He fumbled for his clothes. "I'm leaving. Don't try to stop me."

"Get out," she ordered. Her eyes were dry now, bleak.

"Is that all you have to say? No more arguments? No more propaganda?"

"It's too late now." She shrugged, withdrawn, a stranger. "You wouldn't listen."

He dressed, watching her warily, hating the instinctive wariness. "If you try to stop me," he said at last, finishing with her, "I'll have to kill you."

In the small room the sudden silence had a brittle quality. From the gulf the roll of the surf carried clearly. He turned away in sickness, hoping she would not force the final clash upon them, steeling himself against the quick strong lash of the mind which had so subtly insinuated his own.

Nothing happened. He did not look back. Outside, in the cool night air, in the darkness lifting now to a leaden gray, he felt relief. He stood a moment, motionless, his heavy shoulders slumped. *It must have meant something to you, too,* he thought. *More than a job.*

His thoughts found only silence, closing around him like the heavy, moisture-laden air.

Chapter Eleven

In the morning his headache was back with close to full intensity. Jon Rand put the pain in a kind of compartment and ignored it with stoic determination, just as he tried to ignore the other boxes into which he had put his anger, disappointment, chagrin, resentment—and the occasional uneasy question which asked if he had been too quick to condemn, too sure of the motives behind Taina Erickson's subtle invasion of his mind.

He caught a taxi from La Luz back to Mulege. There had been none cruising in the predawn quiet and peace of La Luz, and Rand had had to find a dispatch office. He wanted a particular cab line, and there was more than an hour's wait before a car with the right markings passed through La Luz, empty, on the way back to Mulege.

The driver, red-eyed and weary from a night's driving, was sullen and uncommunicative. Rand allowed time to lapse before he spoke. "Do you drive out of Mulege?"

"Yeah."

"Then you know another driver named Max Gordon?"

The red-rimmed eyes did not leave the road. "Maybe," the driver said.

"Drives an old gas turbine job." Rand summoned up a show of enthusiasm to cover the head pain which made his eyes narrow.

"Lot of guys drive turbines," the tired driver answered noncommittally.

Rand sensed an irritable suspicion, instinctive hostility. "I guess they're pretty dependable and economical," he said. "What you need in a cab. Yours is diesel, isn't it?"

"Yeah."

"Know where I could find Max this morning? He's on days, I know."

"Look, Mister, I got trouble enough remembering my own schedule."

Rand leaned forward, spoke confidentially. "Max was kind of showing me around, you know? I'm a stranger down here. A man needs a guide, you know?"

The driver didn't answer, but he glanced into his mirror at Rand speculatively.

"Well, Max left me at this club." Rand grinned. "You know the kind I mean?"

"Yeah," the driver agreed wearily.

"Well, to make a long story short, I took this girl down to La Luz, see? Only she had her own car and we went in that, and I never did get together with Max again. And the thing is, I still owe him thirty bucks for yesterday. He was supposed to be waiting for me, and we didn't get together again. So you see, I gotta find him."

The driver's bloodshot eyes were interested now, and his hostile suspicion had faded from his mind. "You owe Max thirty bucks? And he let you get away?"

Rand grinned again. "I slipped out with this showgirl, see? She didn't want her boss to know, so we went out quick and quiet, through a back window. She's not supposed to entertain customers off the premises, or something like that. You know?"

The driver nodded. "Max is probably hunting for you, Mister."

"Well, I want to find him," Rand said sobering. "Don't want him to think I tried to run out on a fare. What the hell! He did a good job for me. You know what time he comes on in the morning?"

The night driver shrugged. "Most of those guys are out early. Lot of 'em check in at the hotels for people going to the airport."

"What about Max?"

"Usually he's on the stand at the Miramar Hotel. The guys there can tell you if he's on a fare."

Rand leaned back, half-closing his eyes against the pain which now did needlework between his temples. "Thanks," he murmured.

"Sure," the driver said, clearly friendly. "Ain't many people would take the trouble to look up a cabbie. Too many guys think they're payin' us too much, anyway. Give nine out of ten of 'em a chance to jump a fare, and you'd never see 'em again!"

Rand nodded, but his eyes were closed. The crease of a frown made a deep indentation in his forehead, and he was no longer listening . . .

Four taxis were lined up at the stand which faced

the entrance to the Miramar, a plush resort hotel. The first two cars were empty, their drivers chatting idly on the walk nearby. But a man was behind the wheel of the third, drinking coffee from a plastic cup. Rand caught a wink of blue fingernails. He saw rounded shoulders and long, wavy black hair. Shoving the pain of his headache back into its compartment, Rand approached the taxicab quickly from behind.

At the last second Max Gordon glanced into the outside-mounted side-view mirror and saw Rand. He had time only to register recognition before Rand's strong fingers clamped over his wrist. Coffee spilled as Max tried to jerk free. His other hand reached for the ignition key.

"Don't try it, Max," Rand growled, keeping his voice low.

Deliberately, his eyes fixed on Max's frightened gaze, Rand projected an image of a fist smashing into a swarthy face—Max's face. Beneath the fist the wide nose crunched and blood spurted. As the vision filled his mind, Max went rigid. Fear jumped into his busy brown eyes.

Rand released Max's wrist. The driver did not move as Rand climbed into the rear seat. "Just so you know where we stand, Max," Rand said quietly, "try to move your head."

Max did. The evidence was in the eyes which rolled toward the rear-view mirror to gape at Rand in panic, and in the stiffened cords at the back of Max's short neck and across his shoulders.

Rand's tone was cold, indifferent. "Now your arms. You can't move them either."

Max was so frightened now that his mouth hung open, and saliva began to drool from one corner. Rand waited long enough for the impression to sink in clearly, for Max to appreciate fully the sense of helplessness and to know the vile taste of terror. Then Rand said, settling back in his seat, "All right, Max. You can start driving now. We made a bargain a couple of days ago. Today you're going to live up to it."

The driver's head shook affirmatively with an almost comic eagerness and relief at the ability of the head to shake at will. "Yeah, sure, Mr. Rand," he croaked. "Sure!"

When they were moving Rand spoke. "Where is the center of Anti demonstrations? Here in Mulege?"

"No," Max said quickly. "Mostly in the towns outside,

112

or in the suburbs. Especially where the workers are."

"The workers," Rand repeated thoughtfully.

"Yeah. They don't get nowhere with tourists—you can see that." Max's brown eyes pecked tentatively at Rand's image in his mirror. "Listen, Mr. Rand, you don't think I had anything to do with those people who tried to—"

"Don't say it, Max," Rand warned coldly. "You fingered me for them. Now you're working for *me*."

"I didn't get anything out of it, Mr. Rand! I didn't know who you were!"

"What did you get, Max—pills?"

The swarthy driver licked his lips, looked uncertain, then appeared to realize suddenly that it was futile to try to hide anything. He seemed to sag from inside, like a balloon losing air. "Yeah—Ortiz, he gets me what I want. Look, Mr. Rand, what's so wrong about that? You're with the Syndicate—you gotta be! I'm on your side!"

"You're on the side of pleasure," Rand retorted half-mockingly, remembering Taina Erickson's heated arguments against PSI-40. What right did she have to preach against an artificial love, he thought bitterly, when she could use a moment of love's crisis, a moment of the greatest yielding of self, for a stealthy attempt to invade her lover's mind?

"Y-yeah," Max Gordon agreed uncertainly. "I guess you could say that."

"And against the Antis."

"That's for sure! Look—Mr. Rand, you out to get somethin' on them?"

"Maybe."

"Why didn't you tell me that? Listen, if I'da known that was what you was after, I never would of . . ." Max's voice trailed off, his nervous brown eyes flicking toward Rand and quickly away. "What I mean is, you just tell me what you want, Mr. Rand!"

A stab of pain through his temples made Rand pause a moment before answering. Then he said, "You know how to put me in touch with the Anti group down here in Baja?"

"Depends on what you mean. Like, they're on the streets all over, passing out pamphlets and things like that. But those aren't the ones you wanta talk to, are they? I mean, they're just suckers who've bought this

113

Anti stuff, like it was a religion. What you want is to get inside, right? To get at the ones who are behind the whole thing."

Through slitted eyes Rand studied the back of Max's neck, where the waves of shiny, oily black hair met and overlapped. "I want to meet the leaders," Rand said quietly. "What I want from you, Max, is a good guess as to where and how."

"Listen, it won't do any good to listen to the speeches in public parks and places like that—they're always doin' that. Kooks! Sometimes there are these demonstrations, and they get outa hand when somebody on the other side, like me, gets sore, and there's a riot, like. That won't do you no good. But I think I know of a place. It's a religious thing, see—like it's all on the up-and-up. This outfit, I mean. They use PSI-40 and they get high, and they see things. There's nothin' wrong with that. But what I've heard is, it's a cover operation for the Antis! I don't mean these religious ones—mysticals, they call 'em, or something like that—aren't on the level. Most of 'em. But the few that aren't straight, the Antis, they can get together at a place like that with nobody the wiser!"

Rand regarded Max thoughtfully, frowning. "Why should they have to be undercover? It isn't against the law to go Anti."

"Not exactly—but they ain't popular, you know? And the police down here don't like the demonstrations—bad for the tourist business—so they make it a little rough on the Antis. Then there's—well, what about you? There's the Syndicate." Max laughed nervously. "Everybody wants to stop them, seems like—the Antis, I mean —so the ones doing all the planning, the leaders, they don't show themselves."

"But you know where I might get a lead on them."

"Well, you understand I can't promise nothin', but you can't drive a hack all the time, long as I been here, without hearing things. A word here, a word there—you know."

"Yes, I know." Rand was silent a moment. Max Gordon was hardly a reliable or trustworthy informant. But Rand doubted that, after the small demonstration of possible consequences, the driver would try to lead him into another trap, or even deliberately mislead him. In any event, Max's rumor was the best lead Rand had. He was tired of being on the defensive. "All right, Max, we'll try it your way. Just one thing. You won't be spreading the word about where I am or what you think I am. Right, Max?"

The head tucked into the rounded shoulders was nodding enthusiastically before Rand finished. "Yes, *sir*, Mr. Rand! You can count on it!"

Chapter Twelve

The Society of Immortal Light met every evening at seven-thirty, with additional daytime services three days a week. Its headquarters was an unobtrusive white stucco building on the fringes of a large suburban shopping district catering to the needs of the date pickers and other workers on the ranches and in the packing houses northwest of Mulege, where a broad and now fertile valley lay between inland mountains and a row of smoothly sculptured foothills separating the valley from the gulf. A signboard near the front doors—handsomely hand-carved wooden doors made by a local artisan, and giving the building its only touch of distinction—announced services for that evening, but none during the day.

Rand dismissed Max Gordon and his taxi after a leisurely tour of the town and its environs, with no further warning than a cold glance and the suggestion that Rand could always find the driver if he needed to. The Taxi raced off with a reckless speed that pantomimed its driver's haste to escape. It was then almost noon. The day was dazzlingly bright and hot, intensifying Rand's headache. He had to drag himself along the baking sidewalks. With half a day of waiting ahead, he checked into an old-fashioned but inviting hotel. Done in the manner of another day, and suffering by consequence in its competition with the modern aluminum and glass cubes rising all over downtown Mulege and along the waterfront, the stucco hotel had large, dim rooms which remained invitingly cool in the midday heat, and a proportionately large, shady, red-bricked lanai where the sun was filtered through a green screen of leafy branches and palm fronds. Here Rand ate lightly, drank one tall, cool, icy tropical drink, and rested quietly, his eyes half closed. There were few people in the hotel, it seemed, and he was left alone.

Afterward he went to his room and tried to sleep. His head was too sensitive for even the soft pillow. Now and then he dozed, only to awake with a start—once in confusion and alarm over a dream in which his mind was exposed, stripped bare while he lay helpless . . .

How long had he lived with these terrible headaches? For at least fifteen years, since he first joined the Syndicate and began to live a regular portion of his life under the influence of PSI-40. There was always a price to pay. Rand had long ago accepted his. The headaches were the cost of the privilege of being a Sensitive and a Syndicate agent. He could, any time he chose, simply resign from Security and the Syndicate, give up the drug, and free himself from the pain accompanying his special talents.

Or could he?

Rand sat up on the bed in his high-ceilinged, thick-walled room, a dim cool haven against the brilliant day with its swords of light and heat. The question had never seriously occurred to him before. What happened when an agent simply got fed up, or decided the price was too high to pay? To his knowledge, Rand could not recall a single instance in which this had happened. Surely it was bound to, one day. What then?

He wondered, with a sudden gnawing doubt, if an agent would be allowed to quit. Would a Sensitive, armed with an intimate inner knowledge of the Syndicate's operation —and with a formidable power should he choose to use it independently—be too dangerous to set free? Would he really be any different from Kemp Johnson, defying the Syndiate with his Anti demonstrations?

A stab of pain drove the disturbing reflection away. When it left him Rand dozed again. He awoke after darkness, his whole body stiff, unrested, the driving pain in his head as savage as before.

He showered in an effort to clear his brain and stimulate his body out of his heavy lethargy. The attempt was only partially successful. He could have taken pain-killing drugs for the headache, but they disturbed the delicate chemical balance which made PSI-40 effective, while producing only minimal results in obliterating the pain. Only one thing ever worked on these headaches—the shots obtainable at Syndicate clinics. Rand didn't even know what they were, but they had always given him relief.

How tempting it was to seek that release from pain! After all, he had accomplished little on his own—he was no closer to Killjoy than he had been when he stepped off the plane at Loreto—why persist as he was?

But the memory of Miguel Huerara rose up again, a sharp reminder of betrayal somewhere within the Syndicate. Resignedly Rand set his teeth against the pain, trying to force it back into its container where it could be, if not ignored, at least endured.

The temperature changed quickly after sunset, though the streets held enough of the day's heat to keep the chill in the air from being uncomfortable. Rand walked slowly through the community toward the temple of the Society of Immortal Light. While the bars and teletheaters and private clubs were thronged—impassive or grinning brown faces watched Rand as he passed—there were few North American tourists here, so far from the pleasure centers of Mulege and Conception Bay. And La Luz, Rand thought, scourging himself with the memory. Here he was among the workers, people who had little, for whom PSI-40 brought a joy, a release, a revelation of beauty and wonder that was completely new.

And completely false, Rand seemed to hear Taina Erickson saying.

He had wondered if there might be a problem gaining admission to a glimpse of Immortal Light, but there was none, for the simple reason that all who came seeking the light had to bring their own fuel. A few, Rand saw, had come with empty pockets. They lounged against the walls or in listless groups, their eyes holding an empty hope as they watched others more fortunate, already lost in rapture. A little surprised, he noticed that, unlike the streets and bars, the attendance here was about equally divided between North Americans and Mexicans, though most had the weatherbeaten look and simple dress of field workers.

The building, like the churches of an older tradition which had lost so many of their adherents to the drug-inspired revelation, was chiefly one large room or hall, a raised platform or stage at one end. Apparently there were other rooms at the back, with doors leading from the stage. A balcony over the entrance housed an electronic orchestra playing a high, trembling theme. Beneath it, and to the right of the entrance, a stairway led to unseen basement rooms. Along the two side walls were rows of paintings, each bathed in its individual cone of light. Rand could not, at first glance, see any continuity in the paintings, other than a uniform brilliance of color. After a moment he guessed that each represented a private landscape of the mind. The vivid play of light and form and color was meant to stimulate receptive minds into creating new landscapes of their own, new visions of the universal glory.

At the far end of the hall, centered over the platform like an altar and speared by a bright blue spotlight directed from the front balcony, was what looked at first like another painting, and quickly turned into something far more complex. Rand stared. It was a startling impression of the strange architectural fantasy he had glimpsed himself, years before, when he first tried PSI-40, before more rational vistas were opened to him by the drug. He was not sure now whether this creation, shining in its blue light, was sculpture or painting or photograph or another kind of illusion. It seemed alive, for the multi-hued shapes and patterns kept changing, growing, diminishing, bursting with color and slowly fading, like fireworks or shooting stars. It was, Rand thought, amazingly effective.

Most of the members of the Society of Immortal Light were staring at this remarkable display, their eyes fixed and unblinking, their expressions remote and introspective. The hall was bare of furniture, and the worshipers of the new revelation were squatting or sitting in small groups on various rugs scattered over the red-tiled floors.

Rand had never scorned or doubted the potential of PSI-40 to induce a response akin to a religious, mystical ecstasy. He had simply felt no need of investigating the experience, since he could not share it.

The mystic, in one guise or another, had always been a phenomenon of society, through countless ages. But a rare phenomenon. PSI-40 had changed all that. The mystical experience was no longer the achievement of a select few. It was no longer even necessary to work for it. It was one of the more common responses to the drug. In all the Immortal Light and similar societies to be found in every suburb of every city across the United States, and other countries wherever PSI-40 was plentifully available, there were untold millions of "mystics." The libraries overflowed with their spiritual testimonials.

Casually Rand took his place among a group placed around a handwoven rug as if they were holding down the four corners. Two of the men were contemplating the display of architectural wonders at the end of the hall. A young woman, her face veiled, her hair covered by a lace mantilla, studied the design woven into the rug, a sun motif in red and gold borrowed from the still dominant ancient Indian culture. The fourth member of the group, a man whose gaze seemed to Rand more alert, was the only one to notice the newcomer.

Studying the rapt faces around him, listening to the discordant but not unpleasing music from the balcony and the occasional mutter or sigh from the worshipers, Rand found remembered words slipping unbidden into his mind. "You've made religion a matter of how many rainbows can be seen." Taina Erickson had not actually said, "you," Rand thought, but the personal application had been implied.

Suddenly a worshiper overcome by his vision leaped to his feet from his place on another rug a few steps away from Rand. Without straining Rand had a clear impression of the man's rapture, a feeling of strong exaltation and happiness in which the sense of self became vague, lost in the overwhelming idea of well-being. The mystic's eyes bulged and his arms reached out toward the shimmering display over the platform. Yet his lips moved in a shapeless way. He mumbled something audible only as one word repeated: "Brightness, brightness . . ."

Many in the hall paid this pronouncement no heed at all. Others looked approvingly at the standing man as if he had voiced a truth of great force and profundity. Serene and smiling, the worshiper sank again to his knees.

His outburst seemed to spark other activity. Exerting a minimal mental effort to clear his mind for receiving impressions, Jon Rand absorbed the flow of wonderment, awe, and fulfillment from all around him, like a chorus of whispers. But there were jarring sensations. One man crawled, abject, into a corner, whimpering. When Rand concentrated on him, he felt an instinctive recoil. He had a glimpse of a boiling sea of torment—the hell of a man whose vision is fragmentation instead of completion, awful aloneness instead of identity with All, darkness instead of light.

And from two or three in the hall, there was—nothing. One of them was the sharp-eyed man whose rug Rand shared. Feeling the eyes on him, Rand swung to gaze dreamily at his companion. Instantly he saw that he was too late. The other man was not fooled. Neither was he enjoying any spiritual rebirth under the impact of PSI-40. His eyes, coolly appraising, were gray and intelligent, set in a businesslike face with a cleft chin, flat cheeks and a mouth that drew a straight line. His sandy hair was cut almost as short as Rand's.

Rand felt a slow tightening of tension. Even that was enough to allow the carefully ignored pain in his head to escape from its imaginary box and flail about like a clumsy boxer. Rand wondered if the pain showed in his eyes. More important, if he was found out, would it again weaken his ability to act decisively or slow his mental responses?

The sandy-haired, cleft-chinned man gave Rand a brief nod—more like a jerk of his head. He muttered through tight lips in a voice so low Rand was not sure whether he had actually heard all the words or read them with the aid of unintentional telepathy. "Downstairs, eight o'clock. Use the stairs but wait for my signal. We don't want to make a parade out of it."

Rand nodded automatically, the impassive block of his face showing nothing of his quickening interest. A moment later the nonworshiper left the group and joined another quartet on the far side of the room near the front platform. An oblique probe, a quick grazing of the minds he confronted, told Rand that a second man of this new group was not preoccupied with any distorted, joyous or terrifying visions. Rand could not attempt a prolonged, concentrated probe upon an alert mind without revealing the intrusion even to a non-Sensitive. Opening his mind to receive useful impressions—an action which did not betray itself in any way—was out of the question in a room full of drugged minds all enjoying hallucinations and fantasies which any Sensitive could pick up as easily as he read violent emotion. Rand contented himself with contemplating the scene around him, taking a visual note of the low-voiced exchange across the way between the two men he had now identified as being mentally and spiritually sober.

Seeing the gray-eyed one turn to stare at him, frowning, Rand guessed that he was supposed to be getting into position near the stairway, waiting for his signal. He rose and ambled toward the back of the hall, drifting over to the stairway, smiling idiotically at anyone who appeared to notice him.

He did not have long to wait. His efficient-looking contact, passing on his way to the street, gave Rand another perfunctory jerk of his head toward the stairs. Without hesitation Rand went down the steps. He moved quickly but without an appearance of haste. He did not look back.

At the bottom he found himself in a low-ceilinged room almost as large as the hall above. It had a dirt floor and was damp-smelling. Rows of chairs were visible in the dimness, which was penetrated by light from the stairwell and by a crack of light at the far end of the basement defining the shape of a door.

It could be another trap—an annoying one set by someone like Ortiz, or a lethal one like that in which Miguel Huerara had died. Or it could be the first doorway of many that would lead Rand to Killjoy.

As he approached the crack of light he heard a murmur of voices. They stopped abruptly when he appeared in the doorway. Half a dozen faces twitched toward him like those of spectators at jai alai. There was a moment's silent appraisal. The faces around the big table in the center of the room—five men and one woman—were not hostile. Neither did they show friendliness. They reminded Rand of a board of directors at a business meeting surveying the new vice president. Or, he thought, the Syndicate's board studying an agent picked for a special assignment. But none of these was a Special.

Kemp Johnson was not among them.

It was the woman who spoke. "You're the new man taking Palmer's place?"

Rand nodded. The man upstairs must have made the same mistake, he thought.

"Take a seat. Kevin will be here any minute."

Just then Rand felt a cool draft at the back of his

neck. Simultaneously he was aware of someone approaching behind him. Rand stepped quickly into the meeting room, turning to face the doorway.

The attentive, tight-mouthed face of the man who had given Rand his signal appeared. His sharp gaze dissected the scene. "You're Jepson?" he addressed Rand.

Without too direct a probe Rand managed to catch the image of another man's face, the sense of sickness, pallor, smell of ether. He guessed that the man before him was thinking of the missing Palmer.

"Yes," Rand said. There had been no perceptible hesitation.

"Sit down."

Room was made for him at a spot before the table next to the woman who had first spoken to him. She was rather a typical member of an underground cell, he thought—plain, pale, straight-haired, the hair a lifeless brown, her face devoid of color or makeup, her figure hidden under a shapeless shift. The analysis led Rand to another observation, pinning down something which had been puzzling him since he entered the basement room. None of the men wore makeup either. Rand was grateful for the good luck that he never chose to wear any himself. The uniform paleness of the group could hardly be coincidence. Eye shadow or painted nails might have made Rand immediately suspect.

He hadn't heard of a prohibition against male makeup among the Antis, but it was possible that Killjoy had introduced innovations of his own. The psychology of it was shrewd. Any movement gained from the establishment of a common code, the setting up of rules and ritual.

"This is Jepson," the sandy-haired man spoke to the entire group. He broke off and waited for another arrival—the second man Rand had identified as sober among the worshipers in the hall—to slip into the room and take a seat. "He'll handle leaflet distribution in Palmer's place. Jepson, this is Radcliff, Dyer, Hughes, Martinez, Blanco. I'm Webb. You won't see them all again before the demonstration, so remember their faces."

Rand nodded. Radcliff was the woman. No "Miss" or "Mrs.," to soften the name, Rand noted. Another piece of psychology.

"You'll have the leaflets ready?" Webb asked.

The woman answered. "They'll be here at four o'clock." She looked at Rand.

"You'll pick them up here, Jepson, promptly at four," Webb said.

"Right," Rand answered briskly.

"You'll need one of the trucks. Martinez?"

"I will have one here," a slight, handsome man with softly accented English replied. "At the hour."

"I'll give you a list where the pickups will be made, Jepson," Webb said. "Before you leave here tonight. Remind me."

Rand doubted that the group leader would need any reminding, but he nodded.

"We'll rendezvous on the northwest field of the Gutierrez ranch at seven," Webb spoke to the assembly in general. "We'll go into town in trucks. Harrison's group will meet us there. Now let's go over assignments . . ."

One by one Webb checked out details of procedure with the individuals around the table. The proposed demonstration, at least in its preliminary planning, was organized with precision and remarkable economy of motion and manpower. A torchlight parade along the waterfront would attract spectators and police—but the latter would not interfere as long as the demonstration remained an orderly and peaceful assembly. As the crowd gathered, Rand's team of distributors would pass out the propaganda leaflets. At precisely eight fifteen the vanguard of the parade would veer away from the beach, cross the main thoroughfare, and march directly into the grounds of the huge Miramar Hotel. As of that moment it would cease to be a peaceful assembly and, in the eyes of the law, would become an unruly mob. There would be time for the chanting, torch-bearing crowd to circle the hotel. By then both police and the hotel's own security force would be converging on the mob. A riot would ensue.

And under cover of this turmoil, a small task force would make a bold, swift strike at the hotel's "unofficial" storeroom containing its entire stock on hand of PSI-40.

Rand examined the plan appreciatively. Chances were that the Miramar operated as the central store for most of or all the major hotels in the Mulege area. The loss from the Antis' strike, presuming it was successful, would be far more than an irritant. It would also be embarrassing to the hotel, to Mexican officials, to the Syndicate.

Even more than the physical wound inflicted, it was Rand's guess, Killjoy was interested in the psychological damage.

"Questions?" Kevin Webb concluded the briefing in his no-nonsense manner.

There were a few. Rand waited until they had been answered before he voiced his own. "I'm coming into this late," he said. "What about Killjoy? Is he leading the attack force?"

Webb looked at him sharply. "That's something you don't need to know."

Rand shrugged. "At least we'd know the plan has some chance of success. Otherwise . . ."

The woman beside him was shocked, and two or three others around the table showed dismay or disapproval. But the remaining men were turning questioningly toward Webb, one of them nodding eagerly. And the gray eyes of the group leader missed nothing.

"Of course he'll be with us," Webb snapped.

"Leading the task force?" Rand persisted.

"Yes." Webb smiled thinly. "Don't worry. The authorities will know he's been there."

Rand nodded, as if satisfied. "Our people have to know, too. It means a lot to them."

He had learned what he wanted to know. As the meeting drew to a conclusion and began to break up, Rand found himself wondering how the apparent efficiency of the Anti force with which Killjoy had aligned himself could have fallen down so completely on the small detail of Rand's easy penetration of this cell. Chance had played a part—the real Jepson had been scheduled to attend the meeting. Why hadn't he?

Webb answered the question when he drew Rand aside while the rest of the group began to desert the basement room at delayed intervals. "Wasn't expecting you until tomorrow," the tight-mouthed leader of the cell said. "If you hadn't taken a place on my prayer rug upstairs and shown me you were sober, I wouldn't have recognized you from the description I had."

"I decided I'd get here as soon as I could."

"Well, yes. A good idea." Webb found a sheet of paper in a pocket. "Here's the list of pickup points. You're sure you understand what you're to do?"

"Yes."

It occurred to Rand that Webb was an extremely methodical man. Rand's appearance in the hall above, his sobriety, his lack of makeup or painted nails, and the perfect timing of his arrival within minutes of a scheduled meeting, all of this had fitted neatly into an apparent pattern. His identity had been accepted without question. The weakness of a too orderly mind, Rand reflected. Like a scholar finding motive and purpose in a set of chance circumstances, simply because he was looking for them.

"Tomorrow, then," Webb said.

"At four," Rand said. But the real Jepson would have arrived by then.

"You needn't bother putting on an act upstairs. We like to disperse as quickly as possible. You're next."

"Right."

He went up the stairway, emerging near the front entrance. In the dark street, hovering in shadows a dozen steps from the temple, the woman was waiting for him.

"You're new here," she said, "do you have a room?"

"I'm at the El Prado."

"Oh." She seemed surprised. "It's expensive."

"It's just for one night," Rand explained.

"There's a room where I'm staying—don't misunderstand," the woman pleaded. "It's quite cheap."

"I see. Well, if I stay on . . ."

"Palmer has a room there. He's ill, but he can talk. I thought you might like to see him—about tomorrow."

"I'll come in the morning," Rand promised.

She gave him the address. "We like to be together when we can. That's one of the things about us that's different. With the drug you're always—alone."

Rand nodded. He felt as if he were mocking her earnestness, trampling on her faith. The pale face in the darkness was innocently accusing, creating in him an odd feeling of guilt. It did not help to remind himself that opposition groups always attracted the earnest and lonely.

Chapter Thirteen

Rand walked slowly back to his hotel in the cool evening. His footsteps jarred in his head, but the pain was bearable. Throughout his bizarre visit to the temple of Immortal Light he had managed to ignore his headache. Idly his fingers touched the top, back, sides of his skull. It felt like some huge, soft, pulpy bruise, sensitive and tingling at his touch.

Twenty-four hours, he thought. In twenty-four hours the pain might end.

The evening's turn of events was almost too good to be trusted. Rand was suspicous of an inordinate amount of luck. Granted that to a large extent he had forced it. He had known the temple was used as a cover by the Antis. And he had expected no great difficulty in infiltrating their ranks. He was not dealing here with trained, disciplined, experienced specialists, but with ordinary people sold on an idea. Most of them probably never expected to do more than march in a parade and carry a placard.

At least, Rand thought, they believed in something. The faces around the table in that ridiculous cellar room had all been—absurd perhaps, pathetically intense—but alive.

While those of the drugged worshippers upstairs, for all their ecstatic visions. . .

Impatiently Rand shrugged his heavy shoulders. It was tempting to push his luck a little further. The torchlight parade would offer excellent cover for his own approach to the Miramar and to Killjoy. And if he could intercept the real Jepson—

With a scowl Rand dismissed the possibility. He had deceived one small group because they were amateurs and too ready to accept him without question. Tomorrow there were certain to be others less susceptible—probably some who knew Jepson. The chance of Rand playing out his role and avoiding exposure was too slim.

And if he didn't show up? There would be some panic,

worry, consternation. But the cell was not to meet again as a unit before the demonstration was scheduled. Even Kevin Webb might not be reached. In any event, there would be no way of determining who Jepson's impersonator was or how important his treachery. And time would be short. Webb—or someone—would have to make a decision. It was unlikely that the word would ever filter up to Killjoy. And on lower levels there was no real appreciation of how big a game they were playing, Rand thought. The decision would be inevitable: plans had gone too far. The demonstration and the robbery would go on as scheduled.

Rand thought of the pale, prim woman who had offered him a room. He shook his head irritably, and his head gave a sharp twinge.

The lobby of the old hotel was almost empty. A guitarist was playing and singing to a quiet handful on the patio, under the wide overhang of the roof supported by thick square beams. Rand stood a few minutes in the shadows, listening. Then he went up to his room.

He almost opened the door and entered the dark room without hesitation. If he had, Killjoy would have ceased to be a problem. It was not instinct or an agent's trained reflexes which made him pause in the corridor just outside his door, but the acute sense given to him by PSI-40 for mental activity nearby, and for the presence of living creatures in particular space. The moment he stopped to concentrate, he knew, not only that someone was in his room, but where the intruder was.

Crouched by the window. To the right. An assassin's position. He would fire a bullet or a poisoned needle, or throw his knife, as soon as Rand presented himself as a target against the light of the corridor. Then out the window onto the roof. Rand's room was on the second floor. It was an easy drop to the garden below.

Noisily Rand fitted his key into the lock. He stood to the right of the door. From the far end of the corridor, through an open window facing the patio below, he could hear the soft strumming of a guitar and the high, mournful tenor voice he had listened to a few minutes before. Rand waited as a final note soared and held. Then he turned the key.

In one motion his hand fell on the door knob, twisted, pushed. One foot lashed out, slamming into the solid, carved wood door. It swung wildly backward, shuddering.

The soft hiss of a needle-gun came from the room, like a snake's warning. With an almost inaudible "tick!-tick!" two needles darted into the wall across the corridor from Rand. He was already moving under the line of fire through the doorway, catapulting across the room with surprising agility, a shape erupting and vanishing in the darkness split by the slash of light from the open door.

There was a scuttling movement near the window. Rand, flattened against the wall opposite the door, half protected by the bulk of a heavy chest, heard the faint rustle. He sensed the vibrations of panic coming from the unseen figure huddled to the right of the window. The man might just as well have been announcing his position, so exactly could Rand place him. With the shrill pulsations of fear to guide him, he knew when the would-be assassin had guessed Rand's whereabouts in the darkness. And when the man't taut finger squeezed over the trigger of his gun, Rand sensed the command as quickly as the man's muscles could translate it into action. Rand was fractionally quicker.

A needle splintered wood from a corner of the chest whose cover Rand had vacated a split-second before. He stormed across the room. The needle-gun swiveled toward him. Rand's palm chopped down like an ax blow. The gun spilled from limp fingers and the assailant's mouth opened to scream. The sound was never born. It was choked off by a knee ramming into the attacker's throat and jaw. He dropped like a wet sack.

Rand was bending over the fallen man, poised for yet another and more lethal blow, when the room lights bloomed around him. He started to straighten and turn. There was a loud crash. It was not until he felt his cheek crack hard against the window sill that he realized, bemusedly, that the crash had been a blow upon his head. . .

He never completely lost consciousness. He was aware of the door to his room ponderously closing. He heard its firm, solid click. He saw knee-length boots, but they were far away. Couldn't have struck me on the head, he thought. Not close enough.

Rand struggled into a sitting position. He put one hand to his head. His fingers came away sticky. Bullet, he thought. Needle doesn't gouge like that. Bullet just nicking. Lucky.

The boots approached. One of them nudged the figure crumpled on the floor near Rand's feet. Rand was having trouble with double vision. He thought without satisfaction that the man on the floor would not trouble anyone for some time.

Tilting his head back, Rand stared up at the owner of the boots. Even with two heads, Lieutenant Juan Huerara was recognizable. He was smiling.

"Even the American businessman can make mistakes," Huerara mumbled. He probably wasn't really mumbling at all, Rand thought. It just sounded that way, as if Huerara were speaking through a filter. "Or should I say the American Security agent with the Mental Freedom Syndicate."

He had blundered, Rand realized. He should have guessed there would be two assassins.

"We all make mistakes," Huerara said generously. "I didn't make sure of you in the first place. But fortunately your mistake proves more serious than mine, Mr. Rand."

Right from the start, Rand thought disgustedly. Huerara had been waiting for him the moment he got off the plane!

Rand groaned. Very slowly he struggled into a kneeling position. The movement brought agonizing pain into his head. Stubbornly he fought against it. "Suspected you," he muttered. "Went to look you up."

But the funeral had thrown him off—that and the fact that he had found Huerara under the influence of PSI-40. The drugged condition could not have been faked. Which meant that Hucrara was neither Sensitive nor Special.

"Ah, yes! I recall your visit. Your second mistake, Mr. Rand. For a Security agent, you are a gullible man."

Perhaps Huerara didn't need extrasensory talent, Rand thought—not with a gun in his hand. And with pain blurring Rand's concentration. Could he summon enough control over his body for one instant to make himself move faster than Huerara's finger could squeeze a hair trigger?

Thoughtfully Lieutenant Huerara set a polished toe against Rand's shoulder and shoved. Rand let himself fall back, making no attempt to resist the push. He fell into the wall, his arm and shoulder taking most of the impact, and slid down to the floor. He did not have to fake the grimace of pain. His eyes were watery with it.

But his vision was getting better. There was only one Huerara looming over him. Rand focused his eyes on the dark, handsome face, ignoring the revolver with its cumbersome-looking silencer in Huerara's gloved hand.

"Are you arresting me?" he asked thickly.

"Arresting?" Huerara laughed. "Why should I do that?"

Rand was silent a long moment, staring up. He wanted as much time as he could get. Forget the pain, he thought. You have known it a long time. It's nothing to think about.

"To embarrass the Syndicate," he said aloud, his voice a little stronger. "But you'd have to charge me with something. What—killing Miguel? No good. Doesn't make sense. Anyway, you could have done that before now."

"But you went to Mr. Taylor, didn't you? I am sorry, Mr. Rand—you have made it impossible for me to arrest you—alive."

Several previously unrelated facts suddenly coalesced in Rand's mind. The abrupt perception struck him so forcibly that he jerked up on one elbow. Huerara reacted to the sudden movement. Just in time Rand sensed the quivering tension which transmitted itself from Huerara's body to the gun in his hand. The black muzzle, staring at Rand's chest, trembled. Carefully Rand sagged back.

"You were very close to death," Huerara breathed.

"That doesn't seem to matter now."

"You are a brave man," the lieutenant said admiringly. "It is true you must die. I think I will arrest you, Mr. Rand—how do you say it?—posthumously. For the murder of my assistant."

The cold-blooded announcement confirmed Rand's guess. "Killjoy didn't send you," he said flatly. "He wouldn't have tolerated killing Miguel to get at me. That must have been your own idea—only someone so drug-ridden that even love and family mean nothing could have done that." He rushed on, ignoring the frown which had erased Huerara's tolerant smile. "And Killjoy probably wouldn't countenance what you're planning here. That man—your assistant—isn't dead."

"You are also a wise man," Huerara said coldly. "There

is a saying, I believe, that wisdom comes when it is too late to use it."

Rand was calculating the razor's edge of time he would have to make his move. He had to increase it somehow. He made a slow half-turn of his body, groaning audibly, as if he were trying to ease pain. The movement turned the front of his body slightly away from the line of fire, narrowing Huerara's target. It also had the effect of coiling Rand's body slightly.

There was sweat on his forehead. "It's not Killjoy," he repeated. "But someone is giving you orders. It's not Garrett. That leaves Pierce."

"It is good to know that you are indeed a worthy opponent, Mr. Rand," Huerara said, a beginning impatience in his tone. "I regret that now I must—"

"Not so worthy," Rand interrupted quickly. "It's obvious enough. Distribution always sets up police contacts. Pierce needs you people. He couldn't distribute without—"

Calling on the full sensitive control his mind could exercise over his aching muscles, Rand uncoiled, snapping his body straight. *"Shoot!"* A soundless scream was projected into Huerara's mind at the instant Rand started to move. Huerara's trigger finger jerked in a spasmodic, uncontrollable response to the violent command —but he fired without aim, without any chance to adjust to Rand's fractional shifting of his body. The bullet tugged at the back of Rand's jacket and ploughed into the floor.

Rand had deliberately provoked the shot, knowing that that involuntary muscular spasm was the one action he could not prevent even with successful hypnotism. It was the last move Juan Huerara remembered. Rand's second command turned Huerara into a statue.

The tensions of the mind are more delicately balanced in some than in others. Just as one body absorbs physical shock while another cannot survive it, so mental shock may stun or momentarily upset the mind's balance—or it may cause a complete rupture. There was no way for Rand to examine the condition of Huerara's mind at the moment of invasion. There was no way of knowing how the man would tolerate the experience of another's unspoken command bursting in his brain like an exploding shell.

Rand did not know how completely Huerara had ceased

to be a menace until he was dragging himself erect, using the window sill for leverage. Then he felt Huerara's mind begin to unravel. It was like watching a set of tightly compressed springs inside a transparent casing lose their tension as first strand snapped, then another, and suddenly the entire mass of coils bulged out, twisted, and spilled over into chaos.

Turning away, Rand leaned against the window frame, fighting nausea. From the green, peaceful garden below, the mellow chords of a guitar drifted up to him. Rand drew in long, shuddering breaths.

Near his feet the first attacker groaned, stirring. He was not seriously hurt. But Huerara stood paralyzed, as inactive as a vegetable, the demoralized brain insistently signaling its flawed state like a cracked record.

At length Jon Rand pushed away from the window. Movement was agony. He stared briefly but without pity at Juan Huerara. Then, his eyes pinched almost shut and his lips unconsciously drawn back over his teeth in pain, he stumbled across the room and found the door, the long corridor, the cool darkness of the night.

Chapter Fourteen

Rand half-fell on the wide steps leading to the street. A taxi was waiting at a stand. The driver, languid against a fender, straightened to attention. A smile turned on like a light bulb. "Taxi, senor?"

Rand pushed by him. No telling what Huerara's cohort would do when he fully regained consciousness. Probably he too was a policeman. While the two assassins had been acting outside the law, Rand could not prove it. An alarm might go out for him. And a taxi would announce where he had gone.

With short, measured, careful steps he made his way along the sidewalk. A couple, avoiding him, stared at his head. Rand remembered the possibility of blood showing. He looked at his image in the window of a darkened store. The reflection was not clear, but he could see a dark patch capping his skull, darker than his hair.

At a variety store still open on the corner to sell souvenirs, Rand bought a straw sombrero, ignoring the curiosity of the clerk and one other customer. He almost regretted the purchase, for even the light pressure of the hatband seemed like a circle of hot steel welded to his head, adding to the jolting shock of each footstep. But he was no longer conspicuous. His wound, which was shallow—the blood was caking over his stubble of black hair—could not be seen.

The best way to deal with pain was to concentrate on something else. Rand fixed his attention on the laborious process of lifting his feet and putting them down again, one after the other. It became a kind of game—and a challenge. He turned corners when he remembered, following a random route which had no other purpose than to remove him as far as possible from the El Prado Hotel, and to confuse anyone who sought to trace his flight. Sometimes he had to stop, and there were moments when consciousness threatened to leave him.

Once he awakened with a start to find himself standing next to an adobe-walled building, leaning against it for support. The effort of pushing himself away from the wall sent a rocket screaming off its pad inside his skull.

He tried detachment, but it had no effect. He could turn off almost any other kind of pain, but not this private inferno where his brain resided.

He felt his knees going soft. Struggling on, at last he came to what seemed to be a park. There was an audience of flowers, tight blotches of dark color, and a chorus of palms moving in rhythm, waving their fans overhead against a dark blue backdrop. Rand staggered off the sidewalk. He could smell grass, cool and wet, and he heard a murmur of water. Longingly he knelt on the grass, and sank down upon it.

The car cruised slowly along the street. Above the stare of its headlights there was another, single light, an orange flame revolving slowly. Passing a darkened square, where in the daytime a fountain made a cool, inviting focal point, one of the two men in the car nudged his companion with his elbow. He pointed. The car nosed in toward the curb and pulled up quietly. The orange light continued to turn in a slow circle. One of the men stayed in the car behind the wheel while the other got out.

Rand started when a flashlight winked in his face, on and off. Each flick of light drove a sliver of pain through his eyes deep into his brain.

"You are all right, senor?"

"Uh—yes."

"You are an American?"

Rand struggled to a sitting position. "Yes."

"It is not allowed to sleep here."

The man with the flashlight wore a uniform. Rand felt a tug of alarm, but his face—the flashlight was steady now, but directed toward the ground rather than into Rand's eyes—revealed nothing. He tried to rise, balancing his head as if he were carrying something on it that might fall.

The patrolman offered his hand and pulled Rand to his feet. "You have perhaps celebrated too much, senor."

"Yeah—I guess I did. I'll be all right now."

"You are staying nearby? Perhaps at a hotel?"

"Uh-no. I can find my way. Thanks."

"I believe it would be better if we took you wherever you are staying."

"No, no!" Rand protested. "It was—just a momentary lapse. It won't happen again."

"It is better if you ride with us." The policeman was polite but firm. He put a hand under Rand's elbow. "This way."

Rand did not resist. He was helped carefully into the back seat of the patrol car, and he sank back against the foam cushions with a sigh of relief. The patrolman took his seat, grinned at the driver, and said to Rand, "Where do you wish to be taken?"

Rand's hesitation was hardly perceptible. He remembered the address he had been given by the pale, earnest woman after the Anti cell meeting. It was the only one he had to offer.

The patrolman who had picked him up nodded. "It is as I thought—you would not find it going this way." He smiled amiably. "It is not good to fall asleep in the square, but you were doing no harm."

It was not good to antagonize the American *turista* either, Rand thought gratefully. It was also clear that no general call had been put out for him. The junior assassin might still be trying frantically to restore Juan Huerara to meaningful existence.

The rooming house could have been an historic landmark. It looked as if it predated the construction of the Rivera Pump by at least a generation. The stucco walls were flaking, and the brick path leading to the entrance had many pitfalls. Rand was more concerned about the Radcliff woman's reaction. When he stumbled going up the path, and smiled wanly, the patrolman put it down to the unsteadiness of drink, and the uncertainty of the brick footing. He did not notice Rand's pain-glazed eyes or read them accurately.

The two-story building was constructed in an L-shape around an uneven courtyard, which was shaded by a single ancient, untrimmed palm. The two policeman looked inquiringly at Rand, who eyed the outside stairway with misgivings. The Radcliff woman's room number was on the second floor. With a resigned shrug he started up the steps, under cover of the darkness using the iron railing like a tow rope to pull himself along. There seemed to be more strength in his arms than in his legs. One of the uniformed men stayed below, brown leather face turned upward, dimly colored by light from a street-level room. The other held Rand's free arm.

At the top of the steps Rand gasped, "I'm—fine now."

"I will see you safely in, sir," the patrolman said with maddening patience.

Rand stopped resisting. He stood slumped outside the door of the woman's room while the patrolman knocked. What would she do? In Rand's pain-oriented universe, the reality of possible exposure seemed less important than it should have been.

The woman, pale and uncertain and shapeless as before, an old cotton robe held tight at her throat, opened the door. Her face remained blank while the patrolman explained. He had found her friend—or husband, perhaps? The patrolman seemed doubtful—who had celebrated too much. It was safer to take drugs, as most did when they could afford it, which was not always the case, of course, the cost of PSI-40 being what it was. She *did* know the American gentleman, didn't she?

Gently Rand tilted his straw sombrero back so that she could see his face more clearly. Her eyes and her mouth made circles of consternation and fright. She recovered quickly.

"Yes! Yes, of course! He is my—my brother." She came out onto the landing to take Rand's arm, neglectful of the frayed cotton robe which parted over a thin gray chest. "I will take care of him."

"Fine! Fine!" The patrolman bowed, smiled, backed away. Rand stared at the woman while he listened to the footsteps click down the stairs and fade out of the courtyard. She tugged at his arm. He started toward the door. His toe stubbed on the rise at the base of the doorway, and his knees buckled. The woman gave a little cry of dismay and clutched at him, but she was not strong enough.

Rand fell into the room, but there seemed to be no floor. He kept on falling, falling . . .

Once he woke to find the white face watching his anxiously. He was lying on a couch with a pillow under his head, which had been sponged clean and dressed. There was perceptibly less pain localized at the point where the bullet had creased his scalp. But the beast still prowled back and forth inside his skull, restlessly back and forth. Rand had the feeling that at any moment he would move his head and the beast would roar with rage, blowing the top of Rand's skull right off.

"Are you feeling better?"

Rand slowly blinked his eyes affirmatively. She seemed to understand.

"Don't try to talk. Sleep."

Not safe, Rand thought.

He must have involuntarily projected the concept. The woman caught it without knowing how. "You're safe here," she said quickly, her eyes pleading for trust. "I haven't told anyone!"

"Anyone?"

"No—no one knows."

That seemed doubtful. When policemen brought a drunken stranger to a woman's room at night in a boarding house, the other tenants generally knew all about it. But even that might be a kind of safety.

At any rate, he thought, there wasn't much he could do about it just then . . .

She spoke to him again. When he failed to answer, she

drew the blanket more securely up around his neck, and once again resumed her vigil.

"What's your name?"

"Radcliff."

"No—your first name."

She hesitated, looking away. "Liz," she murmured. "I was named after a famous movie star, an actress. Famous when I was born. She—she was notorious."

Rand smiled. "Well, you can't be blamed for that."

"No."

"What time is it, Liz?"

"Ten o'clock." She looked away again. Rand caught the sense of guilt. He was suddenly alert. She asked. "Do you want any more soup?"

"No—thanks. What's wrong?"

"Wrong?" She whirled, revealing terrified brown eyes. "What do you mean?"

He studied her for a moment. Then he said quietly, "I think I'd better leave."

"No—no, you can't! You're not well!"

"Well enough, thanks to you."

"No! You'll just make it worse! Your head—"

He pushed back the blanket and carefully swung his feet to the floor. If he moved slowly enough, he thought, the pain seemed bearable. It had to be.

"Who came while I was asleep?" he asked her gently. "Who knows about me?"

Tears rolled silently down her colorless cheeks. She was one of those who never protested out loud, he thought, and consequently never got heard. At least the Anti group gave her a chance to register some kind of meaningful protest.

Then he wondered why he found it meaningful.

"It's Palmer!" she blurted out suddenly. "He came this morning."

"Palmer? But he was supposed to be sick. Isn't he the man I'm replacing?"

"He can get around a little now." Liz Radcliff tried to wipe the tears away. A faint note of accusation crept into her voice. "He said you're not Jepson."

Rand had managed to slip his shirt on. He eyed his trousers. They were carefully laid over the back of a chair

137

across the room. He looked at the woman. "Where's Palmer now?"

She hesitated. "Is it true? What he said?"

"Yes."

She was silent, troubled. Rand wondered if she wished she had not taken him in. The possibility saddened him.

"Then you're a traitor."

"That depends on what you mean by treason."

She turned her back on him as he left the couch and made his way to the chair on legs as awkward as stilts. That little nick on the head had done more damage than he had thought—coupled with the usual PSI-40 headaches. He was in poor shape, but he could console himself with the fact that for the first time he had information genuinely useful to Security. He had specific evidence of an attempt by Pierce to murder a Security agent. Properly used, that information could destroy Pierce. In addition Rand knew when Killjoy could be caught in an act of sabotage.

When and where. And he would be there.

When he was dressed, he asked, "How long ago did Palmer leave? Where was he going?"

She turned, her face for the first time flushed with color. "You expect me to help you?"

"You already have, Liz."

Stiffly he walked to the door. The pain was worse now that he was on his feet and moving about. The thought of the couch was a sickness.

"Wait! He—Palmer left an hour ago! He just came in— I hadn't said anything. He found out who you were— Jepson—and he said it wasn't true. He's seen Jepson. Now he's gone to find Kevin Webb."

Rand nodded. He thought of his assignment, and of the pale face looming anxiously over his during the night. He knew that he ought to silence her. There was too much she could tell—she might even cost him the victory which had already demanded so much of him.

"Who are you?" she asked tearfully. "Why did you come here?"

"I came," he said, "because I needed your help. And because I knew you would give it."

"Tell me you're not a—a traitor."

"Don't worry," he assured her, the answer costing him a painful effort. "I'm not."

138

He turned away from the relief in her face. In that moment he betrayed his creed as an agent, placing the life of a hapless, inconsequential Anti worker above the demands of loyalty to Security and to the Syndicate. He could lie to Liz Radcliff, but he could not harm her.

"Go to your demonstration," he said. "And good luck."

He went out into the morning sunlight and a new agony.

Chapter Fifteen

Montage of pain: Each step a separate test of endurance. Lift, fall, muscles bunching in an uncontrollable cringe, teeth grinding together until they ache. Lift, fall, another step, and another. A chain of agony.

At the end of the chain a yellow bus, sliding over the hot pavement. Rand mingling with the crowd, hot smells and heavy shoulders and high-pitched squeals of delight. Sights of Mulege—look at that! Once a penal colony there! Couldn't keep the prisoners away! Bawl of laughter. The bus jolting along on its sightseeing junket, turning at last toward Mulege. Another street, another crowd, another chain of brutal steps . . .

Near the end of the afternoon Rand reached the waterfront at a point about a quarter mile north of the private beach of the Miramar Hotel. The palisades—a strip of greenery dotted with the ever-present date and fan palms, flanked by a wide cement promenade on one side and the main boulevard on the other—overlooked an apron of smooth white sand. Beyond it was the blue bay with its gentle, curling surf attracting the brown-bodied bathers. There was over everything a dazzle and a glitter that made Rand sway dizzily, shutting his eyes against the hard, bright torment.

Below the palisades Rand found a triangle of shade at the back edge of the beach. Here, among the lovers and the resting swimmers and the elderly vacationers who could not stand too much sun, and the lobster-skinned tourists who had been exposed to too much, here Rand rested, his back propped against the wall which formed a giant's step from sand to cement walk above, his face partly concealed under the straw sombrero which also concealed and protected the sore, throbbing crown of his head.

He appeared to sleep, but in fact he found neither sleep nor restoring rest. He merely waited for darkness, fighting an unending duel with the pain which could no longer be forced into a confined area of his consciousness and held there, but always slipped over or around any barrier he erected.

Stubbornly he challenged the pain. The tent of shade lengthened over him, reaching out over the hot sand to cool it. The water seemed to turn a darker blue as the afternoon waned. The glare softened slightly against Rand's eyelids. At last, when he felt the sun drop behind the inland hills at his back, he opened his eyes to see the sand, the surf and the whole waterfront darken. He felt an exhilarating sense of triumph. He had made it!

Instantly he realized this childish satisfaction was a confession of weakness. But the headaches had never been so bad. He couldn't understand the reason for their violence. He waited for the coming excitement and clamor of the Anti demonstration with a feeling of dread.

When full darkness came he walked slowly to the Miramar. His clothes were wrinkled and soiled. He would be too conspicuous wandering through the lobby or along the hotel's plush corridors. Guards would be sure to notice him. To make matters worse and curious attention even more certain, Rand was forced to walk hunched over and with an old man's cautious, shuffling gait, a pattern of movement designed to cause the least possible jostling of his brain. He perspired freely, though the evening was mild, cooled by a light, pleasant breeze. He knew that he was weakening, and that his only hope of effective action against Killjoy rested upon surprise and a single bold strike.

If that failed, he could hold out no longer. In spite of his misgivings about the loyalty of Baja's Syndicate personnel, he would have to go in for treatment. And report his failure.

Except for one brief check of an emergency stairway, Rand did his reconnoitering from outside the hotel. The building was designed with two large V-shaped wings joined to a connecting core, the whole forming roughly an "X". Where the two wings met on the inland side, there was a delivery ramp at basement level. On this level, one story below ground, a few mall shops, an entertainment lounge and a coffee shop, and men's and women's beauty salons filled out the north wing. In the south wing were some kitchens, linen rooms, utility rooms, other service facilities. And storerooms. The service areas were easily reached from the central delivery ramp.

By eight o'clock, his survey completed, Rand had selected a spot of cover on the hotel grounds near the entrance to the delivery ramp. He remained standing, not trusting himself to lie down, his shadow blending with those of a trio of palms.

The Antis' timetable was accurate. Not long after he took up his vigil he heard a distant murmur, like an answer to the restless mutter of the surf. Staring north, he saw along the palisades a dark snake of movement speckled by orange dots of flame. The murmur grew into a rhythmic chant, the specks of orange into flickering torches, the snake into a mass of marchers four abreast.

Rand wondered if Liz Radcliff carried one of the flames, and if she had spent the day worrying about him and feeling guilty.

Even before the marching demonstrators were clearly discernible, a crowd of onlookers gathered. They lined the parkway which ran parallel to the palisades and they spilled over onto the sandy beach which glowed dimly in the moonlight. Others jammed the balconies of the Miramar and neighboring hotels or thronged its wide verandas and generous gardens. Following the demonstrators—some cruising slowly along the street in patrol cars, others fanning out ahead on foot to form barrier lines, and a few overhead in helicopters—were the Baja police.

Scowling—the deep frown of pain had not left his face throughout that day—Rand tested in his mind the various alternatives of attack. He wished that he had been able to think more clearly when he escaped from his would-be assassins at the El Prado—he would have borrowed Juan Huerara's weapon.

Ordinarily Rand did not carry a gun. It was against the law, for one thing—the result of a celebrated case a decade before when a Sensitive had gone berserk and murdered a dozen people in a bloody trail across Pennsylvania and into New Jersey. Even the powerful Mental Freedom

141

Syndicate had been unable to control Congressional response to the public uproar. After that its agents went unarmed, and—since their mental prowess was little known or understood by the general public—the Syndicate was able to make effective propaganda capital of the practice.

Rand, moreover, disliked using any weapon. He felt it to be an admission of failure. But now he was forced to face the fact that, with his ability to concentrate drastically curtailed and even his physical senses made unreliable by the demoralizing pain in his head, he could not hope to battle Killjoy on anything like equal terms. At best that would have been an uneven contest between a Sensitive and a Special. Now it would be futile.

He had to find another area of vulnerability in Killjoy.

By this time the first rank of Anti marchers had reached the edge of the Miramar's grounds and halted. A solid file of policemen blocked their way, backed up by a reserve line aiming teargas weapons at the marchers. The voice of the Antis had grown shrill, but now Rand found himself listening to that voice more attentively as it became a single dominant chorus, swelling louder and clearer in a heavy marching cadence:

> *"The Antis are calling on the strength in every man,*
> *To find another freedom in a psychedelic ban . . ."*

Moving, Rand thought. And a little absurd. He watched with sharpening distaste the increasing roughness of the police tactics. Authorities everywhere had little sympathy with the Antis. The Syndicate had worked with cunning and cynical self-interest to place itself always on the side of law and right. Those who protested against the widespread dependence on the Syndicate's drugs found themselves in the position of eccentrics on an intellectual level and rabble on a social one.

But there was more to this Anti demonstration than enthusiasm. They were waiting for something. At the prearranged time, eight-fifteen, there should be a signal of some kind . . .

Far out over the gulf a miniature rocket streaked upward and, in a silent explosion, burst into a thousand fragments. There was a kind of sigh from the massed marchers and an expectant stirring among the spectators. A ripple of motion started over the long black column of Antis.

At the end of this ripple the entire mass seemed to surge forward, crashing against the thin line of policemen with ponderous force. A few dark figures spilled through. Others pressed after them, widening the breach. There were shouts, bellowed commands, and from a balcony overlooking the scene a shrill scream. The chant of the Antis went on . . .

"The Antis are marching and the drugs will soon be gone . . .

Two quick thuds were audible above the clamor. Teargas bombs burst over the mob. But at the same time the first line of police was overwhelmed. The orderly formation of the demonstrators disintegrated into a milling mob as they poured over the line of resistance and overran the reserve contingent. Rand heard the first angry crackle of gunfire. More teargas was dumped over the Antis. He saw men and women stumbling blindly, weeping. A policeman lashed out with a club, cracking it off the nearest head. Rand felt a lash of anger.

Then he forgot the anger, forgot the pain which beat in tune with the stirring Anti chant, forgot the puzzle of his own divided sympathies. A gray delivery van coasted down the service ramp to the platform below where merchandise was unloaded. The van made a U-turn and backed up to the platform. There was so much noise and confusion everywhere that Rand doubted if anyone else saw or heard the van arrive. And he doubted that any ordinary van would have persisted in making a delivery or pickup in the face of the spreading violence around the hotel.

A violence which was one-sided, Rand saw, for the Antis made no attempt to defend themselves against the police.

As soon as the gray van stopped, its rear doors opened and a half dozen men jumped out. They sprinted across the platform and through a pair of wide doors into the building. One of the men stayed behind—the van's driver. He was staring up at the sounds of rioting as he climbed from his cab and circled to the van's rear. Beyond him and to his right was a flight of access steps from street level to the loading platform. Rand left his cover.

He had to strike where Killjoy might be weak—through his cohorts. While the driver's attention was diverted by the mob scene, Rand had to get close enough to stop any instinctive reaction when the man saw him. The driver was armed. But if Rand could change places with him, Killjoy would walk or run out of the hotel right into Rand's arms . . .

As Rand started forward, he heard a stifled cry behind him—and sensed Liz Radcliff's anguished recognition! He whirled. The cry might have been a warning. A burly, determined body charged at Rand. He had a glimpse of the close-cropped, sandy-haired head of Kevin Webb lowered as he bore in. There was no time to evade the charge. Rand shot a reflex command at his attacker—*"Sleep!"* Then Webb's driving head and shoulders slammed into him. His straw sombrero flew off.

The impact hurled Rand backward into the trunk of a palm. Webb's momentum kept him driving forward even after he lost consciousness, succumbing to Rand's will. When the two men drove hard into the tree, Rand's neck whiplashed. The back of his head cracked against the trunk.

The effect was shattering. A cork seemed to pop in his skull, letting all the pain bubble forth. For a moment he blacked out. When light and sound and awareness seeped back through the dark curtain, he was vaguely surprised to find himself still on his feet, propped against the leaning palm. Webb, the cell leader for the Antis, had pitched forward onto his face, half lying across Rand's feet. All the babble and turmoil of the demonstration-turned-riot seemed to have condensed and concentrated inside Rand's brain. His vision swam. Through a blur he made out Liz Radcliff's pale, frightened face hovering in the background.

Rand lurched toward her. "Take care of him," he said thickly. "He's not hurt. And stay out of this—it's not a parade any more!"

He stumbled toward the flight of steps leading down to the loading platform. His jaws locked against the pounding pain in his head. His thighs were heavy and his feet clumsy.

With a desperate effort Rand tried to divorce himself from the pain, to detach his consciousness from his body. For a moment he succeeded. He seemed to see from a distance his blocky figure circling the entrance to the delivery ramp, staggering toward the coveted stairway. The image wavered. Control began to slip away . . .

Rand's foot reached for a step and missed. He felt as if he were floating. The cement platform on the lower level seemed to widen, to lift, to rush toward him like a highway glimpsed from a racing car. With his senses distorted and his mind fragmented by the raging pain, Rand's awareness was a kaleidoscope of wind-caught shouts, shots rattling in the distance, pain like shards of glass, the gaping face of the van driver staring at him as he fell, and a sense of urgency from—where? Inside the hotel!

Even in his chaotic mental state, Rand's muscular control was exceptional. He was limp, totally relaxed, when he tumbled onto the platform at the bottom of the steps and skidded forward. Patches of skin were torn from hands and knees, which bore the brunt of the fall, and scraped off one cheek. But cushioned as it was, the impact did something he had thought impossible—stretched the pain in his head a notch higher.

Sickened to the point of helplessness, Rand lay sprawled on his stomach. His head was turned so that he stared toward the gray van and its driver—and at the gun in the driver's hand, pointing directly at him. Instinct—like a contraction of mental muscles—sent a command stabbing toward the driver's crouched figure in an attempt to induce muscles to jerk and deflect the shot. Then a milky darkness engulfed Rand.

He seemed to hear a dull, distant explosion, but no bullet tore into him. He didn't know if he had succeeded in causing the driver's arm to jerk, or if the shot had simply missed. It didn't seem to matter, for Rand's whole attention was now concentrated on a primitive struggle to remain alive and aware, to hold a dwindling prick of light inviolate against darkness and pain. He fought for control, gained, slipped back. Then suddenly the light was a patch growing larger, rushing closer. The darkness slid away.

And Rand saw Killjoy. Lanky figure, slender, quick. Young, Rand thought. A lightness about him. Resilience and agility of youth. But a hard core of force and strength inside.

Sweat blurred Rand's vision. In the cool evening he was drenched with sweat. The pain was not quite all the universe held, but almost. He was a tiny seedling of sanity inside a great envelope of torment. From that position held so tenuously, he was aware of the lanky youth on the platform no more than thirty yards away, busily thrusting boxes into the gray delivery van, snapping out orders,

145

directing his men with cool confidence. Suddenly their job was done. There was shouting, confusion. Another of the group emerged from the hotel, running, his hair flying, his features twisted in the frenzy of haste.

Rand tried to break through his envelope of pain. He was so close to the man he had hunted—so near the goal. And he could do nothing! Nothing!

They were all piling into the van now. The driver, climbing behind the wheel, pointed at Rand and said something. The lean young man looked. For a moment he paused.

His mind touched Rand's.

Pursuers were spilling out of the hotel through the service doors. The driver was yelling at Killjoy. Someone appeared on the ramp above.

Rand waited for the whiplash strike from Killjoy's mind.

It never came.

The young man started to vault into the gray van beside the driver. A shot cracked. Killjoy jerked—and Jon Rand winced as he felt an alien pain.

The youth swayed, clinging to the cab door of the van. The driver grabbed his arm and hauled him inside. Then the van was racing up the ramp, gears whining. Figures scattered before it. More shots spat at the bouncing truck.

It vanished into the darkness. The pulsations which had briefly erupted in Rand's sensitive mind faded. He lay where he was on the platform, heavy with defeat. The blackness encroached once more on his mind. He welcomed it.

Chapter Sixteen

Rand was herded together with a crowd of Antis under arrest. A impressionable patrolman gaped at Rand's Security indentification and hastily released him. Rand slipped away into the darkness. He forced himself to walk.

A long time later the sign of the boat rental came

slowly into focus out of a night mist. He almost groaned aloud when he made it to the door. The place was closed to the business of renting boats at this predawn hour, but a Security branch never really closed.

The agent on duty—an order taker, Rand thought, named Ferris—looked shocked.

"I'm Rand."

"Great Syndicate! Why haven't you contacted me? Garrett has been—"

"I'm sure he has," Rand muttered. Garrett inspired fear across a continent.

Ferris made a point of locking the door through which he had admitted Rand. He pressed buttons that caused shades to slide over the windows. "You're in trouble," he said nervously.

A spasm contorted Rand's face. He regretted letting his pain show. "I need treatment," he said.

Ferris peered closely. "Yes, of course—your face. And what's happened to your head?"

"Never mind. You must have serum on hand—for a PSI reaction."

The agent hesitated. He was too nervous for Security, Rand thought wearily. Then Ferris startled him by saying, "Sorry, Rand. I can't help you."

"What do you mean? You must have the serum—"

"He also has orders." A new voice, cold and quiet, made Rand spin around, an action he immediately regretted as pain sloshed around in his head like water in a bucket.

"I tried to tell you, Rand," Ferris said importantly. "When we didn't hear from you, Mr. Garrett flew out here to take over the case personally."

"That'll do," Garrett said. "You have those guards standing by?"

"Yes, sir!"

"Bring them in." Garrett's heavy lids half-lowered over his gray eyes. His tone did not change. "Place this man under arrest."

Garrett watched dispassionately as an orderly removed the needle from Rand's arm, wiped the puncture with alcohol, and checked it. He nodded at Garrett, who flipped one hand in dismissal.

There were no guards in evidence now, Rand noted —a gesture of contempt on Garrett's part.

Garrett said nothing, staring at Rand like a biologist examing a familiar and not very interesting specimen. Rand waited him out. As one minute ticked by, then another, Rand felt the pressure begin to lift from his brain. He slumped back on the hard cot—the only permanent furnishing to break the four-walled monotony of the windowless cell. Ferris had brought in a chair for Garrett. Rand savored the delicious relief as the serum worked through his bloodstream. His legs and his hands stopped twitching. As the pain eased, he became aware of fatigue washing through him. His eyelids grew heavy. He saw Garrett through a film of gauze. . .

"You will be permitted to sleep when we are through," Garrett said at last.

Slowly Rand sat up. The effort helped to push back the fog of sleep. "Maybe you'd like to tell me why I'm under arrest."

"An explanation hardly seems necessary."

"You have my report," Rand protested. "You know why I had to handle things alone."

Garrett's sensual mouth curved in disdain. "Hardly alone," he said. "You've done your job well, Rand— but not for me."

The remark jolted Rand fully awake. "I didn't know you made wild statements."

"I don't."

"You can check out my report."

"Can I check with Johnson? Can I check with the woman—Erickson? Can I check with Lieutenant Huerara, whose mind is useless by your own admission?"

"Use drugs then!"

"Don't take me for a fool!" Garrett permitted annoyance to disturb his composure. "It will be a week or more before the PSI-40 in your system is sufficiently absorbed to make other drugs reliable."

"Find Taina Erickson. That won't take a week."

"No?" Garrett's voice was silken once more. "Do you suppose she's still waiting in bed for you? We've been searching for her for more than a month already. If you had reported contact with her at once, we'd have caught her!"

Rand sat rigid, a stillness inside him, expectant and

almost fearful, like an animal scenting an enemy. "You know about her," he said.

"Of course."

"She works for Killjoy—Kemp Johnson?"

The mobile lines of Garrett's mouth pulled down at the corners, shaping boredom. "It is late for games, Rand," he declared coldly. "You made love to the woman. Don't ask me to believe that you didn't know she was a defector—formerly one of my agents!"

Excitement, hope—he was not sure what it was— quickened in Rand's mind. As quickly it was chilled. "A defector?" He hated asking the question.

"One of the agents who disappeared!" Garrett was scornful. "One of those who preceded you on the same assignment. What about the other? You didn't mention him."

"To my knowledge I didn't meet him," Rand answered slowly.

He wondered why she had gone over. What would have made Taina betray the Syndicate for Kemp Johnson?

Garrett sighed. "I see that you're going to be unco-operative. The fact is of little importance, Rand."

"I don't get this!" Rand retorted in sudden anger. "You have my report—it's all there! I failed, that's true enough—I let Killjoy get away last night. But failure isn't treason. And we have learned something about him and his organization."

"You've given me nothing!" Garrett snapped. "You think I didn't know Johnson was responsible for that robbery—and the mob demonstration? Your report is worthless, Rand, as it was meant to be!"

"Read my mind if you have to!"

"I already have."

The calm, candid admission brought Rand an uncomfortable chill. He could never get over his dislike for the ability of a Special to invade his consciousness so subtly that he was not aware of the act.

"But I am not sure," Garrett went on, "whether or not you are able to hide things from me, Rand, and to erect plausible imitations of truth. I cannot penetrate completely, you see—not with absolute certainty into the mind of an unwilling Sensitive."

Rand stared at Garrett's cruel, aristocratic face,

representative of a way of life Rand had accepted and shared for fifteen years. He felt a kind of stunned relief that Garrett could not mentally explore every cavern of his mind any time he chose. In that moment Rand didn't stop to think why Garrett felt free to make an admission now which no Special had ever made before. It was simply enough to know that some part of him remained inviolate.

"As I said, it's of no importance," Garrett commented in a tone of indifference. "It doesn't really matter who you're working for. I think not Johnson. Garth Taylor or Pierce. Of the two, Pierce seems most likely. Yes. It must be Pierce."

"And I wrecked a car I was riding in, I suppose, as well as planting assassins in my hotel room."

Garrett shrugged. "Killjoy is not inefficient. But of course I have only your word that such events occurred."

"This is insane!" Rand lost patience. "I've been in Security for fifteen years. Why would I throw that away?"

"You are an intelligent man," Garrett pointed out, as if patiently explaining an answer to a slow student. "You knew things were coming to a head, and you wanted to be sure you would be on the winning side. Unfortunately you guessed wrong."

Garrett leaned forward slightly. The movement subtly suggested a sloughing off of indifference. Rand had a clearer intimation from the taut attention signaled by Garrett's mind. It seemed to sing at a frequency just beyond the range of hearing, like a wire strung tight in the wind.

"That critical moment is even closer than you would imagine, Rand. Pierce thought he could use you against me, but you are still *my* instrument!" Pleased with himself and the drama of the moment, Garrett pushed out of his chair. He examined the pearl-colored coating on his fingernails. Turning, he rapped lightly on the closed door, the only exit from the bare cell. Almost idly he added, "Whether you choose to cooperate does not matter, Rand, because in the end you are still working for me. You always have been. You will do exactly what I wish you to do. And your most important assignment of a not undistinguished career lies ahead of you." He smiled with tolerant amusement. "Get some rest. I want you fresh tonight."

150

Baffled, Rand refrained from asking the obvious questions. It seemed absurd that Garrett could seriously doubt his loyalty, but—

"It is convenient that you've paid one visit to our soon-to-be-lamented Chairman of the Board," Garrett said. "That will make your task easier."

The cell door opened. With a self-satisfied smile Garrett started out. A guard hovered in the corridor outside. Rand could restrain his curiosity no longer.

"What task?" he asked sharply. "And why should anyone lament Garth Taylor yet?"

Garrett's amusement was triumphant. "Because that is your assignment, Rand. Tonight you will kill him."

Garrett returned at six o'clock that evening. Rand had —surprising himself—slept through half the day. His headaches were completely gone, and the combination of rest and freedom from pain had revived him.

"Everything is set," Garrett said. "Taylor is not leaving his place—that was the one possible hitch."

"I suppose this makes sense to you in some way, but I'm not assassinating Taylor."

"Your loyalty is to me, not Taylor. To Security."

"Not any more." Rand was not sure just when he had made the decision. The words came freely and naturally, as if the determination which lay behind them had always been there. "Not to you, not to Security— not to the Syndicate."

"I see."

"Find yourself another killer."

"You'll do," Garrett said blandly.

Puzzled, Rand held back his retort. Garrett was too calm, too sure of himself. Something backed up his confidence.

"You'll use the water approach," Garrett went on. "It's not as well guarded. There is one sentry patrolling Taylor's private dock—you'll have to deal with him. After that there's no one between you and the house. I've seen to that. Taylor has a sundeck facing the water on the second floor with direct access to his bedroom." There was a pause. "I believe you'll find him in his bed. There's a rumor he's had another attack. I've been unable to verify it."

"Why don't you ask him?" Rand suggested.

Garrett was unperturbed by the sarcasm. "He's taking no calls, receiving no visitors. Even most members of the household staff are not allowed to see him. The official word is that he is tired from the strain of the inauguration, and that he is suffering from a slight cold."

"Maybe he is."

"It's more than that." Garrett frowned. His tongue played over his teeth. "Whatever the real situation is, I'm sure you can deal with it."

Rand stared at him. Garrett's unquestioning self-assurance was disturbing. There seemed to be no doubt in his mind, despite Rand's blunt refusal, that his wishes would be carried out.

"There is, of course, more to the assignment than a simple assassination."

"Of course."

"You will also plant evidence that will implicate yourself and the man behind you—Pierce. Once I have that, with Taylor dead, I'll have the Syndicate."

"I'm going to incriminate myself."

"And Pierce."

"Without a protest."

"You may protest," Garrett conceded with a smile. "But you'll do it."

"How much PSI-40 have you taken?"

Garrett laughed. "I am not having hallucinations, Rand."

"How are you going to make me do all this? I don't think you can hypnotize me, Garrett, and even if you could, you'd never be able to force me to kill Taylor against my will."

"You will do it by choice." Garrett's smile was cruel. "I believe you are familiar with pain, Rand? As I recall, you could hardly stand on your feet when you came here this morning so belatedly."

"I hurt," Rand admitted. "Everybody does."

"That was only an introduction to pain." Garrett's silken tone relished the promise. "You have much in store for you."

In spite of himself Rand felt a chill. The threat also angered him. "Any time you're ready," he snapped. "I'm tired of playing games with you. Let's postpone the next talk until you've worked yourself up to standing the sight of blood."

Garrett's long, deeply cut nostrils flared—the only sign that Rand's curt comment had ruffled him.

"This is our last talk," Garrett said coldly. "You will carry out your assignment tonight. I will leave a gun with Ferris. It is standard issue, but the serial number can be traced to Pierce—it was taken from one of his agents. You will also carry on you a disbursement schedule for Baja's December allotment of PSI-40, showing the distribution of the drug for each area with figures indicating gross sales, a breakdown of expenses, and net profit. The figures will be coded, so they will be meaningless to the civil authorities who find them on you—but the Syndicate's directors will recognize them. They are figures which only high-level distribution personnel working directly under Pierce are supposed to have."

"What do I do to make sure I'm caught with the evidence? Shoot myself after I murder Taylor?"

Garrett seemed pleased. "You may prefer that."

The enigmatic statement hung between them. Scowling in bafflement, Rand said nothing as Garrett signaled and the cell door opened for him.

"The weapon and the papers will be waiting for you in the front office. Goodbye, Rand. I shall take over the Johnson case myself." He smiled reflectively. "It will be a memorial to our relationship. It's too bad you learned to betray—you were a good agent."

"Thanks," said Rand sarcastically. "I'll cherish that."

The comment gave him a small amount of satisfaction, but the feeling did not last longer than it took for the door to swing shut. He was left alone in the bare cell with the puzzle—and the vivid memory of the pain which seemed to cause Garrett secret amusement.

Some time later Rand heard the oiled slide of the lock. Ferris, pale and nervous as before, stood in the corridor. There was no guard with him.

"You can go now," he said.

Something in the words and his manner startled Rand. "What do you mean—go?"

"I don't know anything. Garrett just said to unlock the door at ten."

"You mean I'm free?"

"Yes. Look, Rand, I just follow orders. You'll do well if you do the same."

"Yeah." Rand felt reluctant to leave the cell. But curiosity nagged at him. "Any other orders?"

"That's all. Oh—there are some papers on the desk out front. And your gun."

"Garrett isn't here?"

"He left over two hours ago."

Rand frowned. He could just stay where he was. Stick his head under the pillow and pretend it wasn't dark outside, and there was nothing to be afraid of. And no pain. The cell was kind of drab, and the view wasn't much, but it was home. It was safe.

He followed Ferris down the corridor.

In the front office Rand ignored the items on the desk behind the counter. As he started through the swinging gate Ferris anxiously thrust an envelope at him.

"Never mind," said Rand.

"You'd better take it! And the gun!"

Rand shrugged. He did not slip the shoulder holster on. The boat rental was a few steps from the water of Conception Bay. A gun sank fast. As for the papers, perhaps they might prove useful.

He wasn't sure what for, and he did not quite understand the impulse to keep them.

At the door Rand paused. The next step was a big one. It was not just that Loren Garrett had something ugly planned for him, waiting out there in the night's darkness, something he could not yet comprehend. It was not just that the threat of renewed pain was capable of unnerving him. He paused to look back briefly. He wondered how, after fifteen years with the Syndicate, he had come to this turning point. What—besides the severe headaches—had made him ineffective against Killjoy? He wondered why he felt no sense of loss at leaving the security and prestige and power of the Mental Freedom Syndicate, but felt instead something like a sour aftertaste in his mouth.

He went out. Walking slowly across the wharf, he stopped at the breakfront near a short flight of steps leading to a dock. The bay was black with a silver coating of moonlight. Water lapped gently against the weathered piles, scum-slick at the water's edge. Rand made out the letter "J" identifying the dock. He scanned the rows of boats moored along the length of the pier on either side, ranging from small sailing craft to a formidable yacht. He wondered which was the boat he was scheduled to take. A rowboat, he supposed. Garrett might avoid a motor to announce an assassin's approach. There was such a boat tied next to a small cabin cruiser.

From somewhere out on the bay came the rolling clang of a buoy. Farther away the light surf of the gulf spoke in a discreet whisper.

Rand scowled. His muscles were tense. Nerves, he thought. Garrett had got to him with his cat-and-mouse act. Hefting the stubby automatic in its leather holster, Rand swung his arm to hurl the gun out over the water in defiance.

Pain blinded him. He was driven to his knees. His mouth hung open, and he grunted mindlessly, like an animal. He tried to lift his arm and it refused to obey him. He began to shake. The hand holding the automatic dropped limply to his side.

And he was kneeling on the wharf, his breath coming in short wheezes, the pain gone. It left only its after-image, a dull throbbing in Rand's temples.

Shakily he pushed to his feet. He stared at the stubby pistol. The suspicion in his mind was too incredible to accept. He had to test it. Stubbornly blotting out the horror of what he had just experienced, he tried once again to throw the weapon into the bay.

Though he was half-prepared for the pain this time and it did not strike him down as shatteringly, within seconds he was groveling on the wharf with froth forming at the corners of his mouth.

But now he knew how to stop the pain. After some fumbling he managed to drop the loop of the shoulder harness over his head. The automatic hung against his pounding chest. The savage grip of pain slackened.

After a while Rand climbed erect again. He licked his lips. Staring up and down the wharf, he could see nothing. The offices and warehouses lining the waterfront were mostly dark. Within their heavy shadows the sparse streetlights cast a pale glimmer here and there.

Rand probed, searching for Garrett. *"You can't be doing this!"* he thought desperately. *"It isn't possible!"*

He seemed to hear—he could not be sure—mocking laughter.

Chapter Seventeen

The small boat had a motor after all. It was a flat-bottomed, fiberglass craft with a pair of hydrofoil flippers to raise it slightly and give it stability. The motor started instantly, indicating that it had not been waiting long without being primed. The sound reverberated over the water. It would carry a long distance, Rand thought.

When he was far enough out that the wharf with its row of docks projecting like fingers was hardly discernible, and the long line of storage and office buildings was a low, black silhouette against the sky, Rand nerved himself to another test. His throat was suddenly dry. Muscles quivered in anticipation. He swung the tiller to the right. The prow of the boat turned lazily toward the open gulf.

Rand fell off the bench seat, clawing blindly. The pain rose steadily in his brain like the string of an instrument being tuned higher and higher, until it seemed impossible for another notch to be turned without the string snapping. But the twist was made, the pain reached another level of intensity and went on. With his legs kicking out as if he were seized by a fit, and his hands and arms shaking uncontrollably, Rand was a long while getting the rudder righted so that the boat was heading inland down the bay in the general direction of Garth Taylor's estate.

Once the direction was correct the pain diminished. Rand sagged in the bottom of the boat, too limp to crawl onto the seat. This time the pain did not go away completely. It lingered in small, fiery darts, themselves endurable, but each a frightening reminder of the terror that would come any time Rand tried to resist his instructions.

Over and over Rand told himself that Garrett did not have the mental power to induce pain so extreme at such a distance. Rand himself, at short range and with a vulnerable subject, could project an image of pain—he had done it with the kidnapper and would-be hijacker, Ortiz. But an image was not the same thing as actual pain, although it frightened and demoralized anyone who did not understand it. But Rand didn't believe that such a projection could drive him to his knees.

Psychosomatic pain? He did not know the limit of a Special's power. Was it possible that Garrett could cause a weaker mind to create its own physical disorders?

Rand shook his head. He was stubbornly convinced that the pain had an actual rather than psychological origin. For one thing it was completely under outside control. A psychosomatic condition, even externally induced, became subjective. An outsider would hardly be able to turn the condition on and off at will, using it like a whip to herd an unwilling subject, as Rand was being driven. Moreover, the pain was astonishingly like that which he had endured for so many years whenever he used PSI-40 for extended periods. It differed only in intensity, going far beyond any extreme Rand had experienced before. And that earlier torment had been bad enough.

This was what Garrett had meant. This explained why he had been so arrogantly sure of himself. This was the control which rendered Rand helpless to disobey. Somehow Garrett was able to follow Rand's progress at a distance and to read his actions. So far each diagnosis had been immediate and dead accurate. Remarkable as the feat was, Rand did not find it hard to accept, as he did the whip of pain. Under ideal conditions he, a Sensitive, could have followed the movements and motives of a controlled subject. That the power would be developed to a highly sophisticated degree in a Special occasioned wonder, but not disbelief.

With a sick feeling Rand acknowledged to himself that in the end he would do Garrett's bidding. A point of pain could be reached where no effort of will would overrule the body's demand for relief.

Rand slapped one hand viciously against the seat bench in anger. Garrett was making him a tool—less than human. And he was helpless!

When he had calmed down he coolly weighed the possibility of suicide. Garrett must have anticipated the move. Suppose Rand jumped into deep water in the middle of the bay and made no effort to swim? Would any attempt to goad him into action with pain so immobilize his body that he would drown even faster? More likely, Rand decided, Garrett would use lighter flicks of pain, lashes strong enough to force him to swim for his life but not violent enough to paralyze and sink him.

Anyway, he had no real wish to die. Not yet. Not while there was the smallest hope of last-minute resistance.

The boat nosed slowly out to the center of Conception Bay, well over a mile across at this point. While he kept the prow pointed approximately toward Taylor's estate along the southwest shore, Rand also set the motor at its lowest speed. He wanted as much time as he could get.

Deliberately spacing them to minimize the punishment of mind and body, Rand made a series of tests. He found that there was a margin of time—one and a half seconds was the longest interval—between any act of defiance, such as altering the boat's course, and its answering sentence of pain. But the pain ceased just as quickly when a cooperative move was made. Thus Rand was able to face up to brief exposures to the bite of agony. He learned that Garrett—it must be he—could not be fooled. Surreptitious, slight or seemingly accidental changes of direction brought the same result as a bold move, though sometimes with a fractional delay. Somehow Garrett was able to sense resistance. It must announce itself by some kind of mental activity, just as fear or joy or anger were readily perceptible. Rand's Sensitive's mind could not detect subtle reactions clearly, especially in a mind capable of raising a defensive shield against invasion. But Garrett enjoyed a higher power, a greater perceptive.

Unhappily, Rand proved to himself by painful demonstration that his mental shield could not prevent detection or block the blow of pain when it came.

When he was still a mile from the stretch of shore where he had placed Taylor's house—the attacks had provided a specialized kind of navigational aid—Rand cut the motor. The boat drifted toward shore. Soon he could make out the bulky profiles of the estates lining this fashionable shore of the bay. Feathery palms leaned against the sky like drunken sentries. The sea grass which grew dense near the shoreline slowed the boat's progress, and it began to swing about as it drifted. Rand hastily picked up the oars.

The Taylor estate was closer than he had estimated. He was almost on top of it before a vague familiarity about the outline of the big house, and a chance glimpse of a sentry moving out along the private dock, warned him. Rand dipped the oars deep and shot in close to shore behind the protective shadow of a neighboring dock.

He rested there for several minutes. His arms were weary, and he had a slight cramp in one thigh. The sentry walked out to the end of Taylor's dock, surveyed the placid silver mirror of the bay, glanced in a cursory inspection toward Taylor's yacht in its berth next to the dock, and turned to retrace his steps. Rand clocked him. He reappeared at the foot of the dock in eighteen minutes.

A glancing probe of the sentry's mind revealed something unusual to Rand—a kind of nervousness. Did he suspect something? Was Rand walking into a trap? No— the nervousness was of another kind. Tinged with guilt.

Thirty-five minutes later, after two more of the sentry's rounds, made at intervals of thirteen and twenty-one minutes, Rand guessed the factor behind the man's erratic and guilty behavior. He had taken a moderate dosage of PSI-40. Probably to alleviate the wearisome boredom of his watch, Rand thought. For nights on end it must be a completely uneventful vigil. And the temptation to escape into timelessness through the drug, in small amounts which still left the man capable of going through the motions of sentry duty, had been too strong.

And perhaps he had been helped along this night.

The Syndicate claimed the drug was not habit-forming, Rand reflected—and suddenly remembered his defense of it to Taina Erickson on the plane carrying them to Baja. Her accusation had been blunt. When something proved almost universally irresistible, any distinction about its being addictive or not became largely a matter of semantics, with the only real difference being the lack of withdrawal complications. In a real sense PSI-40 was psychologically addictive.

Rand turned away from the argument. It brought other and more unpleasant memories of Taina.

Once he had made certain of the sentry's condition, Rand acted boldly. As soon as the man disappeared from the dock, Rand rowed quickly across the open stretch of water. He tied his boat beneath the pier where it would escape anything but a sharply vigilant scrutiny. He went up a wooden ladder onto the dock, paused in the shadow of Taylor's large cruiser, and examined the house. Curtains were drawn over the large windows on the second floor which Rand readily identified as those of Taylor's bedroom. Light glowed behind the curtains. Most of the ground-floor level was dark, at least at the back of the building. Lights from the entry and from the front bedrooms would not be visible from Rand's location.

The sentry was quite careless. He stumbled a little as he returned to the wooden dock, and he made more noise than necessary. Given ample warning, Rand waited in a crouch on the deck of the yacht tied alongside the dock. The sentry passed within six feet of him without noticing him. Rand jumped onto the dock. Lost in misty visions of extraordinary freedom from spatial and spiritual limitations, the sentry was slow to react to ordinary earthly sounds. By the time he started to turn, Rand's arm was encircling his throat and a hand muffled his outcry.

There was a brief, silent struggle. Hypnotism would have been faster and easier, but it would also have warned Taylor or any Sensitive among his staff. After a moment the sentry's struggles weakened. He sagged in Rand's arms.

Rand locked the sentry, bound and gagged, in a storage room of Taylor's yacht. When he returned to the dock he noticed the sentry's small carbine. Thoughtfully he picked it up and examined it with a professional eye. Deciding it was no more effective at close range than the automatic and more cumbersome to carry if he had to climb, Rand started to throw it aside.

He grunted as the pain struck. With luck he caught the carbine before it fell out of reach. The quick action cut off the jolting pain. Rand gasped in relief.

Then he stared at the carbine more thoughtfully than before. He had learned something new. Garrett could not gauge his motives for an action accurately. He had misunderstood the discarding of the rifle as an act of resistance. Might he also misread an apparently cooperative action?

There was no certain answer, but the faint hope buoyed Rand.

He reached the ground-floor patio without incident. He let his consciousness open. He had talked to Taylor and felt the imprint of his mind. Rand knew he could recognize it as readily as he could identify a tone of voice in another man. Cautiously Rand narrowed the focus of his attention to the rooms overhead, having found no audible activity on the lower level. His mind was like an empty vessel, capable of receiving impressions without revealing its presence through overt activity of its own.

Rand frowned. The familiar stamp of Garth Taylor's strong ego and assertive power was missing. Instead Rand felt a mental sensation not unlike putting out your hand in the darkness and touching a smooth, impregnable metal surface, cold and hard and featureless. He started to relax. That must be Taylor. Asleep, perhaps, with a protective shield erected as a routine precaution.

Then he sensed a second shield.

Crouching motionless on the dark patio, his own mind carefully blocked against a sudden probe, Rand examined his discovery. Although the texture of a mental shield revealed little of the consciousness behind it, Rand assumed that the second mind he detected was that of a Sensitive. One of Taylor's palace guard—it would be surprising if he did not have more than one within warning distance at all times.

Well, Rand reflected with irony, Garrett had probably not planned that he should survive the assassination attempt anyway.

Rand left the shadows of the patio, moving away from the house to examine the open sundeck above. That movement answered any doubt in his mind about how closely his activities were being monitored and blotted out his faint hope. The grinding pain seemed as if it would crush him. He lurched helplessly. Only the presence of a date palm kept him from collapsing. He slid off it. In desperation he lunged back toward the house.

The pain fell away.

He stood panting beneath the sundeck. Once again Garrett had misinterpreted an action. And wouldn't Taylor and his guard have detected Rand's pain? Anything so totally obsessive must surely have communicated itself in a shrill message to any Special or Sensitive nearby. To Rand the fact indicated a major flaw in Loren Garrett's plan. To proceed with the plot seemed suicidal.

But Rand had no choice.

He began to search for a way to climb to the second-story sundeck. He felt that his chance of survival, if it had ever existed, was now not worth considering. The conviction left him unmoved. Better death or capture than dumb submission to Garrett's will.

He found a strong iron light fixture attached to one of the heavy wooden beams able to support his weight. He hauled himself up until he could reach the railing of the sundeck. From there he climbed onto the deck—not gracefully, but quickly and quietly.

Somewhat to his surprise there was no reaction from inside the house—no sign of sudden activity or alarm. Rand stood frowning on the open deck. Something was wrong. Something didn't make sense.

But one of the sliding glass doors to Garth Taylor's bedroom was invitingly—and conveniently—open. Only a screen door intervened.

The screen slid readily at a touch. Its latch had not been secured. The draperies floated away from the window under the caress of a slight breeze. Through a gap in the drapes Rand saw Taylor in his bed, apparently asleep.

Rand stepped through the draperies into the soft light of the bedroom, the carbine in his hands.

An alarm rang in his brain even before his foot sank into the plush carpeting. Taylor was not sleeping. Rand had sensed that total stillness before. Here was no shield erected to prevent invasion. Here was darkness. Infinite darkness.

Taylor was dead.

Rand stood rigid before the sliding door. A figure stepped from the cover of a wardrobe door at the far end of the huge room. A second was not immediately visible, though Rand could feel the shielded mind in the bathroom on his right.

Then she came out. Rand stared. The small hairs at the back of his neck had risen, and now a chill passed along that nape like a feathery caress. Blue eyes returned his stare with a level, unflinching gaze.

"You!"

"Yes, Jon."

Rand turned from Taina Erickson to peer sharply at the lanky figure regarding him from the other end of the bedroom. "And you, I've been looking for you."

"I know," said Killjoy.

"Taylor?"

"He's dead."

"You killed him." It was a flat statement.

"No!" Taina Erickson broke in. "That's not true!"

Rand smiled without mirth. "You were just visiting?"

Drily Killjoy said, "We'd a better reason for being here than you, Rand."

Rand shrugged. His eyes were cold. "One man's murder is no better than another's."

"Taylor wasn't murdered." Taina's voice was convincing.

Rand's attention jerked toward the bed. He frowned. Taylor might have been sleeping. He had not been dead long. There was no visible mark on him, no sign of violence about his person, the bed or the room.

"His death was convenient for you in that case," Rand pointed out.

"No! It came at the worst possible time!" Killjoy exclaimed. "If he'd lived, we'd have been able to expose Garrett—through you!"

Killjoy, the man who had fled Garrett's vengeance seventeen years before as a boy, took a step forward, bringing his face from muted shadow into clear light. Rand's first thought was that he was remarkably youthful. He was more believably a young man named Kemp Johnson than the militant and adroit Anti leader called Killjoy. He carried his left arm awkwardly, a bandage wrapped around his upper biceps and across his shoulder. The bullet fired just as Johnson was escaping at the Miramar must have creased the fleshy part of his shoulder.

"If you didn't kill him," Rand demanded, "how did he die?"

"A stroke. They don't even know on the household staff yet—that is, most of them. I have a man planted here—he let us in. Taylor was supposed to be sleeping. We found him dying."

"I don't suppose you just let him die."

Johnson flushed. "No, we didn't! He was beyond help."

"Where's his secretary?" Rand demanded. "He was never far away."

"He sleeps. Unharmed. You're right, he's loyal to Taylor, so we had to make sure he wouldn't interfere."

Rand's uncertainty deepened. And he guessed that his allotment of pain-free time was surely shrinking. The carbine he carried was pointing toward Johnson. How long before Garrett demanded that the trigger be pulled? Could the Security director know that the rifle was pointing at someone other than Taylor?

"You must have had a reason for coming here tonight," Rand said. "You seem to be quick with reasons."

"We had a good one," Johnson replied. "I've already indicated it. We came to warn him about you—protect him against you if necessary—and prove that Garrett was trying to take over the Syndicate."

"How could you know I was coming?"

"We know quite a bit—in some ways more than you know about yourself."

Rand glanced at Taina. Her lips compressed during his cold appraisal—those full, soft lips which had once been bruised by his kisses. "You have excellent sources," he admitted.

"We know you were forced to come here." Killjoy spoke rapidly, brushing past Rand's questions. "We also know how it was done! There's something else you should be told. Garrett has an agent planted on Taylor's staff—"

"Everybody seems to," Rand interrupted caustically. "Pierce, too, I suppose."

"Probably. Never mind that! The point is, the moment you fire that rifle, alarms will be given. The police have been alerted about a possible summons. They'll be here within three minutes. In less time than that a patrol boat will be charging across the bay. And another signal will bring a VTOL down on the roof. The warning will also touch off an automatic system which will floodlight the grounds, front and rear, and let the guard dogs loose. You see, you weren't meant to escape."

"I never expected to," Rand said. "But you'll be caught in the same trap. This will be Garrett's big night."

"Only if you pull that trigger."

"Why shouldn't I?"

"Because you don't want to," Johnson said quickly. "Because you don't believe in what you've done any more. Because you wouldn't have been able to shoot Taylor, no matter what it cost you. Hadn't you planned to warn him in the split second of time available to you before the pain forced you to shoot?"

"What if I had?" Rand rasped angrily.

"Don't you see, Jon?" Taina Erickson pleaded. "You've started to change. I know—it happened to me. Garrett didn't put me through what you've had—only because he never had the chance. I was lucky. But he doesn't have to control you any more—you can be free! Believe me, Jon, you can be complete!"

"Why should I believe you?" Rand retorted. He turned away from her stricken expression, shutting his mind against her pain, refusing to consider why the pain was there.

"You're wrong, Rand," Kemp Johnson protested, for the first time speaking sharply. "I'm sorry things worked out the way they did between you two. If I'd know Taina would fall in love with you I'd never have put her on you. It seemed like a good idea."

Still Rand closed his mind against her. He had to. She had violated his trust in a way he could never forget—

"That wasn't a violation!" Johnson exclaimed, revealing that he could read Rand's thoughts with ease. His tone was impatient. "Don't you see it yet, man? That was an act of love! The most complete kind of union a man and a woman can know! And you ran away from it!"

Rand stared at him. Understanding came slowly, then burst upon him full blown. He swung toward Taina. His arm relaxed. The barrel of the carbine tilted toward the floor. The rigid barrier in Rand's mind fell away, and he felt joy sing in him as a smile began to bloom on her lips.

Then the pain struck, driving him to his knees. His mouth went slack. His whole body jerked as if he were being manipulated by invisible wires, each red hot and crackling with a high-voltage charge. In the final extremity of pain there was repeated the feeling of withdrawal of his essential self into a tiny core of sanity which held out against the onslaught of chaos. From that retreat Jon Rand saw Taina staring at him in compassion and anguish. He saw Kemp Johnson advancing toward him across the bedroom past the brown carved posts of the huge bed where Garth Taylor lay dead. And slowly, inevitably, Rand raised the muzzle of the carbine because that was the only way to ease the pain, because when he tried to resist he began to jibber like an idiot. He could no more help lifting his hand than a drowning man can keep his lungs from opening.

The muzzle centered on Killjoy's lean chest. The young man did not stop. He was a half dozen steps away. Rand fought against the terrible compulsion to tighten his finger on the trigger. His hand was rigid, the bones sticking out, aching. Pain blinded him. Hoarse bleats erupted from his throat.

"You fool!" Rand shouted in his mind at Johnson. *"Strike! Or I'll kill you!"*

Taina's mouth opened in a soundless scream. Johnson halted six feet away, hesitating. Rand's finger tightened—

Something jelled in Rand's mind. Hope flared. With a snarl he hurled the gun at Kemp Johnson's face. Then he leaped after it, his strong, square hands clutching for the other's throat, his knee driving forward for a crippling blow.

The blow never landed, and his hands found only air. An invisible wall seemed to rise up before him. He slammed into it. Stunned, he reeled back on clown's legs. A red veil dropped over his eyes. Soft hands seemed to cover his mouth and his nose. Very shortly he could not breathe. His heart hurled itself against the bars of its cage, again and again and again . . .

Until it grew tired, and labored, and finally stopped.

Chapter Eighteen

Rand woke to a whitewashed room, cool and dim, a soft bed, bandages over his upper chest and wrapped about his head—and an indescribable feeling of well-being.

He turned toward a stir of movement. Blue eyes—at once eager and anxious—searched his. "Jon?"

"I didn't expect to wake up in the same world."

Taina smiled. "It's a better one. Better than you've known."

"I feel that, but—I don't know exactly why."

"You will." Her expression sobered. "You may have a headache for a little while, but a normal one. Nothing like those you've been having. All that's over."

He didn't quite believe her, but he was in no mood to argue. The sunlight beyond the curtained window of his room was a slanting light, sharp rather than dazzling. He guessed it was late afternoon, near sunset. But what day?

"Tuesday."

He heard the answer in his mind. Two days since the aborted plot to assassinate Taylor.

Suddenly he pushed up on his elbows. "That was different!" he exclaimed. "The way I heard you!"

"Yes."

"Direct telepathy—verbal, not just images, impressions."

"That's right."

Rand propped up his pillow and fell back against it. He was not ready for this new wonder—not yet. There were too many unanswered questions. He chose the most important one.

"What about Johnson? Did I do much damage?"

"He's fine," she said quickly—too quickly, Rand thought.

"The truth," he insisted.

"You didn't hurt him. His wound was opened again when you jumped him, but it's a shallow wound, and he heals quickly like all Specials." She hesitated. "He's . . . up and about already."

"I'm glad of that." He wondered about her nervousness.

"You did that deliberately, didn't you?" she asked. "Threw your rifle at Kemp, I mean, and then attacked him."

"Yes."

"Kemp said it was the only way you could keep from shooting him—to make another kind of attack, one that would momentarily fool Garrett—and one you knew would fail."

Rand shrugged. He said nothing.

"I'm proud of you," she whispered.

Rand closed his eyes, embarrassed—and pleased. Then he realized that he could probably hide neither the embarrassment nor the pleasure. He looked at her again. "How did you get me away from there? And yourselves?"

"There was no alarm, thanks to you. We went out the way you arrived—we even borrowed your boat. Kemp had his agent discover Taylor dead and rouse the staff after we were safely away. Taylor died of natural causes, so there's been no formal investigation other than the medical one."

"Kemp?" Rand's tone carried a deeper question.

"No, Jon. I admire him, but that's all." She smiled wryly. "He's young."

Unwillingly Rand thought of another question. He hesitated.

"Kit was part of a job," Taina said.

"Following me?"

"Yes." Now it was her turn to voice a wonder. "Was Liz Radcliff part of a job, too?"

"You know about her? Is she all right?"

"She's been released. Most of them are out on bail, or were let go for lack of evidence."

"Good."

"Is that all—just good?"

"Yes." Rand smiled. "I think I would frighten her."

The questions asked, they faced each other with love's uncertainty and hope. At last Rand asked, "Was Johnson right about what happened between us that night in La Luz?"

"Oh, Jon!" Her uncertainty fell away. "You can see for yourself!"

For the first time in his life Rand looked into the immense region of another human mind opened to his unblurred mental vision. In his awe he did not probe deeply. But he saw the melting warmth of her love. It was like a hot liquid in his mind.

Aloud he said, "I should have known right away."

"You had no way. It—it was new. It never happened to either of us before." To his surprise her neck and cheeks were pink. "I was—can I say I lost my head?"

"Why not?" Rand grinned. "Next time I'll know."

"Maybe you won't want another time."

"How about right now?"

Her blue eyes danced. She kissed him lightly, but drew away when he reached for her.

"You're an invalid, remember? You're recovering from an ordeal and an operation."

"That's another thing I wanted to ask you. Why do I feel so different? What's been done to me?"

"How do you feel different?"

He considered. "I'd say that I feel light-headed. Except that I don't mean intoxicated or dizzy or anything like that. It's as if a weight had been lifted—pressure of some kind removed. And I have insights I never had before. Like a moment ago with you."

"You've described pretty much what's happened. I'll show you that weight off your mind."

From a table beside the bed she picked up with the aid of small tweezers two tiny dark specks. She handled them with delicate, patient care. Placing the specks on a piece of white tissue, she handed them to Rand. There was a magnifying glass on the table. She gave it to him.

"Look through this."

Rand peered through the thick glass. The specks, many times enlarged, assumed specific, orderly, meaningful shapes. They turned out not to be black at all. Tiny divisions of color were clearly visible.

"One of them looks like a miniature radio, if that makes sense."

Taina Erickson nodded. "It's a subminiature transmitter and receiver. Part of it was destroyed when it was removed. This is an electrolytic modular structure."

Rand studied the tiny objects. The skin felt tight across his face, but he spoke calmly. "Removed?"

"You were operated on. Not a serious operation, though you'll find some minor scar tissue under those bandages where the electrodes and corrosion-resistant wires were buried under your skin—upper chest and underarm areas, and of course your scalp. The transmitter and receiver, the primary control apparatus, were planted in tiny depressions in your skull. All undetectible, except by a thorough physical exam."

"But I had one just before I got this assign—" Rand broke off.

"Yes. At a Syndicate clinic."

Rand's face took on its angry scowl of concentration. "In the skull," he said. "That explains the headaches, I suppose—but how does it explain the way Garrett was able to use pain as a control?"

Taina waited, letting him work it out for himself.

"He must have planned it from the beginning—back in New York." Rand's thoughts raced. "When I slept—right after the briefing before the Board of Directors. It could have been done then. And it was Garrett's order that I get quick-sleep!"

"Garrett might have been thinking of the assassination plot then," Taina said. "But it all began long before. The control factor was built in—from the time you joined the Syndicate and had your first physical and mental examination." She paused. "You've always had the headaches, Jon. Don't you see why yet?"

Rand stared at the tiny objects on the white tissue. Suddenly he remembered a dream, a sense of panic, and cool, antiseptic words: "He's yours now."

"That's it!" Taina cried.

He shook his head. "It doesn't make sense yet."

"It goes all the way back—to the real beginning, Jon. The way PSI-40 affected people. There were two basic reactions. One was hallucinogenic. It took many directions, but it was essentially the same response to the drug. Then there was another—the reaction which opened a whole new dimension of awareness, tapping the mind's power in areas which had never been accessible before."

"The Special," Rand cut in.

"*Only* the Special. Like you, darling."

Rand looked at her as if she had lost her senses.

"There's no such thing as a Sensitive, Jon, except a man-created one. That's what the conflict really was about when the Syndicate began. That's why Powell Johnson tried to disappear, and why the others had to find him and murder him. The controlling group wanted to exploit the drug for themselves alone. To do that, to be sure of it, they had to keep the power the drug released exclusive to themselves. They found a way."

Rand stared at the instruments on the tissue, specks of dirt to be carelessly blown away on a breath. "That way?"

"That gave you fifteen years of headaches. That interfered with your PSI-reaction, restricting it. Limiting what you were and what you could do. And that gave Garrett his whip to use if the time ever came when it was needed."

"But how could it remain operative all these years?"

"Your body's electricity, small as it is, can keep these instruments running indefinitely."

For a long time Rand lay motionless. He was staring at the woman beside his bed, but his thoughts were not of her or of the immediate events which had brought him to this quiet, whitewashed room. They ranged a long way back. He saw himself acting the role the Syndicate had charted for him, unquestioning and obedient. The vain young man, so proud of being chosen, being "different." The eager young agent, fresh from training, enjoying the daily discoveries which showed his superiority over ordinary people, growing a little more arrogant as time went by. The increasingly confident senior agent, advancing through the ranks of the Syndicate's Security section, getting the "plums" and thinking how well he was being taken care of. Always living apart from society, as befitted one of the chosen few. Separate and safe in the knowledge that the world was becoming ever more Syndicate-oriented, and that what was good for the Syndicate was good for society—and for Jon Rand.

Safe, he thought with bitterness. As a work animal or a machine is safe, kept in good health or working order because it is useful, fed and exercised, or cleaned and oiled, but kept firmly within bounds so that it could do no harm—and aspire no higher.

And he had *chosen* the role!

No force had been applied—although it now seemed that Anti propaganda about accidents and mysterious disappearances involving Specials who refused to join the Syndicate might well be true. Quite simply, Rand had been bought.

In a way he had done what the religious fanatics, the sexually enslaved, the naturists had done. To obtain the glories offered through PSI-40, Rand had sold his independence. He had given up part of his humanity. And he had been cheated in the bargain! His talent had been deliberately warped so that he would remain tame!

"We were all tricked," Taina declared. "You no more than the rest of us. That's why we have such a big job ahead of us—to find the others like ourselves, one by one, and show them how they've been used."

"Used," Rand muttered.

He made an effort to shake off the bitter anger, the sense of so many wasted years. His need fastened on her words—"find the others."

"You're right." He was vehement. "There are probably hundreds walking around with little instruments in their heads to drive them into line. If we can reach them, get them on our side—" He broke off. "Why didn't you try to tell me some of this when we first met?"

"Because you weren't ready to listen," she answered. "We had no way of knowing how you'd react. But there was a good chance you'd simply notify Garrett. We didn't want him to know what we were planning. We weren't ready for that."

"He knows now," Rand said. "He knows you've gone over to Johnson."

"You're sure?"

"He learned it from me," Rand admitted, scowling.

"Don't blame yourself." Taina hesitated, and Rand once more caught a flicker of worry from her mind. But she went on quickly, as if she did not want him to detect her concern. "Given time, we can break the Syndicate's power and destroy its monopoly of PSI-40. But we need time."

"Garrett won't let you have it." Rand studied her closely, sensitive to the currents of her thoughts and emotions.

He detected the flicker again, smothered. Then she realized what he was doing. A shield suddenly barred his mental scrutiny.

"Don't do that," she protested angrily.

She avoided his eyes and drew away slightly. Rand noticed that the sun had left the room without his being aware of it. It was dusk.

"Have I the full powers of a Special?"

The question surprised her. "Yes—that is, you will."

"What does that mean?"

"When did you have your last PSI-40 intake?"

Startled, Rand made a quick rundown of the days. "If today is Tuesday, it's been almost three days."

She flashed a brief smile. "Then your PSI-reaction isn't very strong. You don't usually have full power for three days, do you?"

"No. But I can do things right now I could never do before!"

"That's only a shadow. All you've ever had is a shadow of what you can know and do."

Rand looked at her quietly. After a moment he pushed the sheet back and swiveled his legs toward her. "I'll need a pill now," he said.

"You can't get up!" she protested. "Jon, darling, you need—"

"I like the darling," he cut in. "But before you get started on what I need, I might as well say now that I know you're worried about Johnson and I can guess why."

"But you're weaker than you think, Jon—there's nothing you can do."

"Where is Johnson?"

"I—I don't know. I'm not even sure but that I'm dreaming up a dragon that isn't there."

"The dragon is there, all right," Rand stated bluntly.

"The question is, has Johnson gone after him? What makes you think he might have?"

Abruptly Taina stopped resisting. "I'm afraid, Jon. He canceled a meeting scheduled for tonight without any reason. And he's disappeared."

"That's not much to go on."

"Since Garth Taylor died, he's been acting strangely. I think Taylor reminded him strongly of his father. And he hates Garrett. Up until now he's been against unnecessary violence—he doesn't believe in it. But I think what Garrett did to you, and tried to do to Taylor, has affected him deeply—touched some hidden core of feeling that he can't control. That's what I'm afraid of."

"You should be. Now get me that pill."

"What can you do?" Taina demanded. "We don't even know where Kemp is—or Garrett."

"I'll find them. Listen to me. Garrett is totally ruthless. Johnson isn't. No matter how much he hates Garrett, Johnson won't be able to overcome that. Human life is important to him—he can't forget that even when his own life is at stake. Garth Taylor said the same thing, but I learned it for myself in Taylor's bedroom that night you were there to stop me. I could have shot Johnson. He couldn't quite bring himself to use his powers in any way that might destroy me." Rand paused, then went on relentlessly. "Garrett has no such scruples. I don't have to tell you that the man who'll win a life-and-death struggle is the one who won't hold anything back—who'll use every weapon he has, no matter what."

Taina was silent. He experienced her fear with her, and he saw that it was not only for Kemp Johnson but also for him. And the fear for him was colored by an inexpressible longing, melting, fusing. Their minds touched in something like a quick embrace.

"I have to try," Rand said gently when they had withdrawn. "I can fight Garrett on his terms."

"But he's been a Special all these years! He's learned to use his power!"

"Then I'll have to learn fast. If I ever get the drug."

She gave in. "What kind?" she asked.

Rand looked puzzled. "Is there more than one?"

"Oh—I forgot. You knew that Kemp got the PSI-40 formula from his father?"

"Yes."

"He perfected a delayed-release capsule. It's the same thing, but it releases the drug into the bloodstream at intervals. He can remain active for weeks that way on a single intake."

Rand remembered his study of Johnson's record in the Security file and the puzzle over the youth's apparent ability to exercise a Special's talent at any time. Another question was answered, and his respect for the young man grew.

"I think we can forget about a delayed release," he said slowly. "Tomorrow doesn't matter right now. I need a straight, massive dosage." He smiled at her worried expression. "How about hunting it up while I dress? A man's entitled to some secrets, even from a woman who curls up inside his mind."

Chapter Nineteen

Taina Erickson's fast little car raced through the night, following the sweep of the scenic parkway which overlooked the dark expanse of Conception Bay. Rand sat beside her in a silence broken by the whistling wind and the rasp of the engine, and by a thousand tattered fragments of thought, like billboards glimpsed and gone.

He was a little like a bat, Rand thought, flying through the dark with a special kind of radar to guide him. He did not need to bounce mental signals off objects around him. The signals flicked out at him as he passed, his mind recording them in the same way his body felt the thump of each irregularity in the road. Soon he found that he could tune in snatches of thought or filter them out at will, like a radio selector dial moving from station to station. With a little experimenting he learned that he could employ a kind of selective screening, in effect cutting off all but a single communication.

"You'll get used to it," Taina assured him breaking the silence.

"It's the verbal thing that's strange. Being able to pick up *anyone's* thoughts."

She nodded. "But you'll still have to communicate with

an average person vocally or in basic thought-images. The receiver, in that case, hasn't improved, even though your power to transmit is immensely greater. It's a question of —usable power."

Once again Rand felt a kind of awe at the still uncharted range of a Special's abilities. He thought of the exhilarating experience of immersion in another's consciousness, as he had been able to merge with Taina, a communion possible only between Specials.

Her eyes left the road and rested on his face. A mental bubble of mirth formed, and he knew she had caught his thought. The bubble teased him, floated away, burst, Rand wanted to chase her down an endless labyrinth of laughter, but she sobered quickly.

"Other changes aren't so easy to predict," she warned.

"Such as?"

"Clairvoyance, for instance. Some have, some don't. Have you experienced it before?"

"Yes."

"Then it'll probably increase. But—oh, damn! There's so much we don't know! So much that's uncertain! Like telekinesis, making physical objects move. Or dominance, the power to direct another mind. There's no way of measuring your powers yet."

"How about teleportation?"

She shook her head. "Not that we know of, though it's possible."

"Are you afraid Garrett might have some surprises waiting for me—that he might have had some for Johnson?"

Reluctant to confess it, she could not hide her fear. "I shouldn't have let you come!" she burst out.

"We had no choice," Rand reassured her quietly. "Especially after that newscast tonight."

He had already made his decision; the evening news had merely confirmed it. They had tuned it in while waiting for Rand's heavy dosage of PSI-40 to take effect. When Garth Taylor and the Mental Freedom Syndicate were mentioned, Rand and Taina had both jerked to attention. They watched somber filmed coverage showing Taylor's body being carried to the plane waiting to fly it to New York. Many of the nation's leading dignitaries, the announcer had said, would be present for the funeral of the former powerful head of the Syndicate.

"We have no choice," Rand repeated, "because Garrett

has none. He'll have to be in New York for the funeral."

"Maybe he's already left," she said hopefully.

"Then where is Johnson?" When Taina made no reply, Rand pointed out, "Garrett will want a showdown tonight—before he flies back. There's sure to be a directors' meeting scheduled for right after the funeral. Garrett has to go into that meeting with this Baja business behind him. We're loose ends he can't afford. We know he tried to kill Taylor by using me. If that got to Pierce . . ."

Taina banked the low-slung car fast into a steep curve. As it leveled out, she spoke above the whine of the tires. "Pierce tried to have you killed—he's no better than Garrett!"

"Pierce is a fighter," Rand admitted. "But I think he can be influenced where Garrett can't. I think Pierce is ready to believe the Syndicate has to change." Rand paused. The dim light from the dashboard penciled in his pensive scowl. He thought of Miguel and Juan Huerara. He held no friendly feelings for Pierce, who would use men as callously as Garrett. The difference between the two men might come down to the fact that Pierce's area of self-interest conceivably would also allow society to survive. Garrett's would not. Forcefully Rand said, "We can't let Garrett take over the Syndicate. Not if we can stop him!"

The steering wheel gave a brief jerk. The sensitive car, responsive to the slightest action of the driver, did a wavering dance before Taina straightened it out.

"You promised you'd only try to save Kemp," she reminded him. "Not go after Garrett yourself!"

"Yes," Rand agreed with reluctance. He found himself regretting the impossibility of lying to her. "If that's possible. It may not be. We still don't know what's happened."

After a moment's silence Taina said fiercely, "I won't be left out of it—I can't let you go alone!"

"You have to! We've been over that. You're the only other one who knows about Garrett and about Taylor's death—knows all the facts. And the only one who can keep Johnson's organization together if something has happened to him—and if I don't come back. We can't risk all three of us. If Garrett could eliminate all of us, no one would ever stop him. So you have to stay clear. That's *your* promise!"

There was a clash of wills. She wanted to resist his argument, to refute his logic, to deny her promise. In the end she bowed before his insistence.

A cocoon of silence enveloped them once more, while beyond it the wind buffeted and the car's engine sent out its staccato roar as they sped toward Mulege.

The main streets of the city were a babble of light, sound, flashing mental images. Rand had to screen out most of them. The little car cruised slowly toward the center of town, then jogged right in the direction of the waterfront.

"How close do you want me to get?" Taina asked.

"Not much farther."

"Why are you so sure Garrett will still be using that boat rental as a base?"

"I'll ask you something first; how far is communication possible?"

"Between Specials?"

"Yes."

"Under ideal conditions, a mile or more."

"What's ideal?"

Taina frowned. "Isolation. No electric engines or atom smashers or high-frequency radio or television or X-rays. No people. Especially no people."

Rand nodded. "The closest you can come to those conditions in Baja is along the waterfront. There's little if any interference over water. Garrett's already shown that when he drove me across the bay that night. And the commercial dock area by the boat rental is far enough from the major resorts to be relatively deserted at night."

"But he knows you'd look there!"

In the emotional urgency of the moment Taina slipped unintentionally into telepathic exchange. Rand responded automatically in the same way. It was like putting on an old slipper.

"That's just it. The battleground is to his liking—and he knows I'll come. So that's just where he'll be, waiting for me. Johnson must have guessed as much. Garrett is arrogant, egotistical. He doesn't fear me. He has no reason to—he doesn't even know my control factor has been removed unless he managed to get that out of Johnson. He'll figure he can brush me aside like a bug, or bring me to my knees any time he wants." Rand's smile was meant for her. *"Maybe I can give him a few surprises."*

177

A block farther Rand started to tell her to stop the car. Her foot was already pressing down on the brake. Rand squeezed out of the little car's crowded compartment.

Peering through the window at her pale face, shadowed by anxiety, Rand thought, *"Stay out of range. I have to know that."*

"Yes." The whispered response was like a mental caress. *"You're not fooling me, darling—I know what you're going to do. But you must come back!"*

Chapter Twenty

When the mutter of the car's engine could no longer be heard reverberating along the narrow, silent street, Rand turned to face the bayfront. Fish smells were strong on the wind.

For the first time Rand let his mind open fully. An ingrained habit of restraint had held him back while Taina was with him. The new experience was like looking at the sky through a telescope when you had always seen it before only with the naked eye, or putting on corrective lenses when you hadn't known that you were nearly blind —had believed that the blur of objects was normal. Suddenly a whole new universe was there inside Rand's brain. What had been faint and distant was bright and clear. Where there had been random perception, there was order.

And there was the Enemy.

"Rand?" The tone of mind was cold.

Rand did not reply.

"The other is alive—I have not done with him. But I've been waiting for you, Rand. And you no longer serve any useful purpose. It is death you hear—waiting for you. Come!"

Rand felt his leg muscles tug and lift without his volition. The street was abnormally hushed, as a forest teeming with life grows still with the sense of impending battle between two giants. In the silence Rand's unresisting footsteps echoed down the narrow canyon.

The dock area was only a short distance away. As he neared it, Rand saw orderly rows of boats defining the grid

178

of a private marina. The stripped masts of sailboats were black against the night sky, like a ravaged forest of naked trunks.

A quarter mile east was the dock which faced the boat rental.

Rand felt Garrett's nearness strongly as he reached the waterfront. There was no sensation, no mental activity he could detect—just a presence. He wondered what strength or ruse Garrett had used to overpower Kemp Johnson. Perhaps he had begun by forcing Johnson to walk toward him. As Rand walked now, his legs continuing to obey an external command.

Rand kept his mind well shielded, and he was certain that Garrett had not yet directly probed his consciousness. Apparently he was able to communicate in another way. It was as if he could bypass Rand's brain and strike directly at his body, influencing its intricate network of nerve ends and muscle groups, giving it orders—the order to walk, and now the order to turn along the wharf toward the boat rental.

It was time, Rand thought, that he accepted the challenge. He stopped.

His legs quivered. His muscles went into spasms. Quick, hot needles of pain. A burning sensation spreading from his feet past his ankles and into his calves. Then a convulsive contraction, a hard cramp which knotted both calves in intense pain.

Grimly Rand held his ground. The weight of his body on his cramped leg muscles was agony. The pressure abruptly increased. Rand swayed but his feet remained rooted. Tiny flecks of color began to dance before his eyes.

Suddenly the pressure was gone. His leg muscles relaxed, the pain eased, his vision cleared.

"So you are a Special!" Loren Garrett's thought reached out to Rand.

Rand was silent. He had dropped to one knee, then shifted to the other, quickly massaging his calves, kneading away the tension.

"So was Killjoy!" Garrett conveyed his contempt. *"But he was more clever as a boy than as a man."*

Rising, Rand moved away from the water's edge. As he did so a length of rope lying at the foot of a pier uncoiled and slapped viciously across the spot where he had been.

Weapon two, Rand thought. Telekinesis. Could he do the

same? Or did the power take time to develop and control—time which Garrett had had and Rand had not?

He hugged the wall of a warehouse—a wall of ribbed aluminum. Would the nearness of buildings, or numbers of them, or metal, affect Garrett's aim or control? There were so many unknown factors, as Taina had argued.

Abruptly he knew where Garrett was. The intuition surprised him and brought with it a nagging reminder which he could not pin down. But he definitely placed Garrett over the water. With concentration he pinpointed the exact position. Garrett was standing in shadow on the deck of a twin-hulled hydrofoil yacht moored to the end of the dock by the Syndicate's boat rental. The yacht was probably the Syndicate's property, too, Rand thought. And useful for transporting prisoners—or carrying bodies out to sea.

And Kemp Johnson was on it, alive. Alive and *awakening*.

Hastily Rand turned his attention away from the boat. If Garrett did not sense Johnson's return to consciousness, he might yet be surprised, caught off guard and off balance.

Suddenly Rand remembered what had teased his memory a moment before when he located Garrett on the yacht —the Security director had a weak directional sense. Once again Rand remembered that Baja briefing in Garrett's office—Garrett had been unable to determine the whereabouts of that eavesdropper.

Instantly Rand's long training to spot the exploit weakness came into play. Without even analyzing what he was doing, Rand acted upon the potential advantage. He sent confusing stabs of thought toward Garrett, like a clever boxer circling around a heavier and stronger opponent, flicking light but stinging jabs. Rand's jabs were muscle twinges, mocking laughter, darts of imagined pain, an electrical charge that made Garrett's hair crackle and stand on end. Rand felt an answering anger and a heavy, threatening probe.

Physically and mentally Rand kept moving, presenting no fixed target. His probing brain was never silent, never lingered on any one prong of attack but shifted quickly from objects glimpsed—a furled sail, a cabin door, a pair of oars, a scudding cloud, a smear of oil on the wharf—to the projected barbs and taunts. At the same time he ranged in and out among the waterfront buildings and the mounds of stacked goods being loaded or unloaded. Climbing, jumping, running this way and that at changing speeds, Rand worked closer to the pier where Garrett lurked. He was never still.

Behind him a sailboat's thin mast snapped and crashed across the boat's deck. An oar tilted on end and slapped at air. A door flew off its hinges. An invisible weight seemed to graze Rand's mind, like a ponderous blow glancing off a fighter's cheek, awesome but harmless.

Garrett was striking late and off target.

A sudden, warning intuition flared in Rand's mind. He was approaching a battery of fuel pumps in a service station supplying gasoline and oil to boats with the old-fashioned engines. In a flashing clairvoyant image Rand saw himself engulfed in flames.

He threw himself to the ground behind a stack of boxes. An explosion rocked the waterfront. Gasoline-fed flames shot a hundred feet into the air, and smoke billowed up.

A scream was almost lost in the thunder of the flames. Rand saw a blackened figure tottering at the edge of the holocaust—the man whose image he had mistaken for his own in his saving moment of clairvoyance. An innocent passerby, a watchman, a wharf bum, he would never know which—someone who had wandered onto the scene unnoticed by the two combatants, so total was their concentration upon each other and their maneuvers.

Without hesitation Rand put the stranger mercifully under hypnotic sleep, and—from twenty yards away —hurled the charred body clear of the flames as easily as a child tosses a rag doll.

The instant's action exposed Rand to Garrett's unceasing, searching probe. And the towering column of flames threw a sunbright glare over the whole waterfront, painting everything with stark clarity. Rand sensed the triumph in the Special's mind as Garrett simultaneously spotted him near the flames and located him mentally. There was no chance to evade or escape, no longer any question of Garrett's directional weakness.

Garrett's mind locked with his like train cars coupling, clashing together.

At first Rand panicked. A red glaze seemed to coat his brain. The crackling inside his head was frighteningly soundless, yet more real and truly audible than the snap of twigs breaking. Rand's jaws opened and clashed shut without his volition. His eyes bulged. His hand jerked up, the arm swiveling at the elbow, and lashed him across the bridge of his nose. His heart beat like a great drum in his chest, and his loins turned weak.

Under relentless pressure Rand staggered toward the flaming furnace Garrett had ignited from the tanks of gasoline.

The panic passed. Anger returned. Rand fought the powerful command surging across the waterfront from the deck of the yacht. His knee twisted, trying to pitch him forward, but he braced it firmly. His stomach knotted, doubling him over in pain. He planted his feet wide and stood hunched over, seared by the heat of the fire—but immovable.

"I'm—used—to—pain!"

His thought defied Garrett, who was physically visible now, a dark, menacing figure silhouetted above the sleek profile of the yacht.

Garrett's response was a more violent attack. Stubbornly Rand held out against it—and knew suddenly that he could take anything Garrett threw at him. In the same moment Garrett knew it. Rand grinned ferociously into the red glare of the fire. But Garrett remained unperturbed. There seemed to be no reason for his continuing, arrogant assumption of victory.

Suddenly Rand realized that, while he could withstand Garrett's attack and resist his commands, the effort took all the strength and will and concentration he had. There was nothing left over for a counterattack. And in time—there were signs already, brief spasms of weakness which Rand had to shore up hastily—his defenses would begin to slip, to falter, to fail.

As if he sensed Rand's vision of defeat, Garrett stepped up the fury of his onslaught. Bright crimson lines danced through Rand's brain. He blocked them, pushed them back, squeezed them out—and in desperation struck back at Garrett for the first time with all his power.

There was a moment's confusion. Rand thought his power must be greater than he knew. One blow had Garrett reeling.

Then Rand felt the quick, savage pressure of another mind. Staring out toward the yacht, he saw Garrett entangled in a physical struggle with a second figure. They teetered on the edge of the deck railing. The second man pulled back abruptly. Loren Garrett plunged over the side, his arms flailing wildly as he hurtled toward the water.

Rand felt the cold impact with the water as if he were in Garrett's place. He didn't need Kemp Johnson's urging to join in a concerted attack against the floundering enemy. There was a strange new pulsation in Rand's mind, and it was a while before he identified it as Garrett's fear.

There was no reticence now in Kemp Johnson's aggressive action. Evidently Garrett had taught him a hard lesson. His quick mind sought out a vulnerable spot in Garrett's defenses. Garrett's stomach muscles contracted. A cramp pulled him under water.

At the same time, in the dark depths of the bay, a shark answered a primitive summons, reacting to the imaginary scent of blood. Rand recalled the story from Johnson's past when he had saved a swimmer's life by routing a shark.

Shortly Rand and Johnson were working effectively as a team. When Garrett tried to block Johnson's attack, Rand struck in his place. They probed different areas of weakness, but in the end came back to the stomach and the crippling cramp.

The shark slid swiftly through the dark water, and he was joined by another.

The second time Garrett went down, he was under for what seemed a long time. When he came up there was water in his lungs and fire in his chest and a wild animal of fear prowling through his brain.

He saw the sharks.

The third time Garrett did not surface.

After a while, when there was no more resistance, Rand diverted his awareness. He felt nauseated. Kemp Johnson held his tight grip on the cold, dark emptiness which had been Loren Garrett's mind.

Exhausted, Rand sat on the stump of a projecting pile at the edge of the wharf. Kemp Johnson walked slowly toward him along the dock. Behind him the yacht where Garrett had fought rolled gently on the water.

"You did fine," Johnson thought. *"You kept him so busy he didn't detect me until it was too late."*

Rand understood many other things that came unspoken from Johnson's mind into his—gratitude, warmth, friendship, and most of all a dull, tired emptiness that comes with the final achievement of a long, bitter and arduous mission.

In the end there was no vengeful triumph, not even satisfaction. There was only an old sadness and the knowledge of a promise kept.

Johnson paused at the foot of the dock to stare at Rand. His face no longer seemed young.

"It won't bring your father back," Rand thought, *"or change the Syndicate overnight, but it had to be done."*

Kemp Johnson nodded wearily. He turned to look out over the calm water. The savage image of violence had faded. There was no sign on the placid surface of the bay of the strange duel which had been fought. "It took two of us," he said aloud.

The words were a tribute, and a kind of epitaph.

In the distance sirens wailed. There had been a timelessness about the struggle with Garrett, but Rand knew it had all taken place within a few minutes. Through the screams of the sirens and over the rumble of the flames fed by the fuel tanks came the bark of a small car's engine. Jon Rand stood as the car's growl became louder, closer, fiercer in its haste. He began to smile.